THE HUNGER HEROES

Missed Meal Mayhem

BY JARRETT LERNER

Aladdin
NEW YORK   LONDON   TORONTO   SYDNEY   NEW DELHI

In a seemingly ordinary city...

Atop a seemingly ordinary building...

Live a group of EXTRAordinary heroes...

ALADDIN / An imprint of Simon & Schuster Children's Publishing Division / 1230 Avenue of the Americas, New York, New York 10020 / First Aladdin edition October 2021 / Copyright © 2021 by Jarrett Lerner / All rights reserved, including the right of reproduction in whole or in part in any form. / ALADDIN and related logo are registered trademarks of Simon & Schuster, Inc. / For information about special discounts for bulk purchases, please contact Simon & Schuster Special Sales at 1-866-506-1949 or business@simonandschuster.com. / The Simon & Schuster Speakers Bureau can bring authors to your live event. For more information or to book an event contact the Simon & Schuster Speakers Bureau at 1-866-248-3049 or visit our website at www.simonspeakers.com. / Designed by Jarrett Lerner & Karin Paprocki / The illustrations for this book were rendered digitally. / The text of this book was hand-lettered. / Manufactured in China 0422 SCP / 10 9 8 7 6 5 4 3 2 / Library of Congress Control Number 2021931258 / ISBN 9781534462823 (hc) / ISBN 9781534462809 (pbk) / ISBN 9781534462816 (ebook)

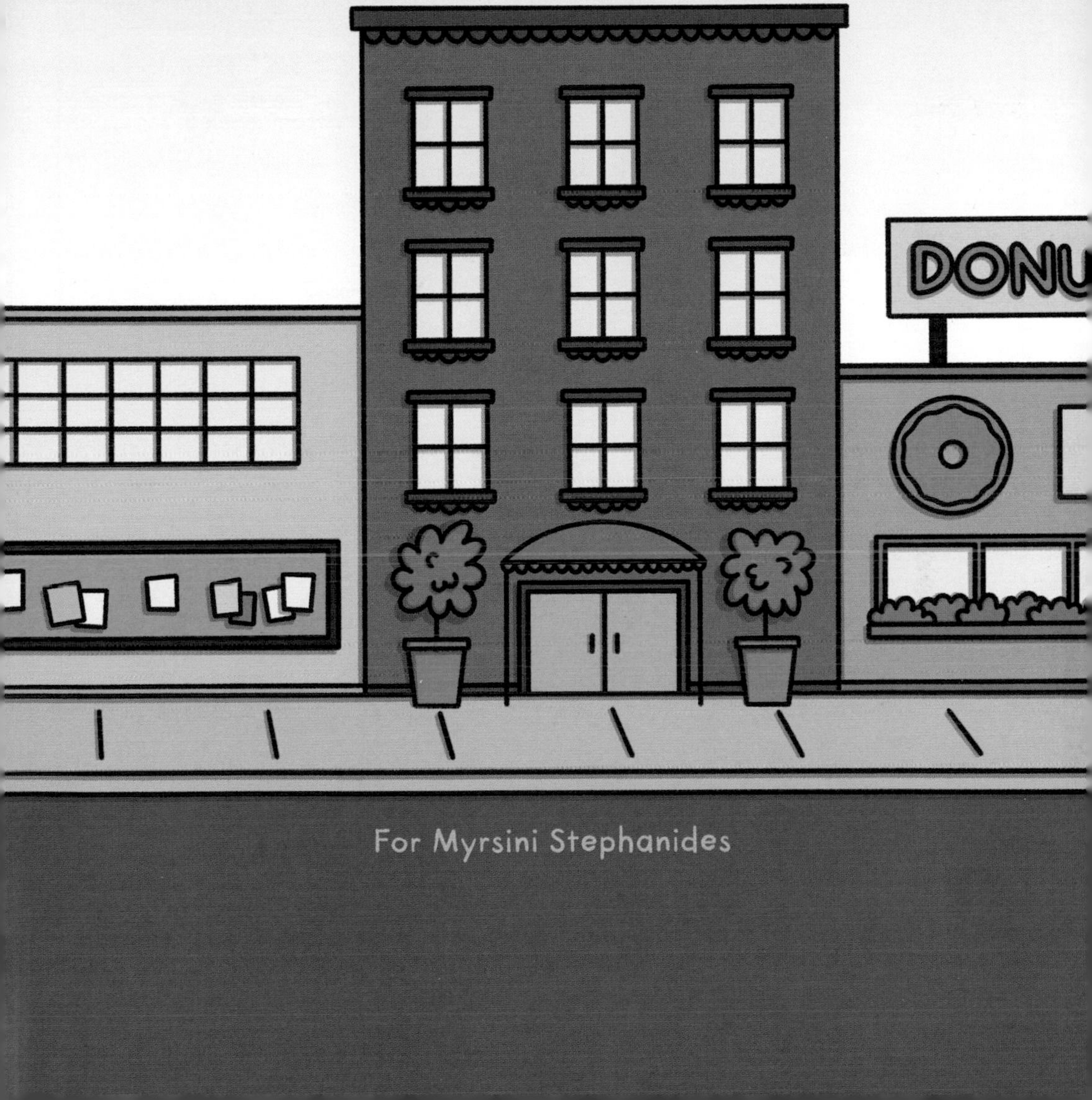
DONU

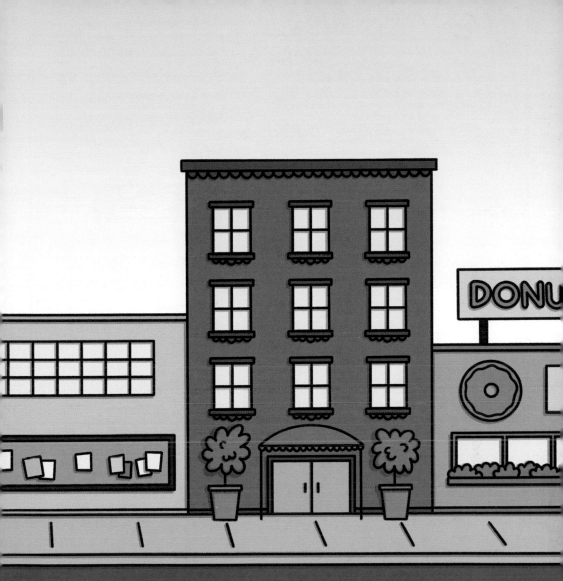

For Myrsini Stephanides

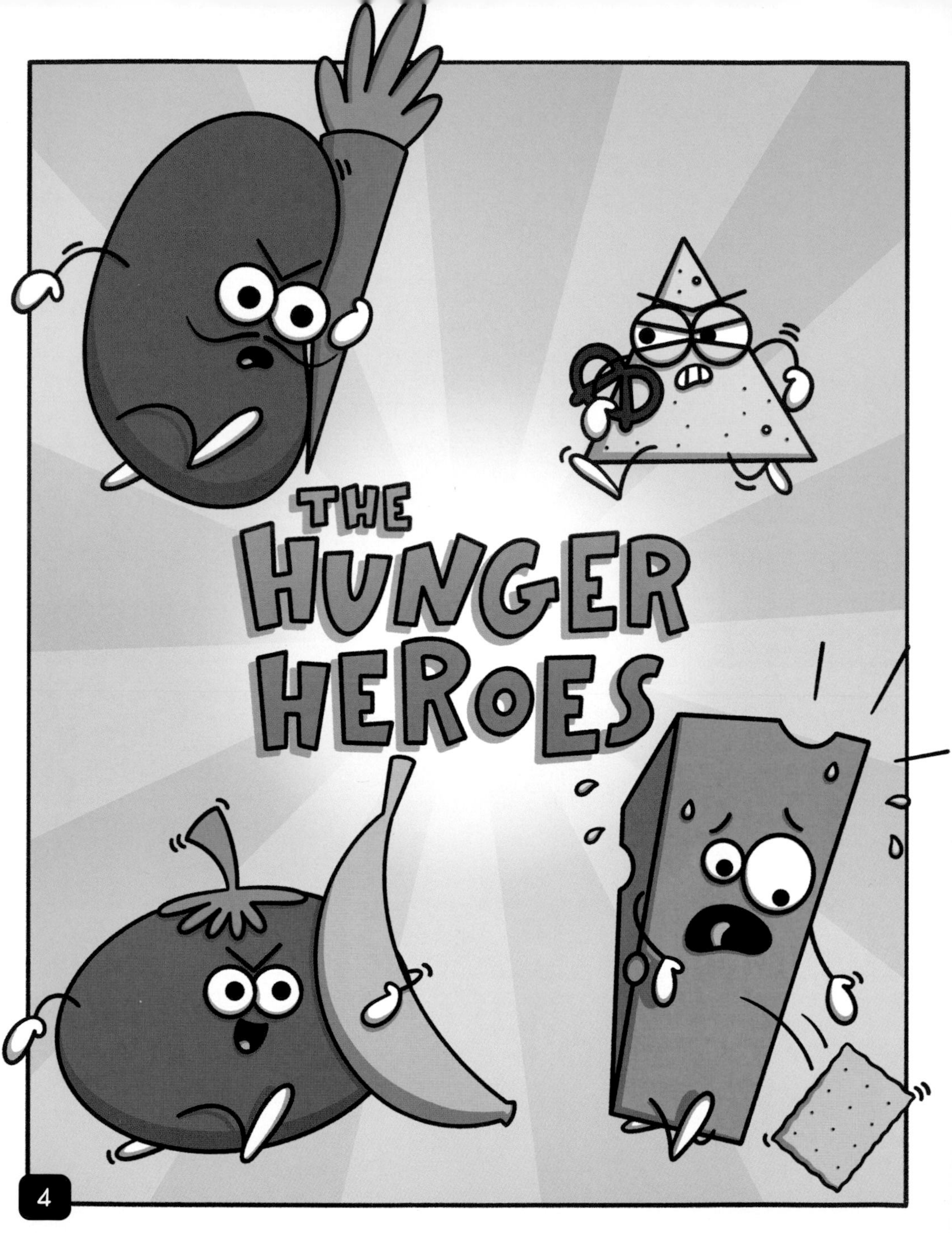
THE HUNGER HEROES

The Hunger Heroes are superpowered taco ingredients who help the kids of their city whenever they need a snack!

Just look at these happy campers!

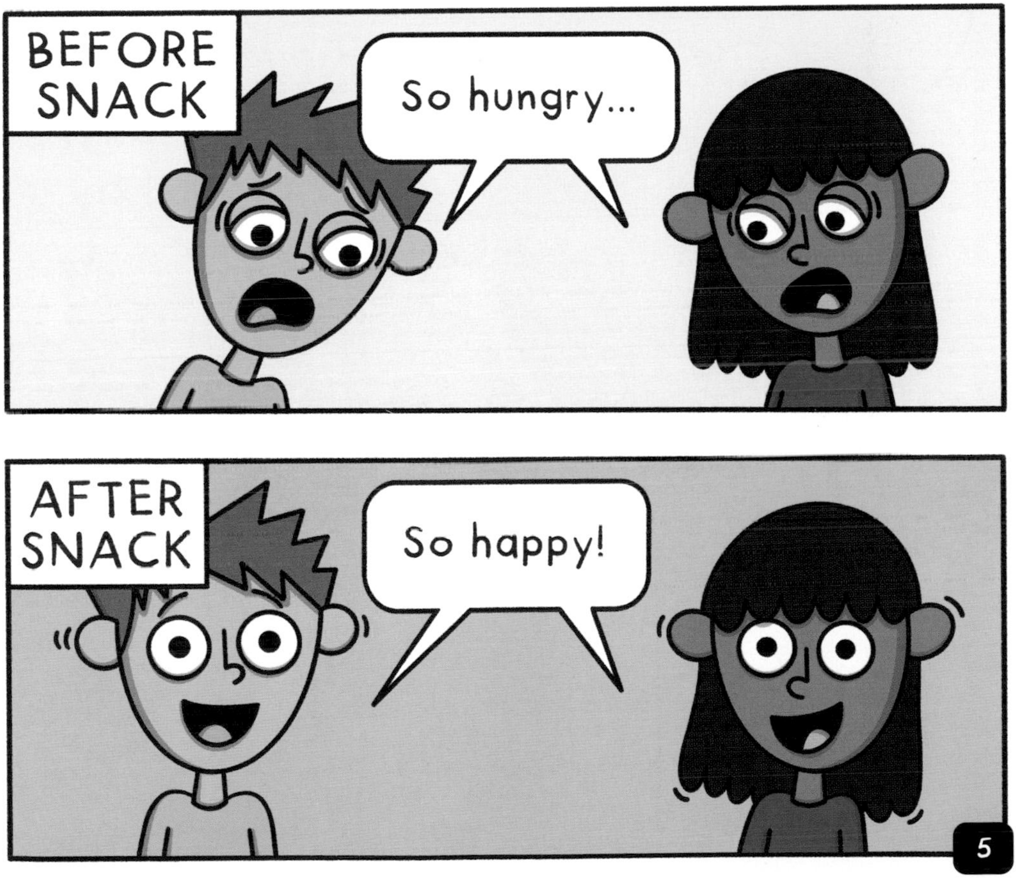
BEFORE SNACK
So hungry...
AFTER SNACK
So happy!

First up, it's

MR. TOOTS!

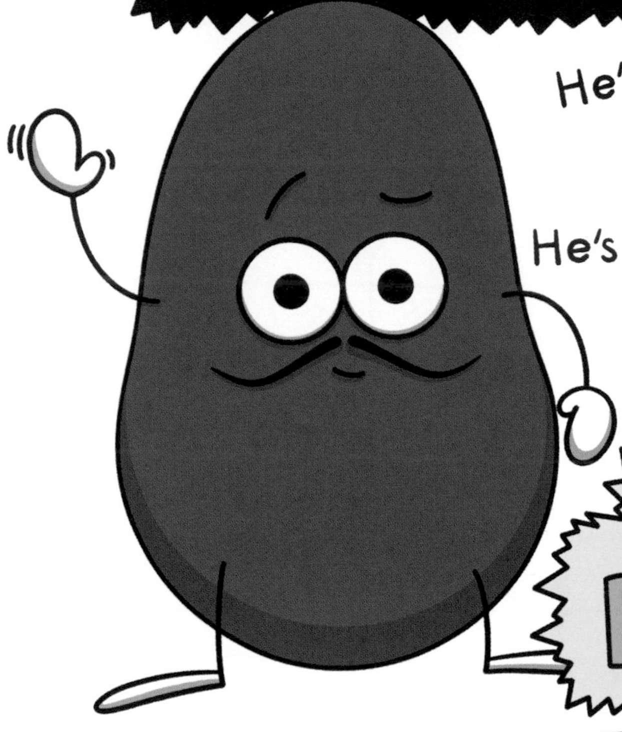

He's bold!

He's brave!

He's a big huge BEAN!

PLUS:

he's fueled by

TOOT POWER!

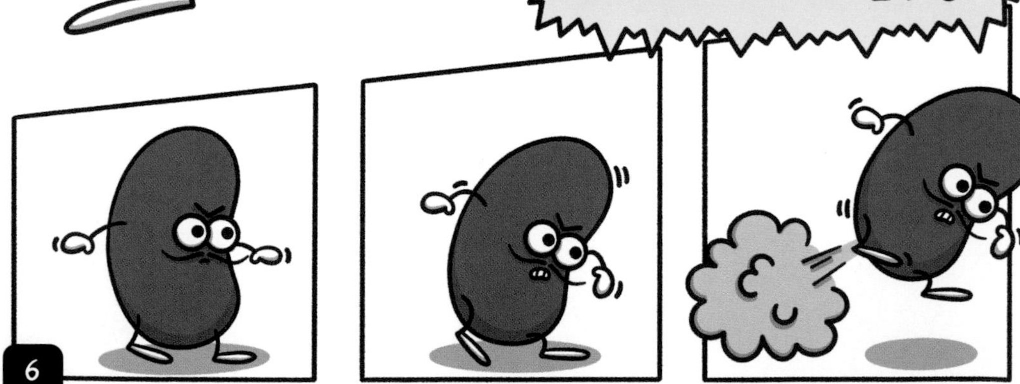

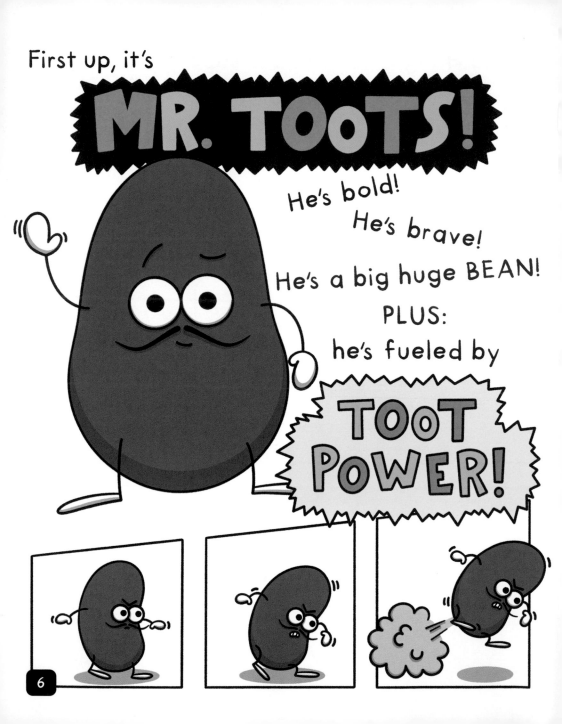

Next up, there's

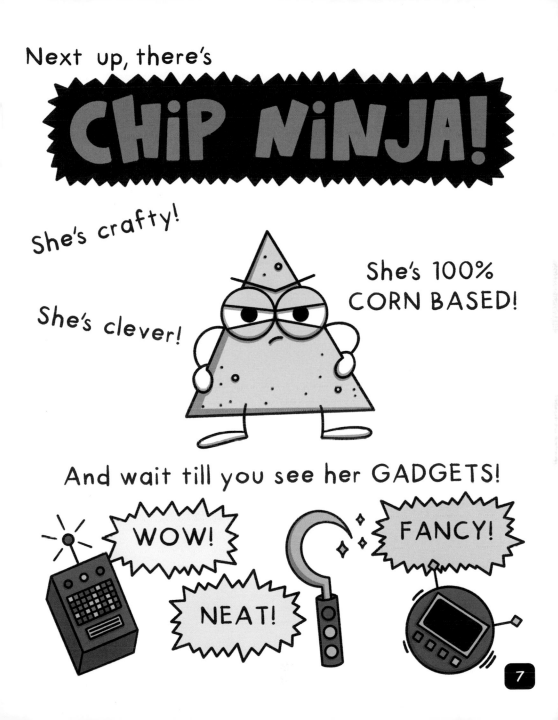

CHIP NINJA!

She's crafty!

She's clever!

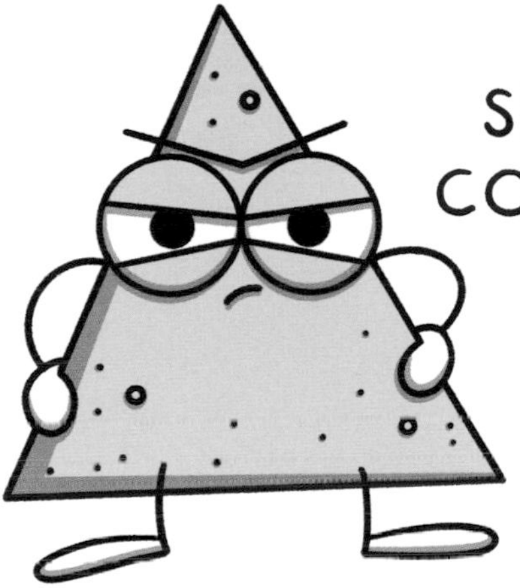

She's 100% CORN BASED!

And wait till you see her GADGETS!

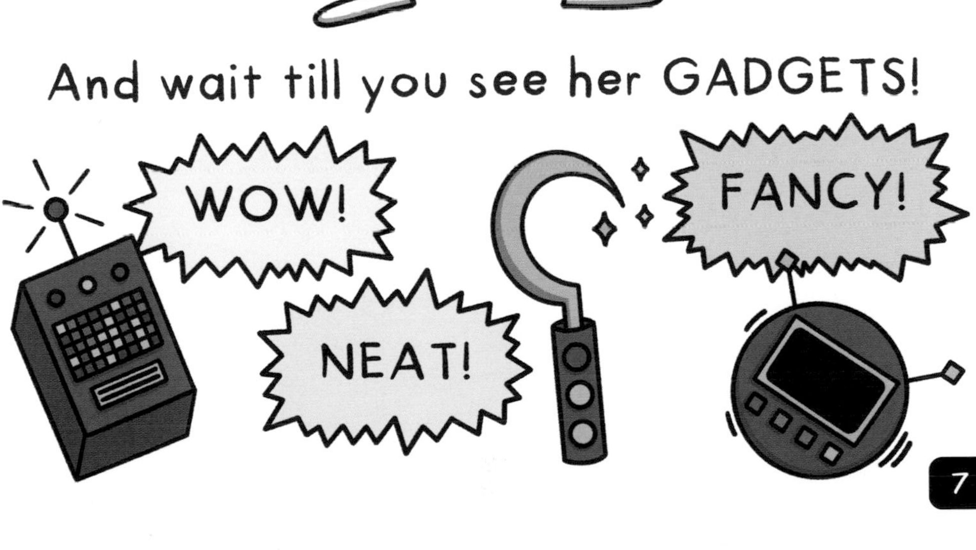
WOW!
NEAT!
FANCY!

And now, meet

TAMMY!

She's strong!

She's sassy!

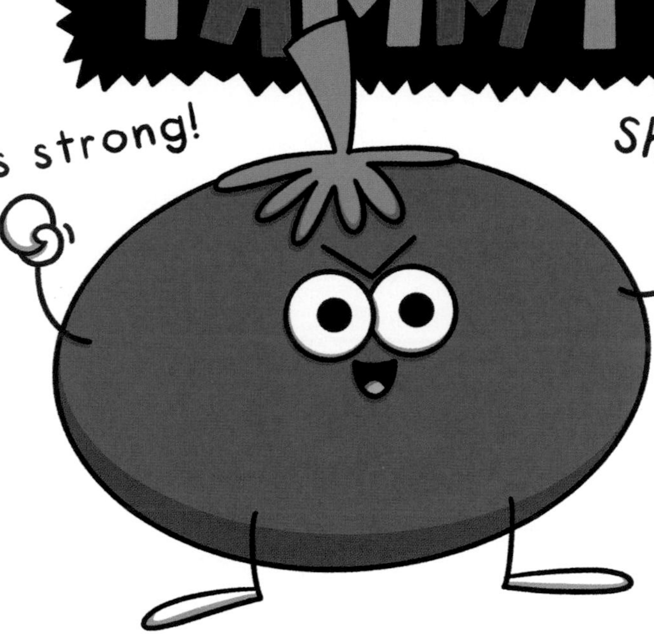

She's packed full of seeds!

Hunger Heroes,
When you're hungry,
We're your heroes,
Yeah!

And she SINGS!

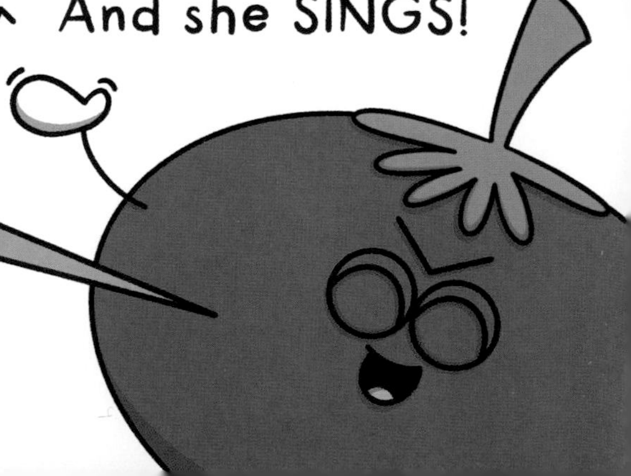

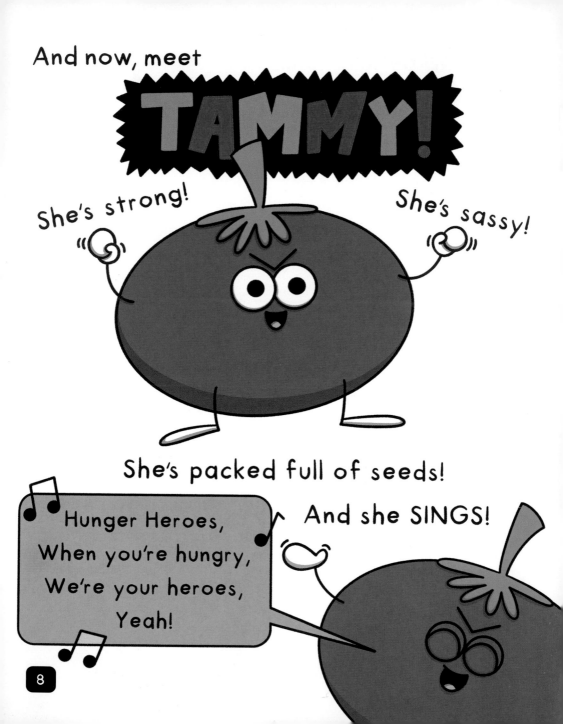

And last but not least...

Leonard?

Where's Leonard?

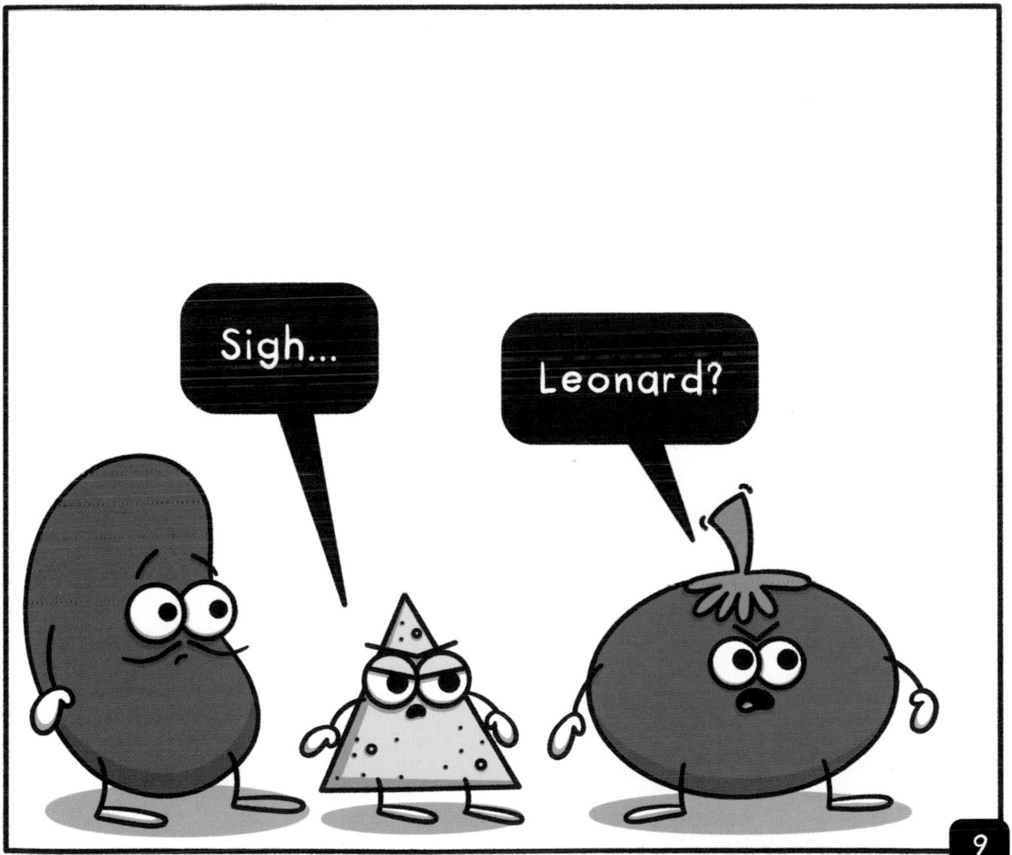
Sigh...
Leonard?

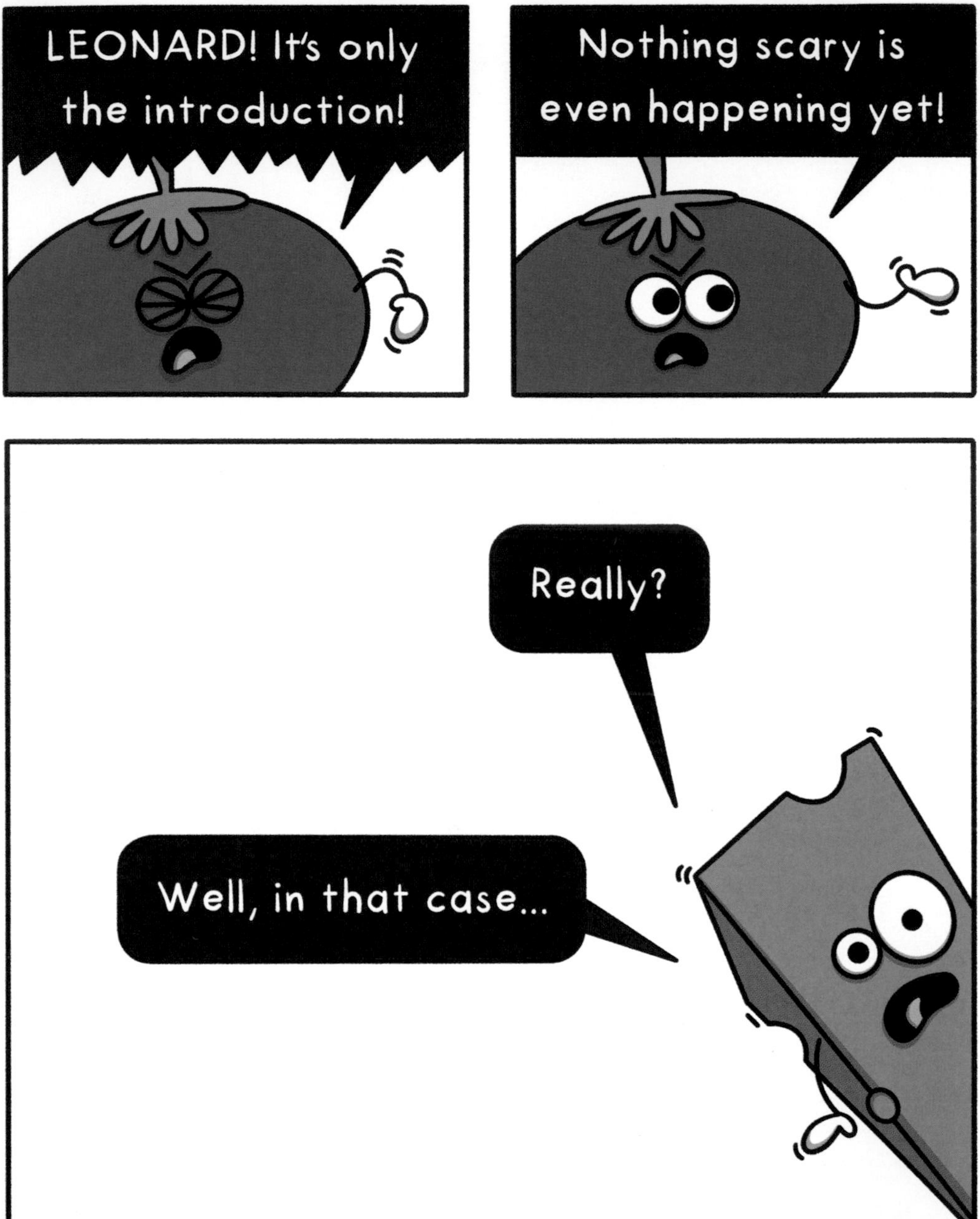
LEONARD! It's only the introduction!
Nothing scary is even happening yet!
Really?
Well, in that case...

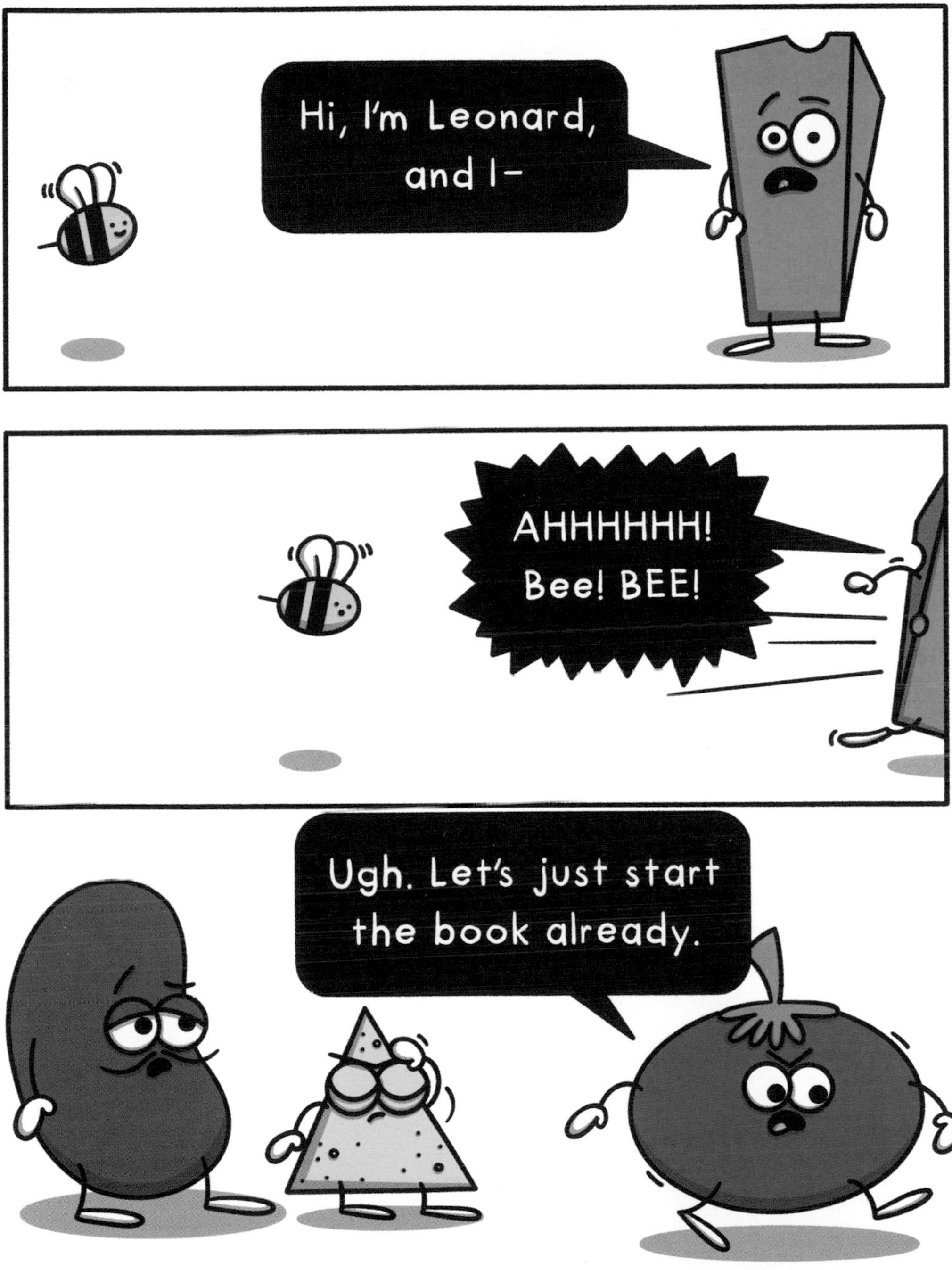
Hi, I'm Leonard, and I-
AHHHHHH! Bee! BEE!
Ugh. Let's just start the book already.

CHAPTER 1

It was a regular Tuesday morning at Hunger Heroes headquarters.

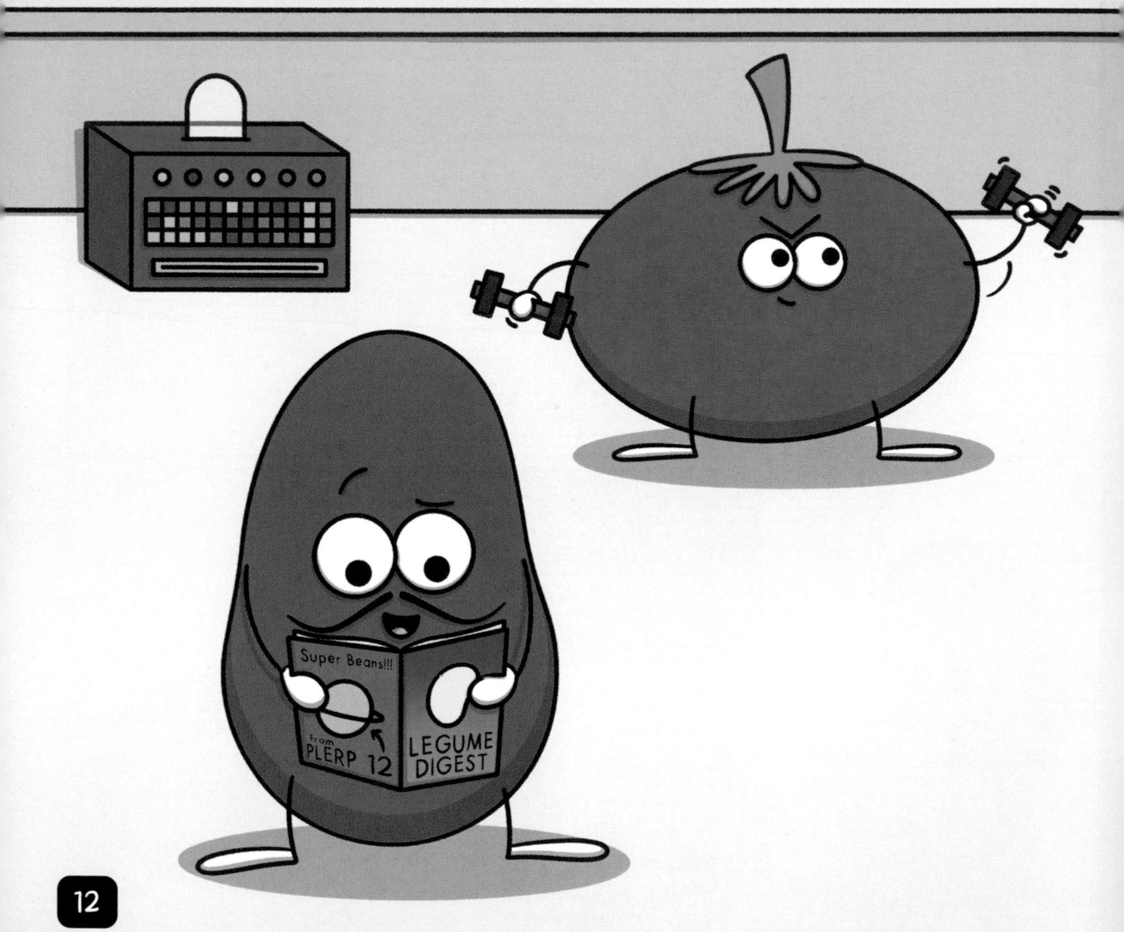

Super Beans!!!
from PLERP 12
LEGUME DIGEST

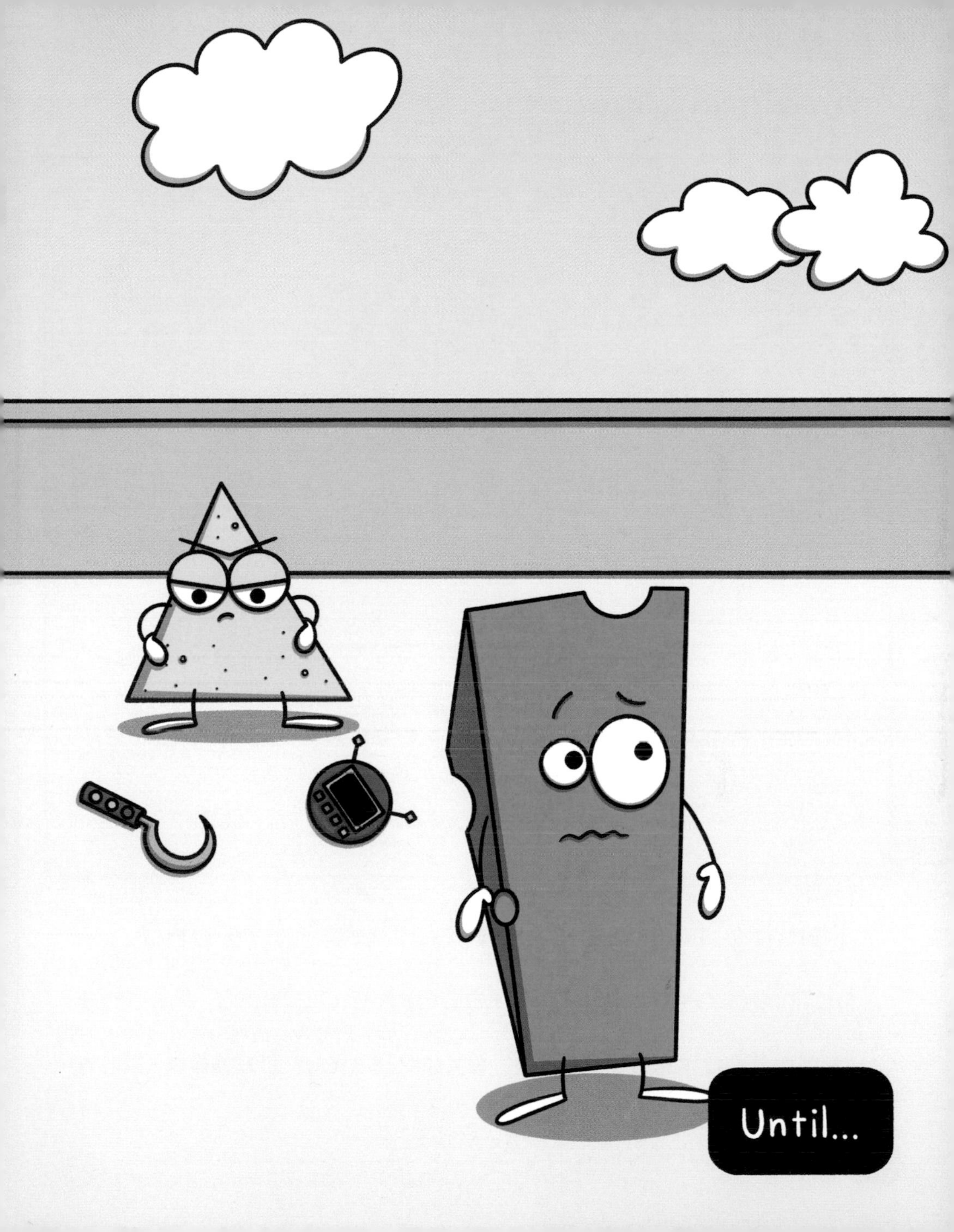
Until...

an alarm sounded!

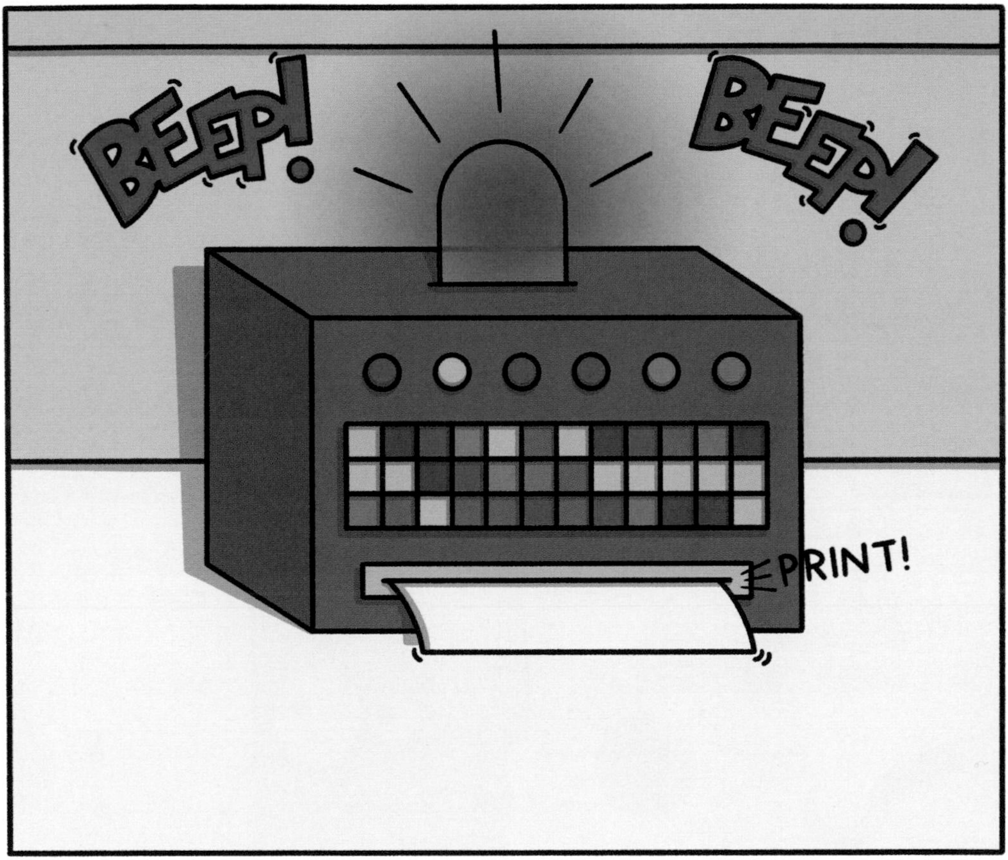
BEEP!
BEEP!
PRINT!

Tammy tossed aside her weights and hurried over to the report machine. As she read the report, her expression turned grim.

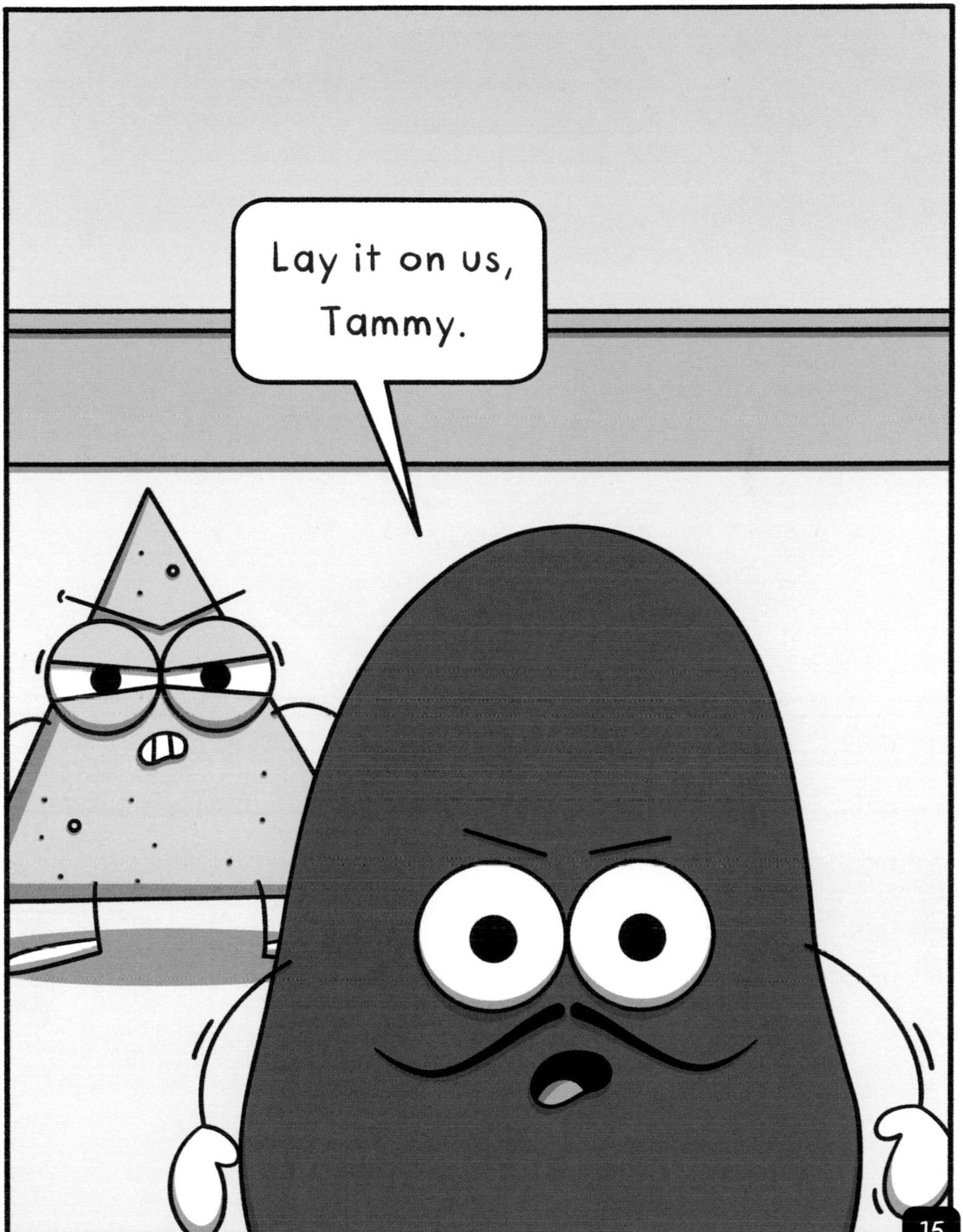
Lay it on us, Tammy.

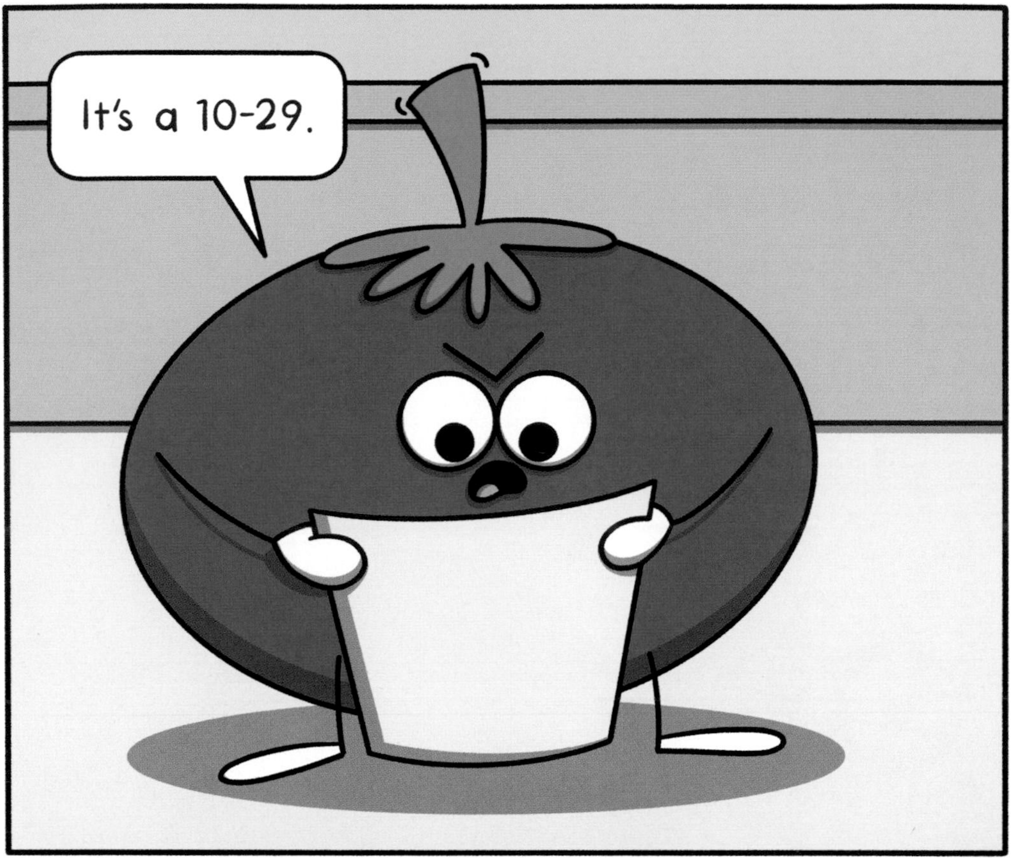
It's a 10-29.

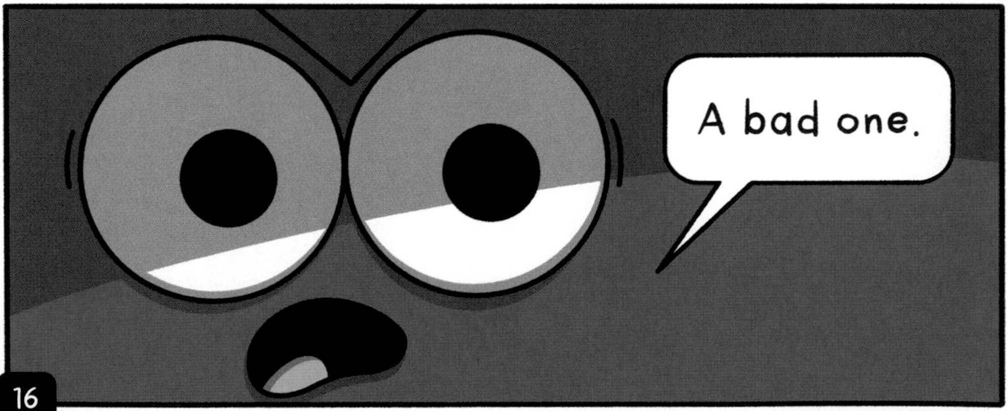
A bad one.

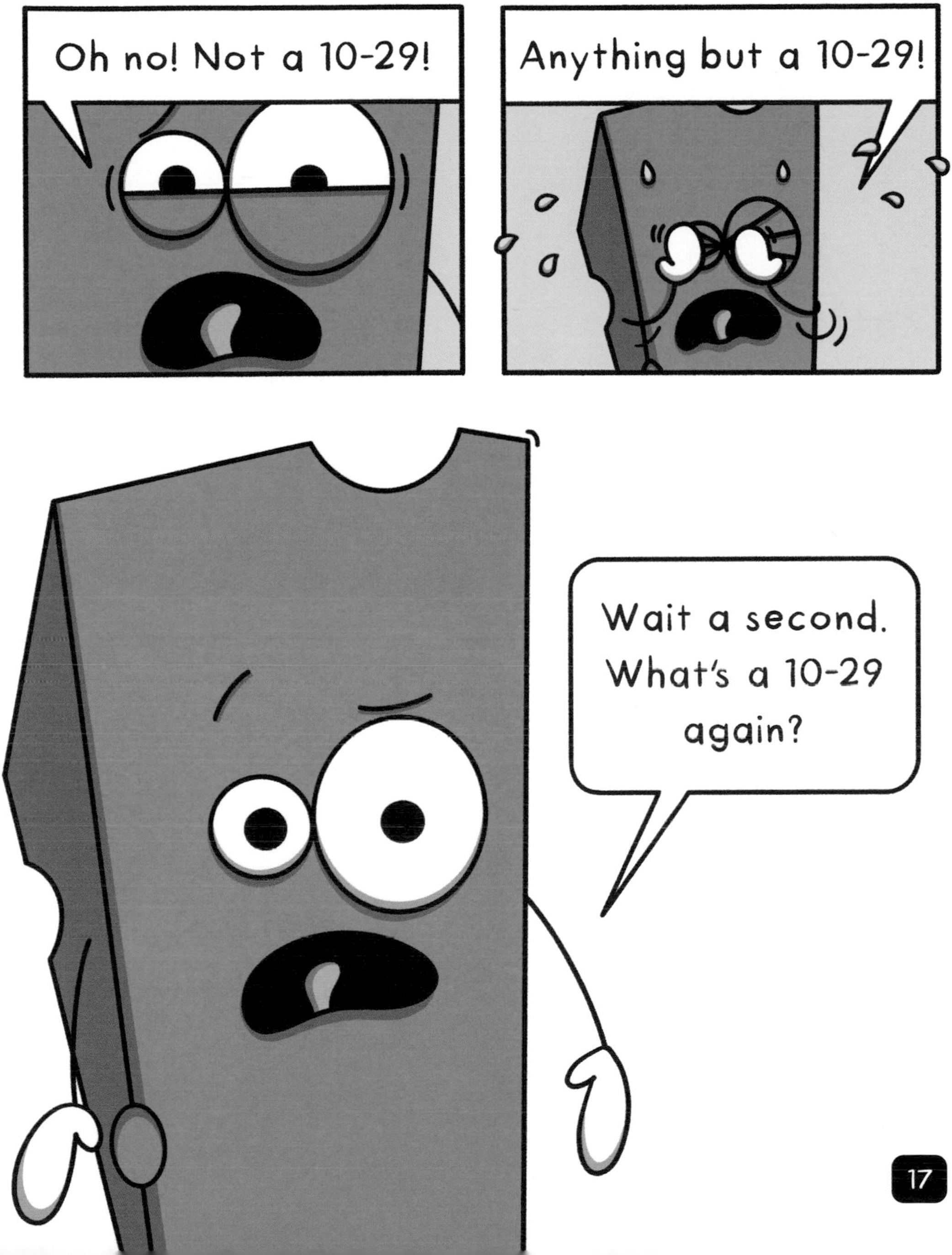
Oh no! Not a 10-29!
Anything but a 10-29!
Wait a second. What's a 10-29 again?

"It's a missed meal," Chip Ninja said.

She snatched the report out of Tammy's hand and looked it over herself.

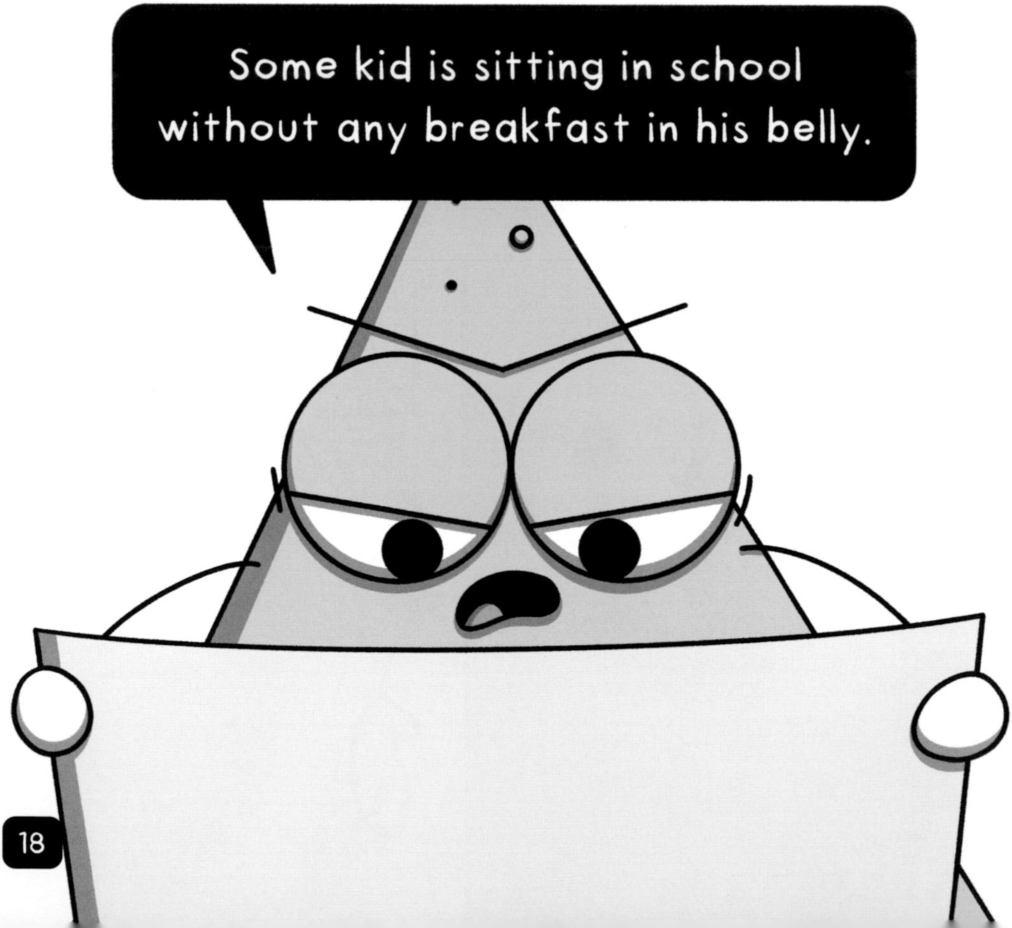
Some kid is sitting in school without any breakfast in his belly.

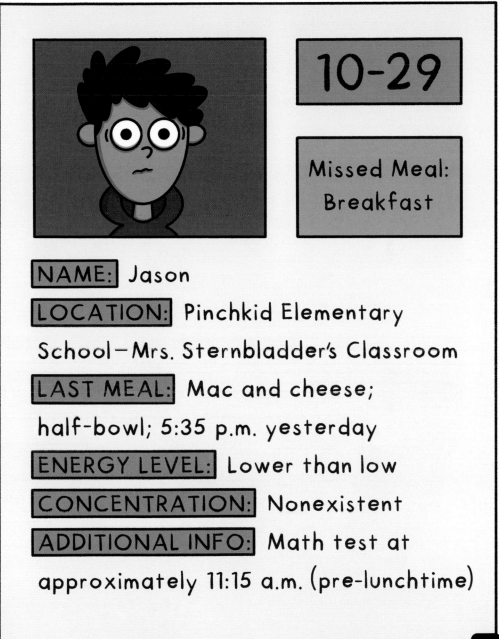

10-29

Missed Meal: Breakfast

NAME: Jason

LOCATION: Pinchkid Elementary School—Mrs. Sternbladder's Classroom

LAST MEAL: Mac and cheese; half-bowl; 5:35 p.m. yesterday

ENERGY LEVEL: Lower than low

CONCENTRATION: Nonexistent

ADDITIONAL INFO: Math test at approximately 11:15 a.m. (pre-lunchtime)

There was no time to lose.

The Hunger Heroes had to get to the school—and FAST!

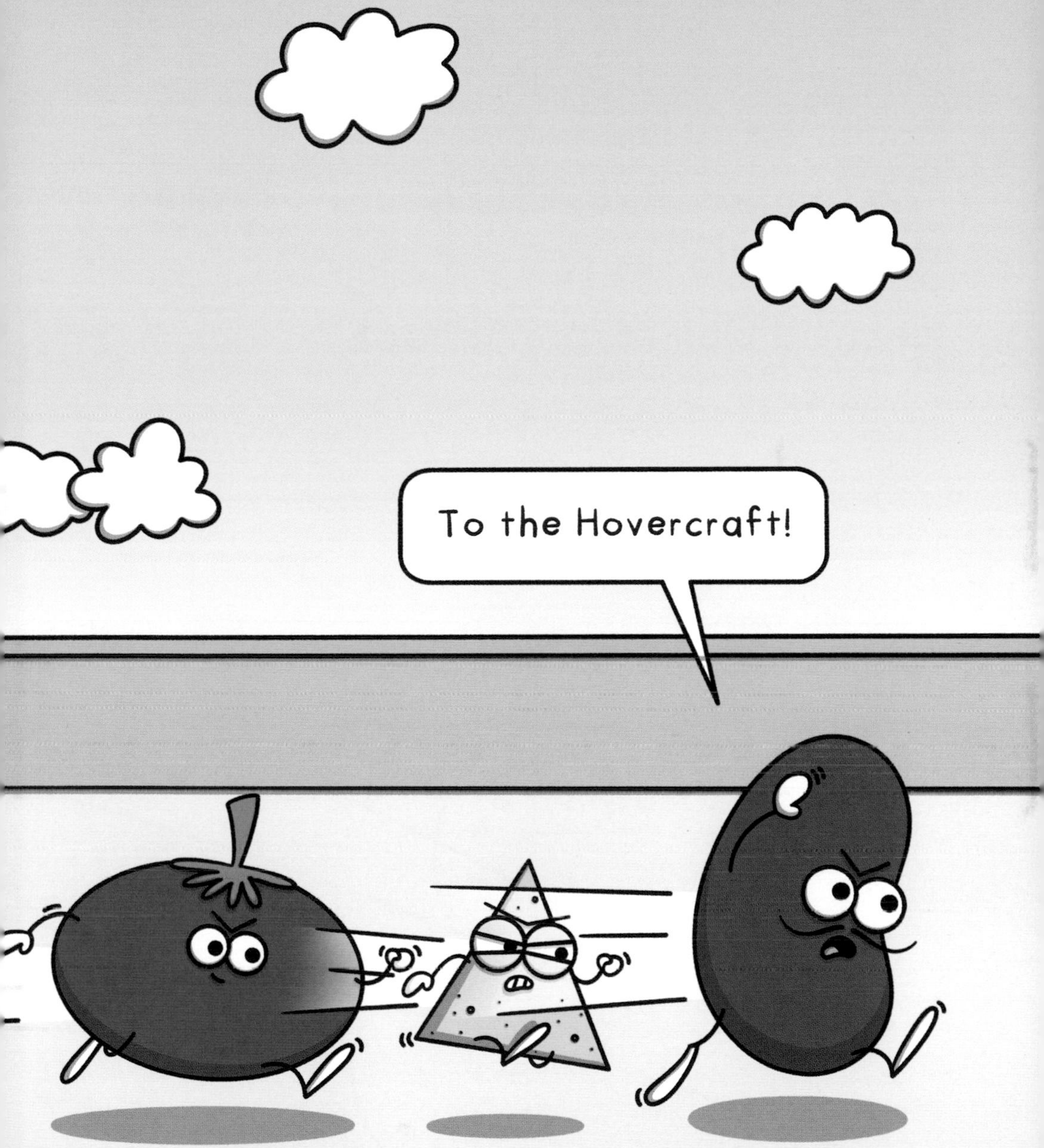
To the Hovercraft!

CHAPTER 2

The Hunger Heroes Hovercraft soared through the sky toward James H. Pinchkid Elementary School.

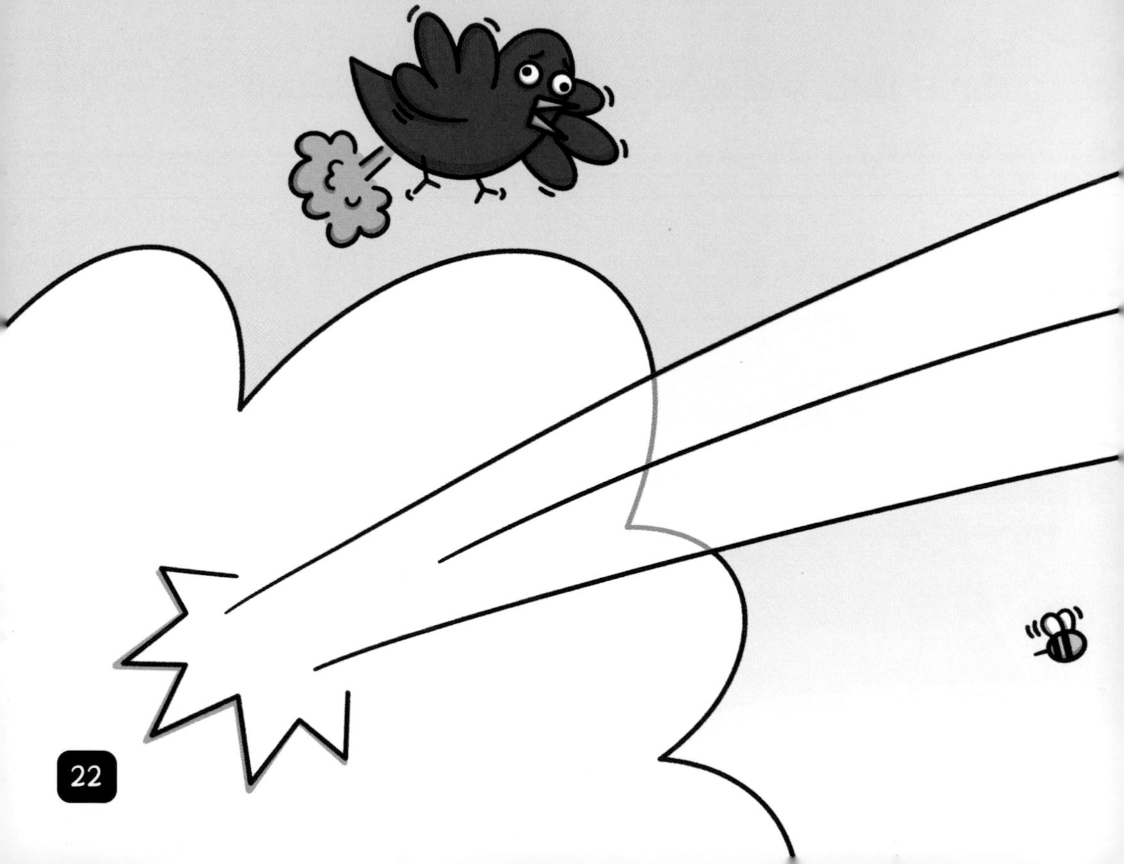

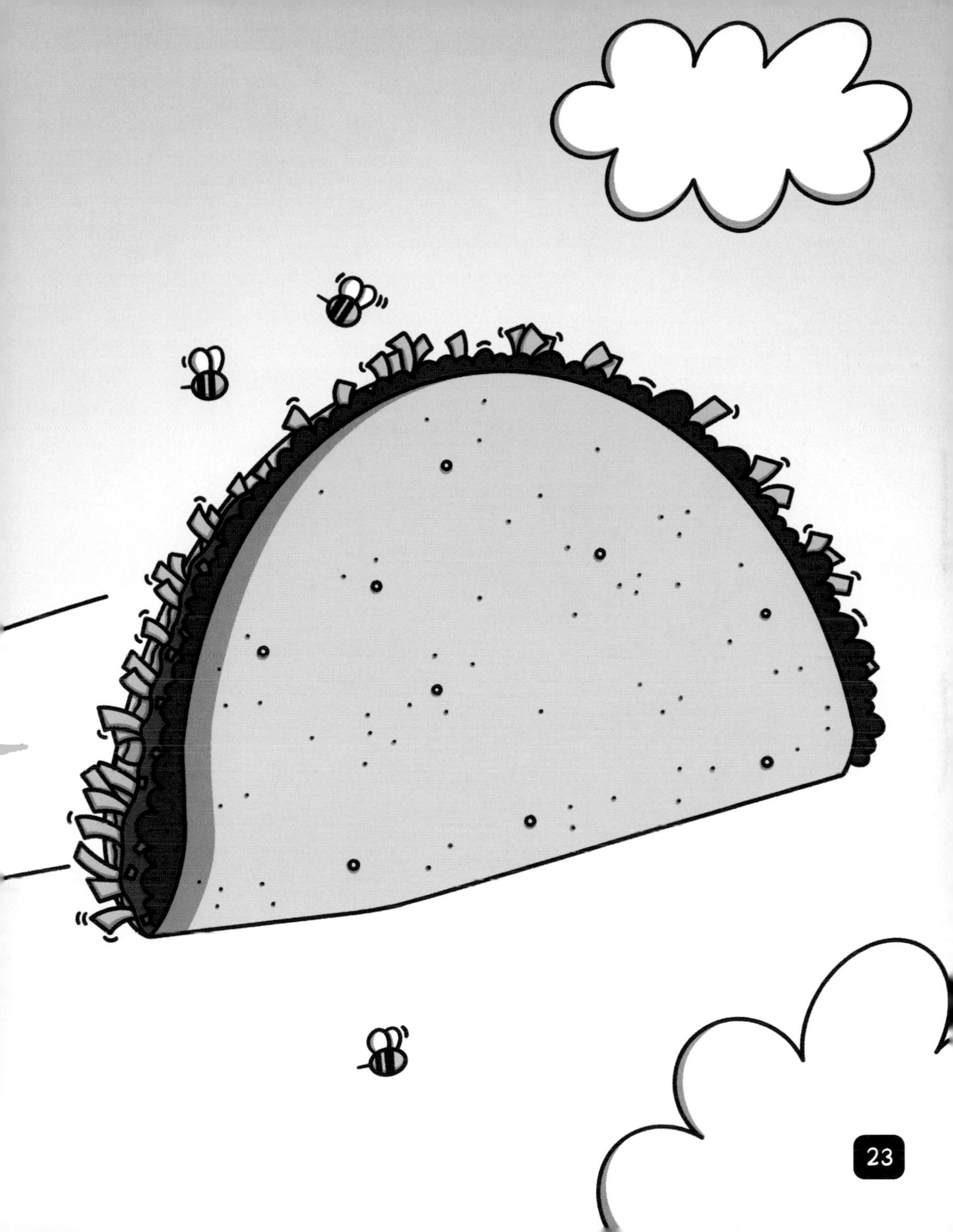

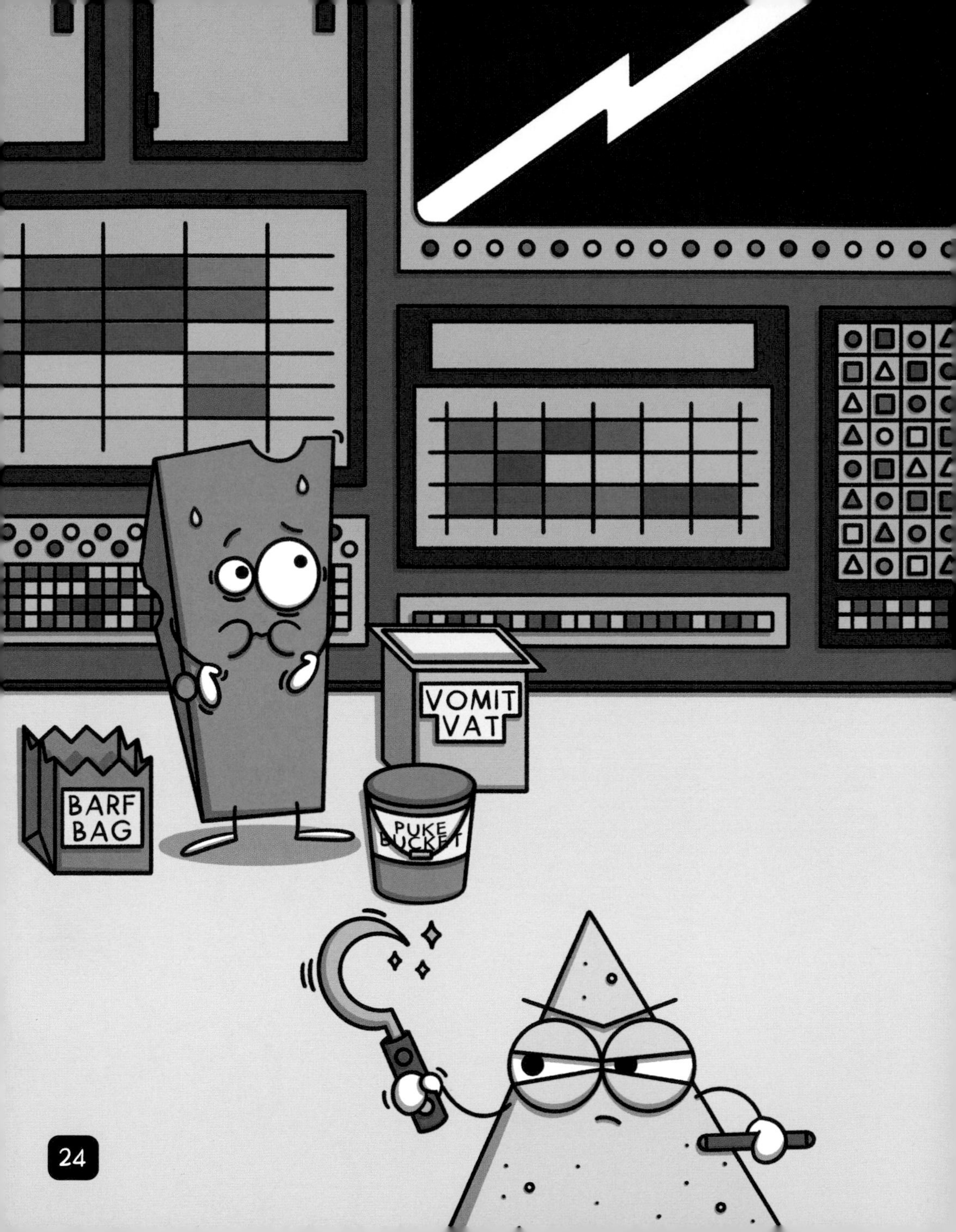
VOMIT
VAT
BARF
BAG
PUKE
BUCKET

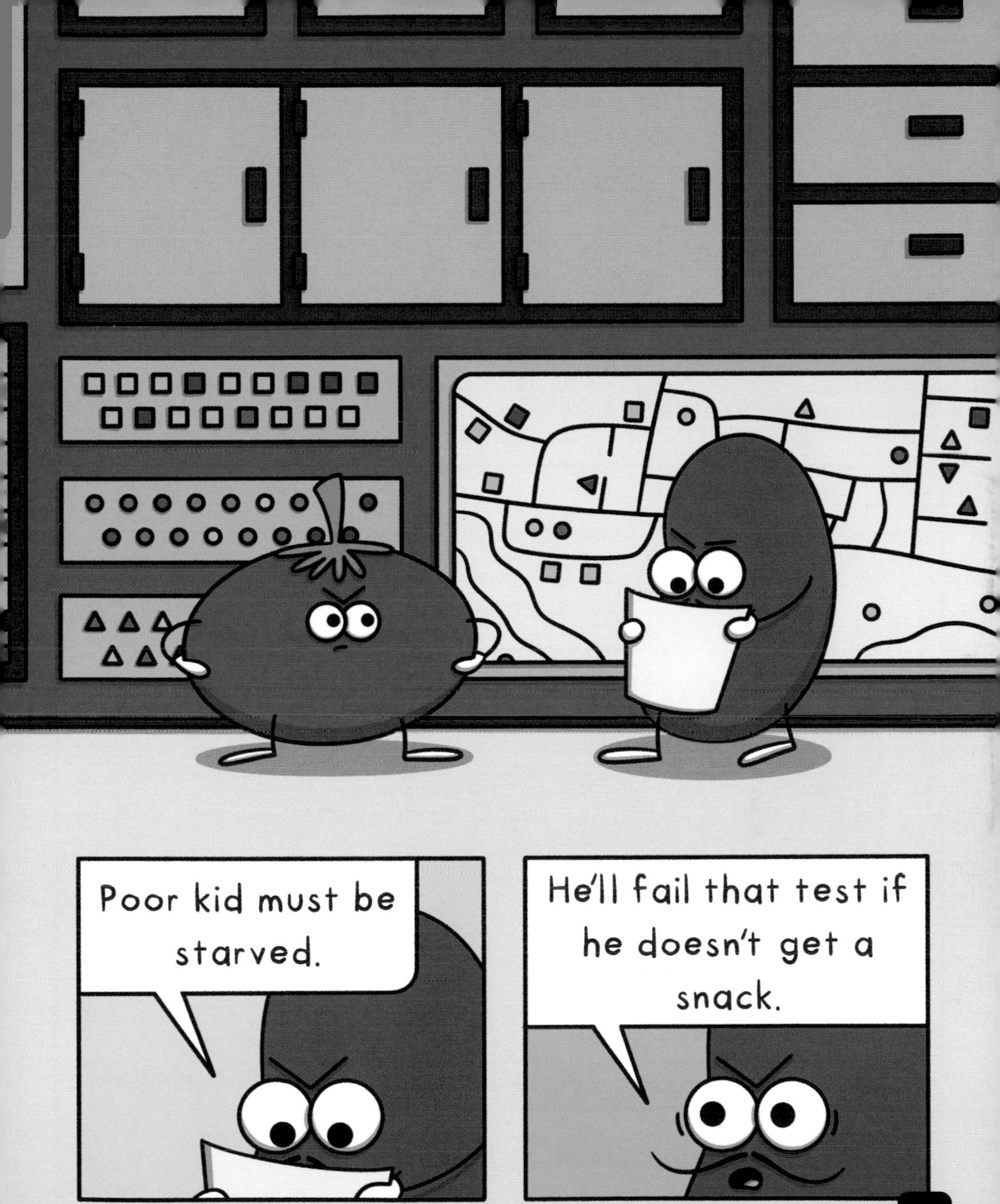
Poor kid must be starved.
He'll fail that test if he doesn't get a snack.

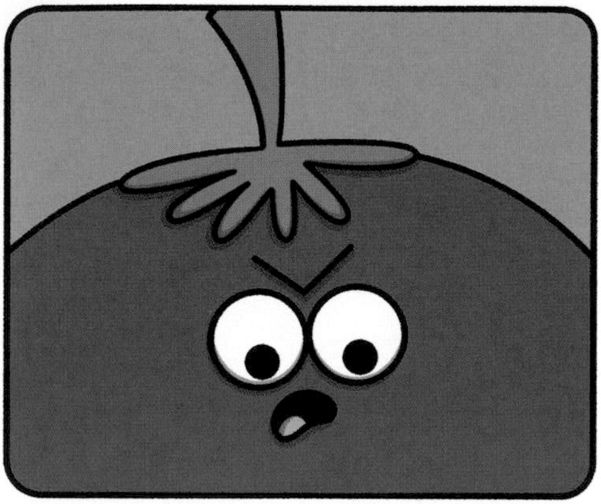

"Well," Tammy said, "we know he won't be getting any snacks from Mrs. Sternbladder...."

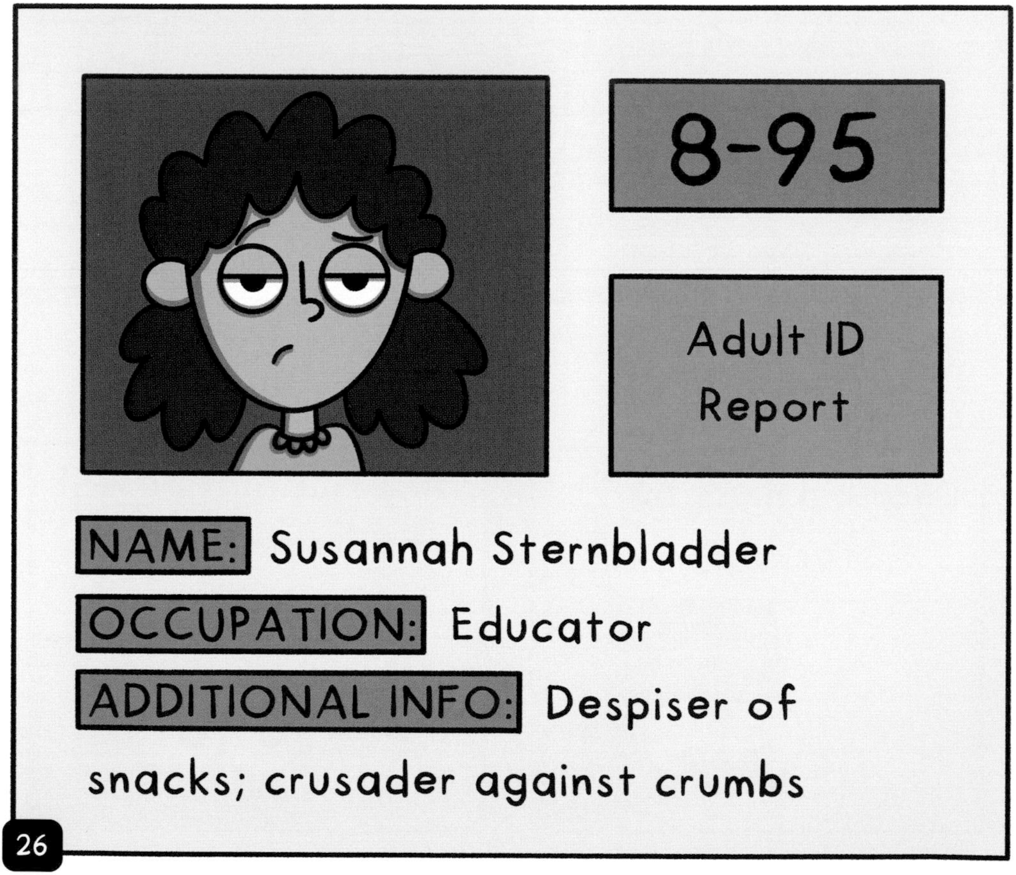
8-95
Adult ID Report
NAME: Susannah Sternbladder
OCCUPATION: Educator
ADDITIONAL INFO: Despiser of snacks; crusader against crumbs

WISE WORDS

ALERT!

"Now, Tammy," cautioned Mr. Toots. "We shouldn't be so quick to judge Mrs. Sternbladder. There's always more to someone's story than meets the eye."

"For all we know, we could help two people today—Jason AND Mrs. Sternbladder."

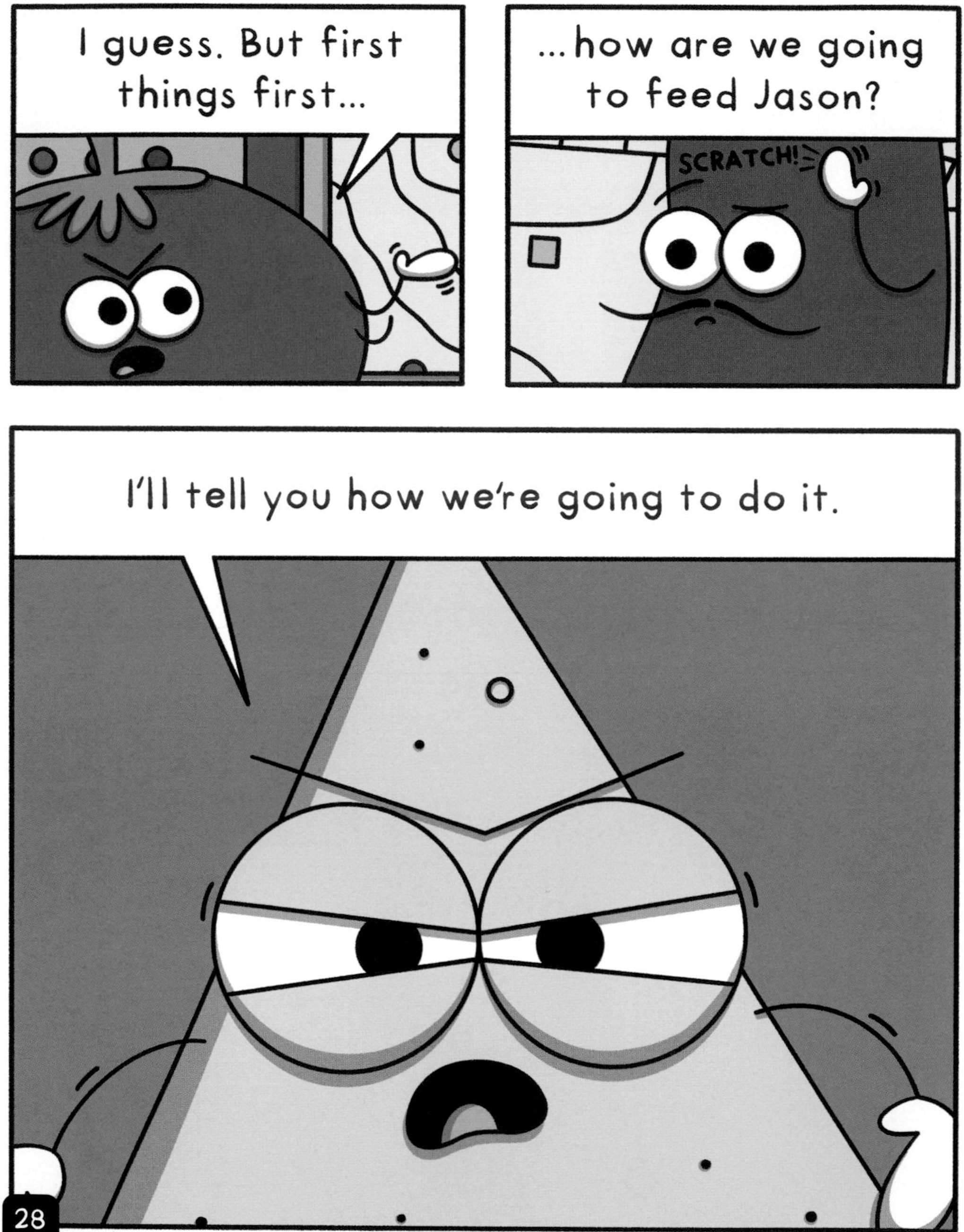
I guess. But first things first...
...how are we going to feed Jason?
SCRATCH!
I'll tell you how we're going to do it.

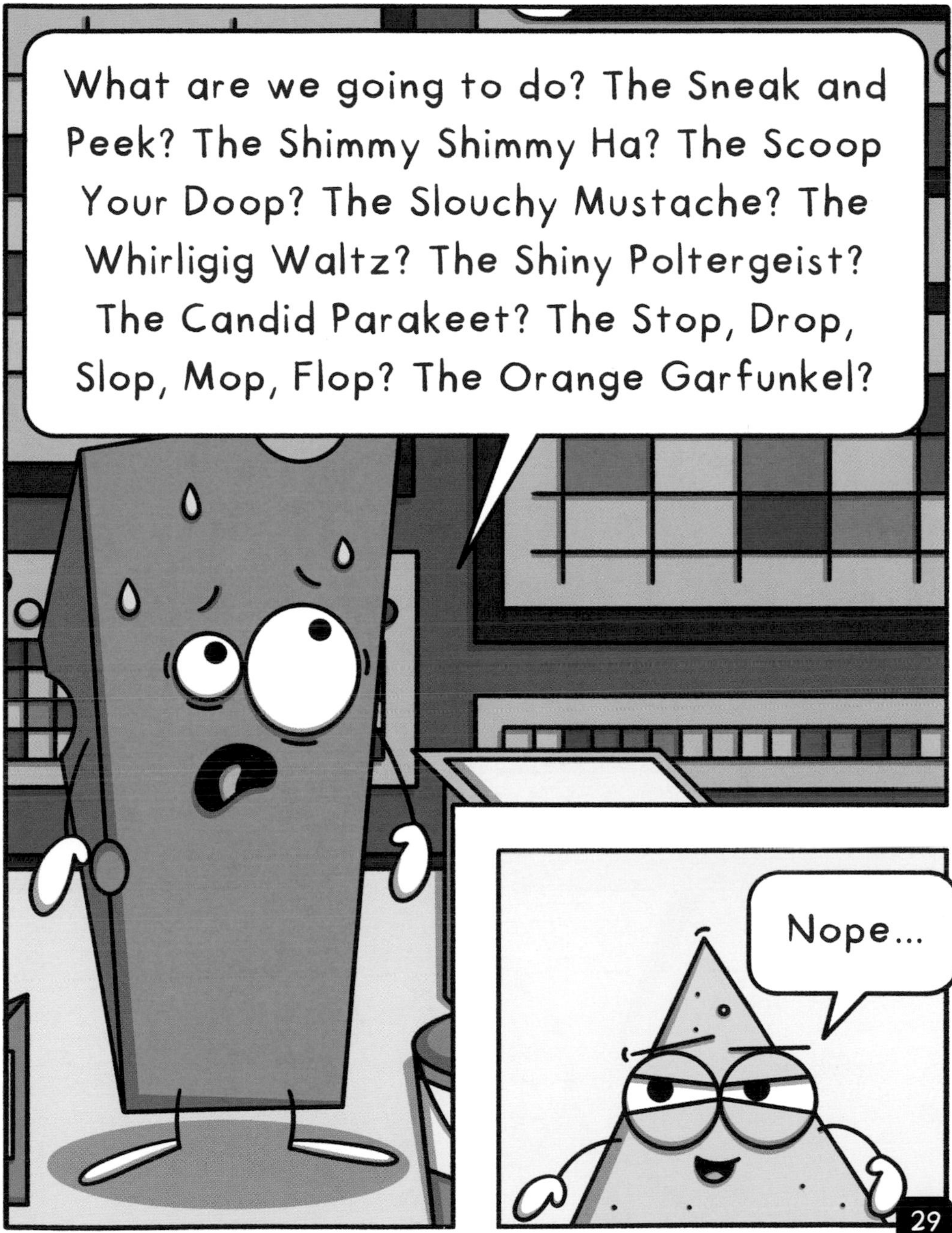
What are we going to do? The Sneak and Peek? The Shimmy Shimmy Ha? The Scoop Your Doop? The Slouchy Mustache? The Whirligig Waltz? The Shiny Poltergeist? The Candid Parakeet? The Stop, Drop, Slop, Mop, Flop? The Orange Garfunkel?
Nope...

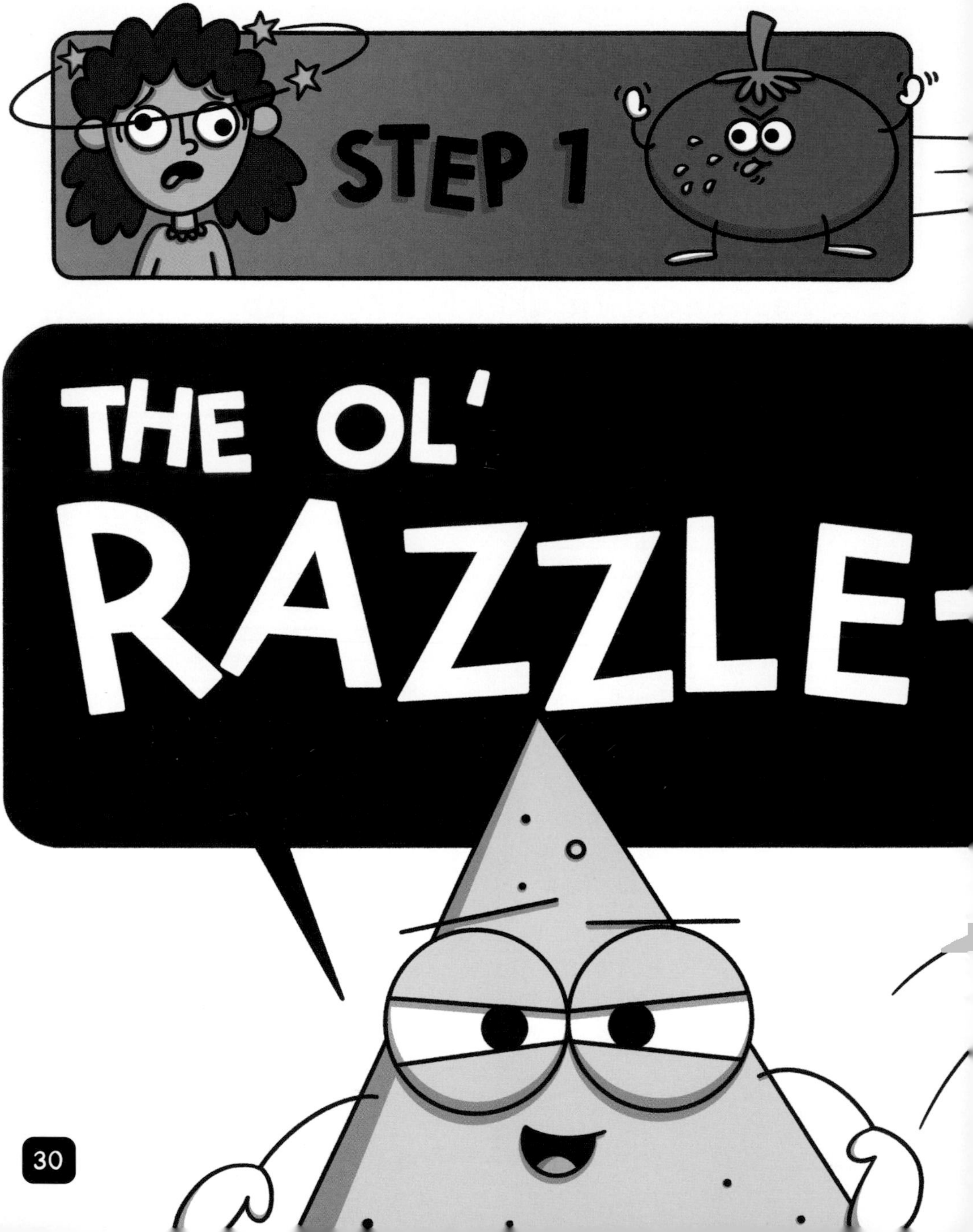
STEP 1
THE OL'
RAZZLE-

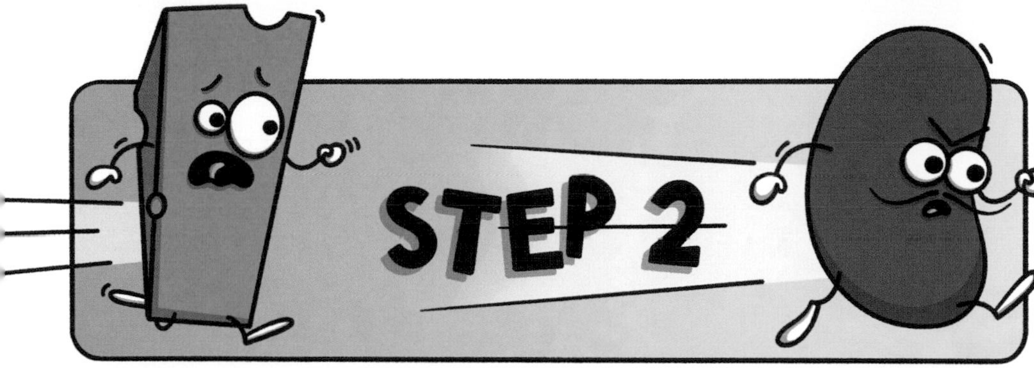
STEP 2

-DAZZLE

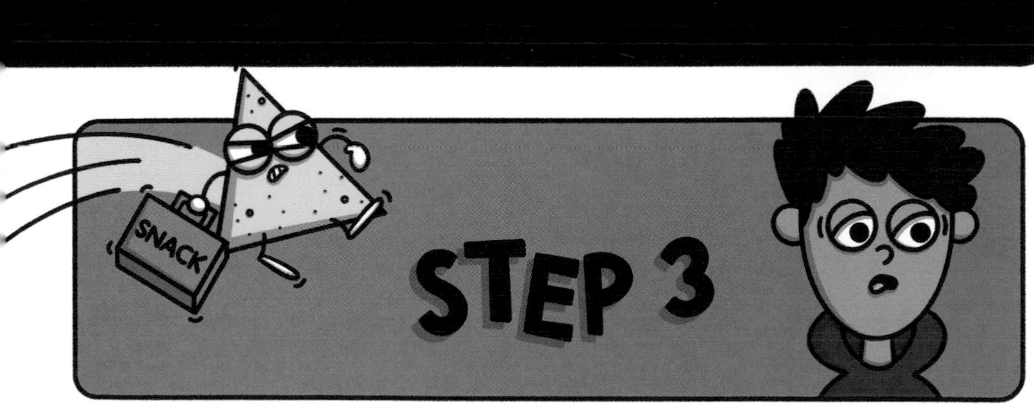
SNACK
STEP 3

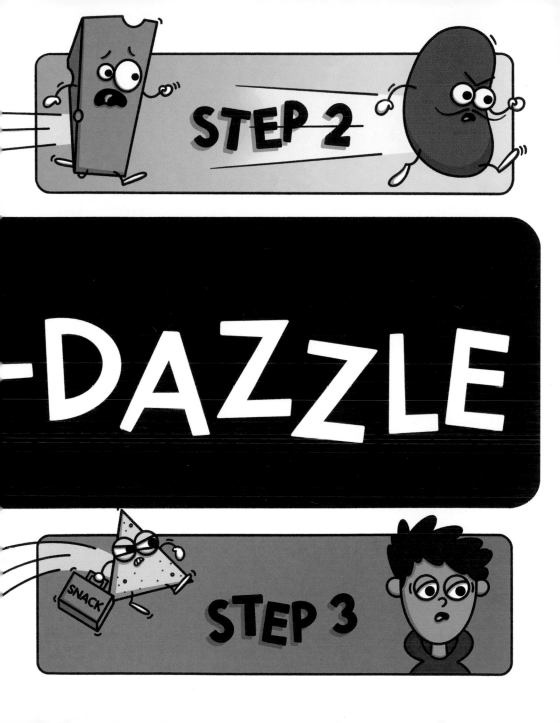

CHAPTER 3

The Hunger Heroes made it to the school in record time. Tammy lowered the Hovercraft and landed on the lawn.

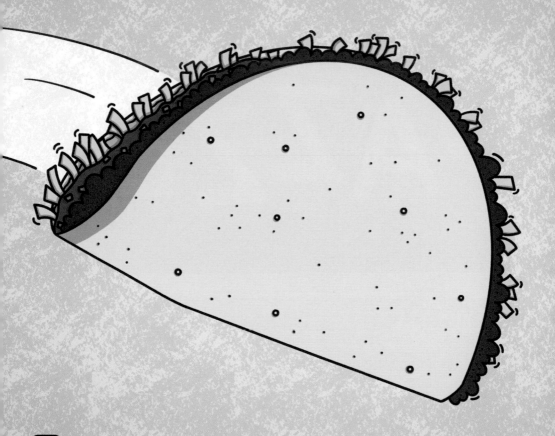

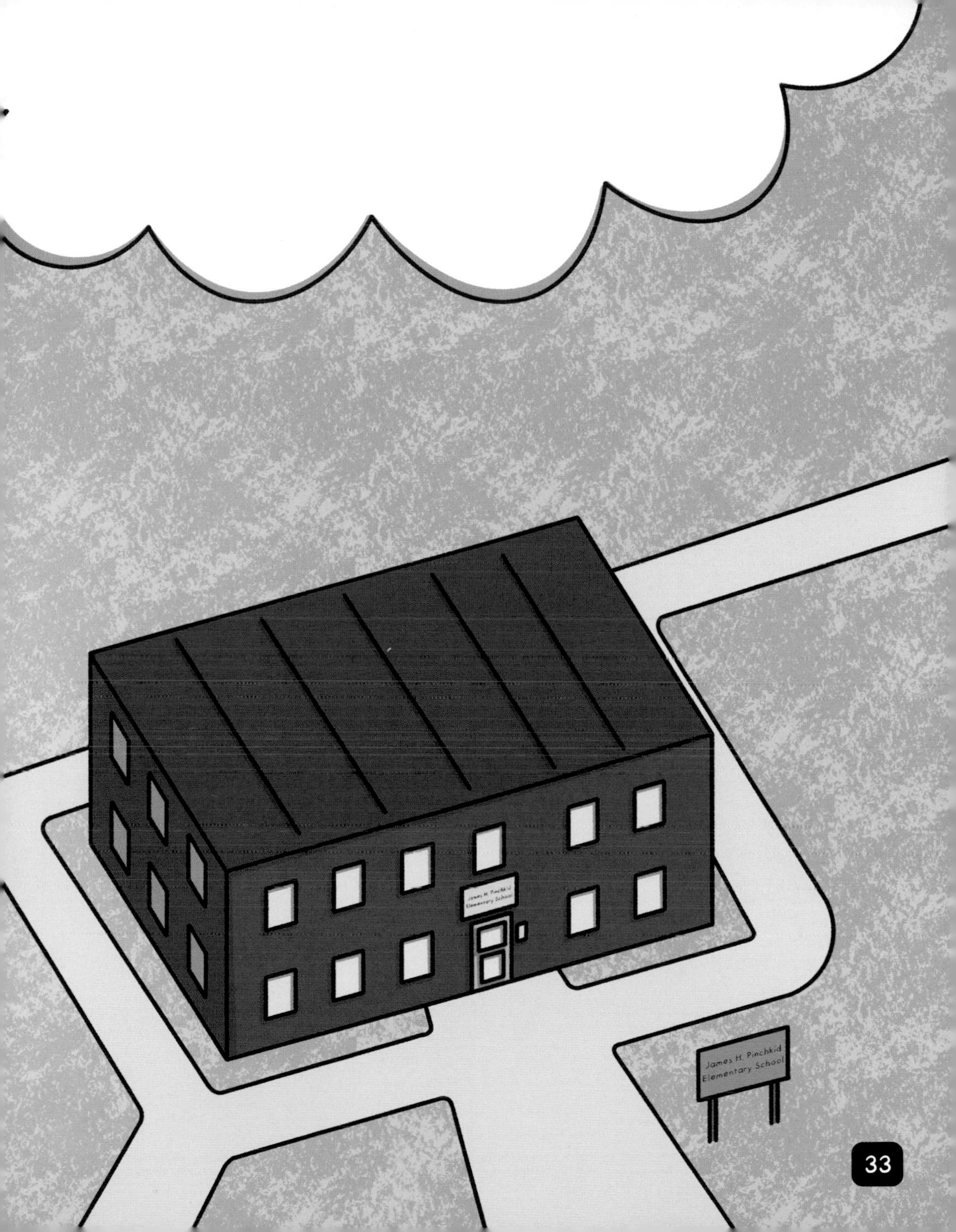
James H. Pinchkid
Elementary School

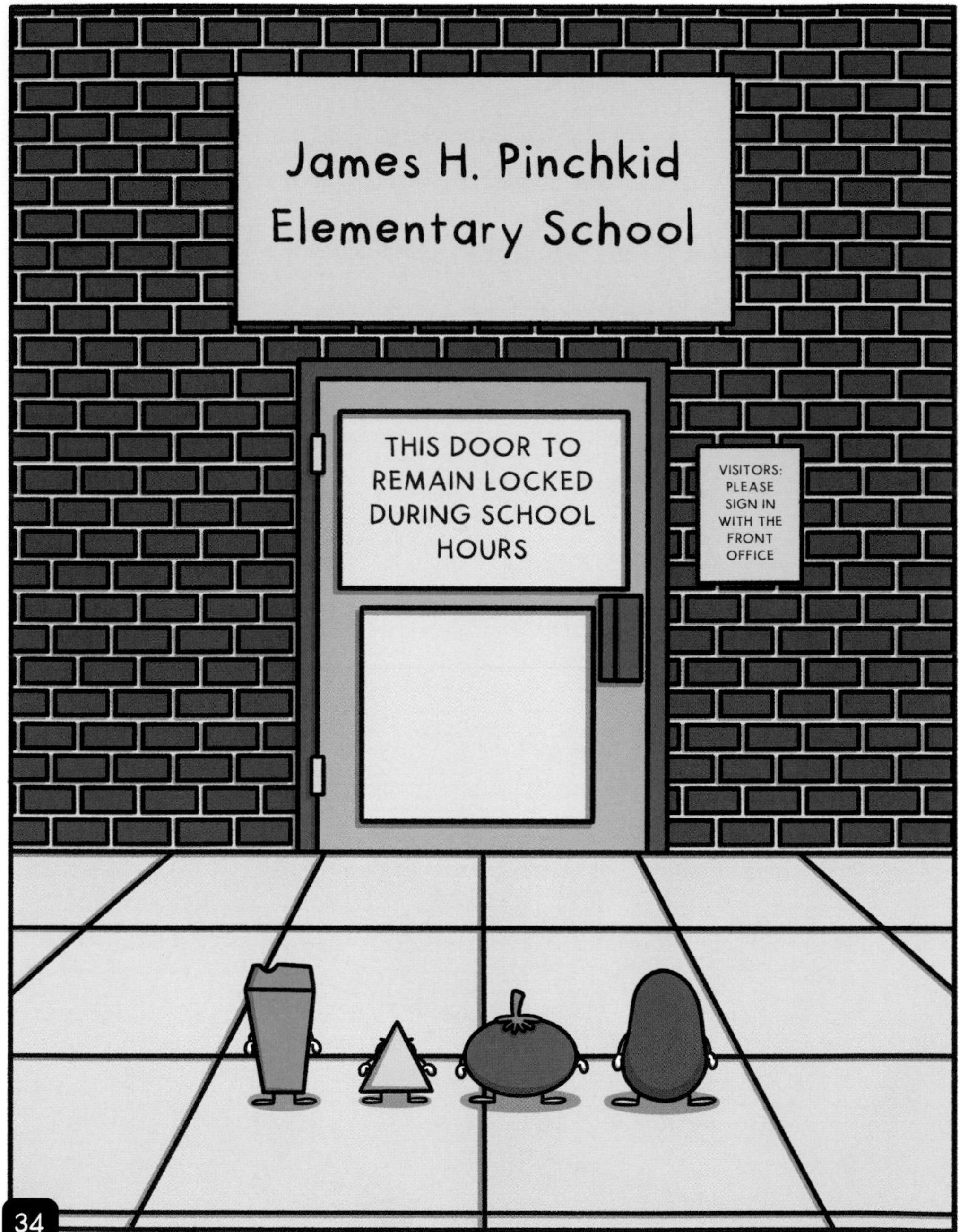
James H. Pinchkid
Elementary School
THIS DOOR TO
REMAIN LOCKED
DURING SCHOOL
HOURS
VISITORS:
PLEASE
SIGN IN
WITH THE
FRONT
OFFICE

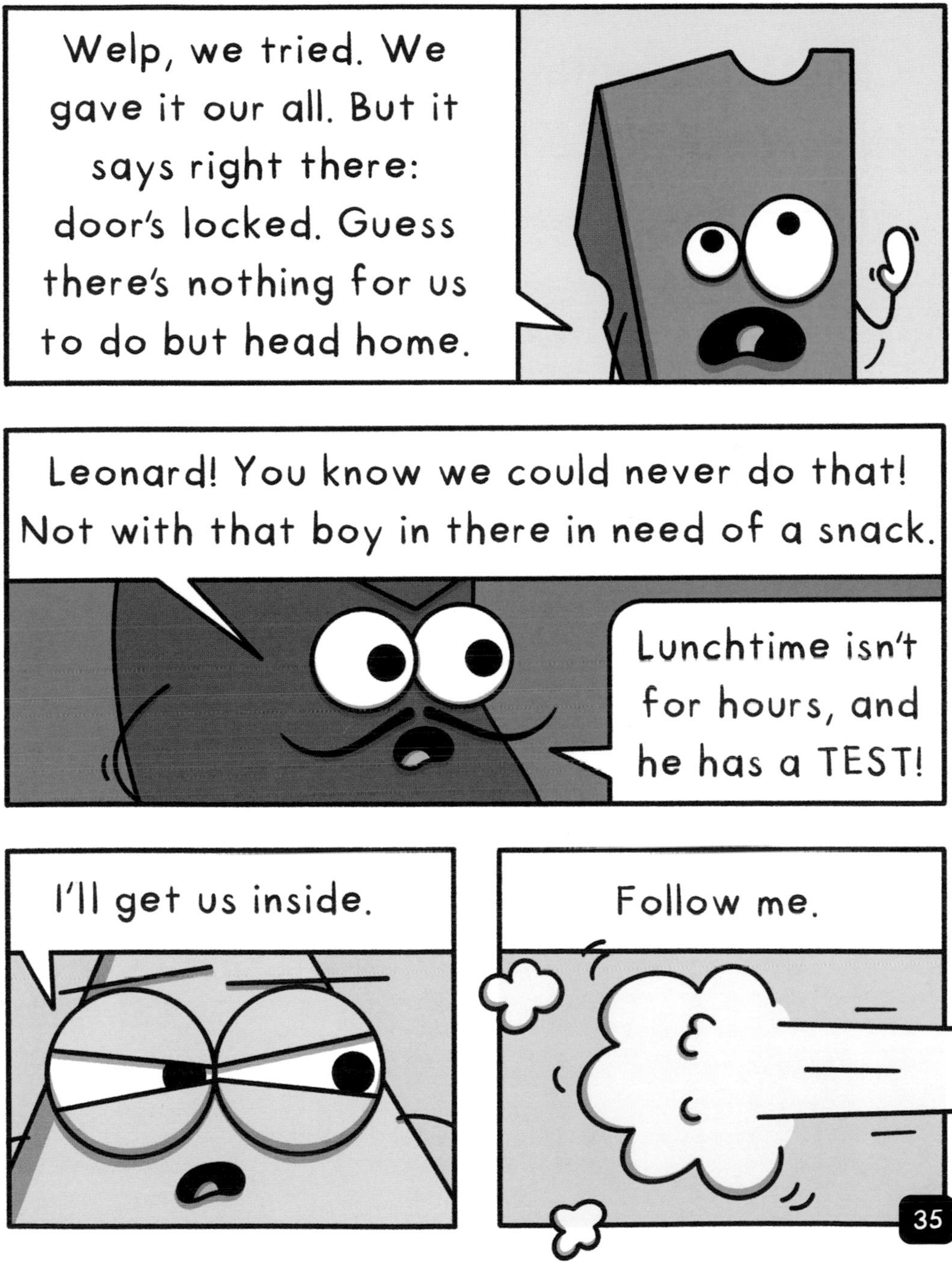
Welp, we tried. We gave it our all. But it says right there: door's locked. Guess there's nothing for us to do but head home.
Leonard! You know we could never do that! Not with that boy in there in need of a snack.
Lunchtime isn't for hours, and he has a TEST!
I'll get us inside.
Follow me.

Chip Ninja led the others around to the side of the building until she found what she was looking for.

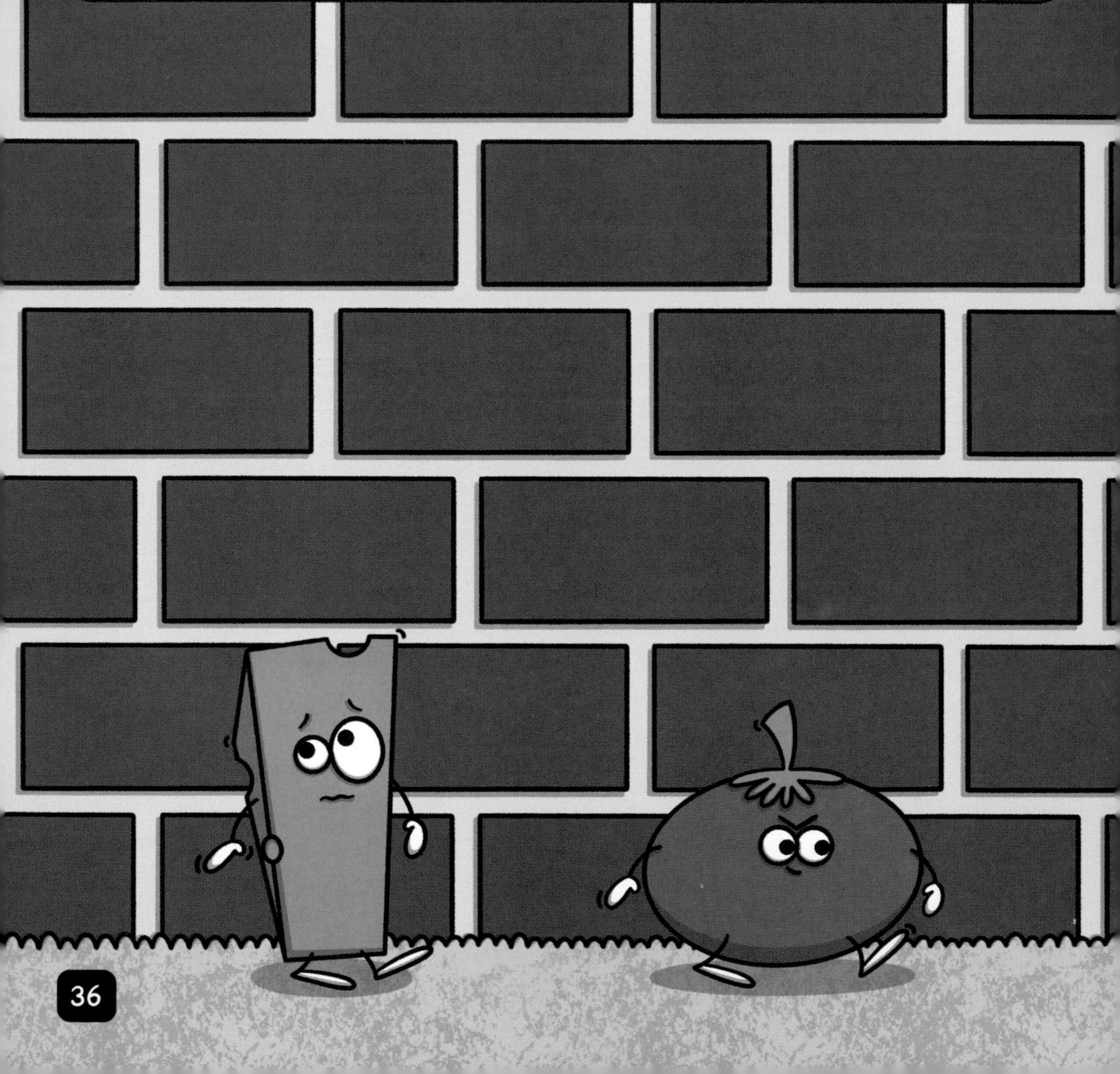

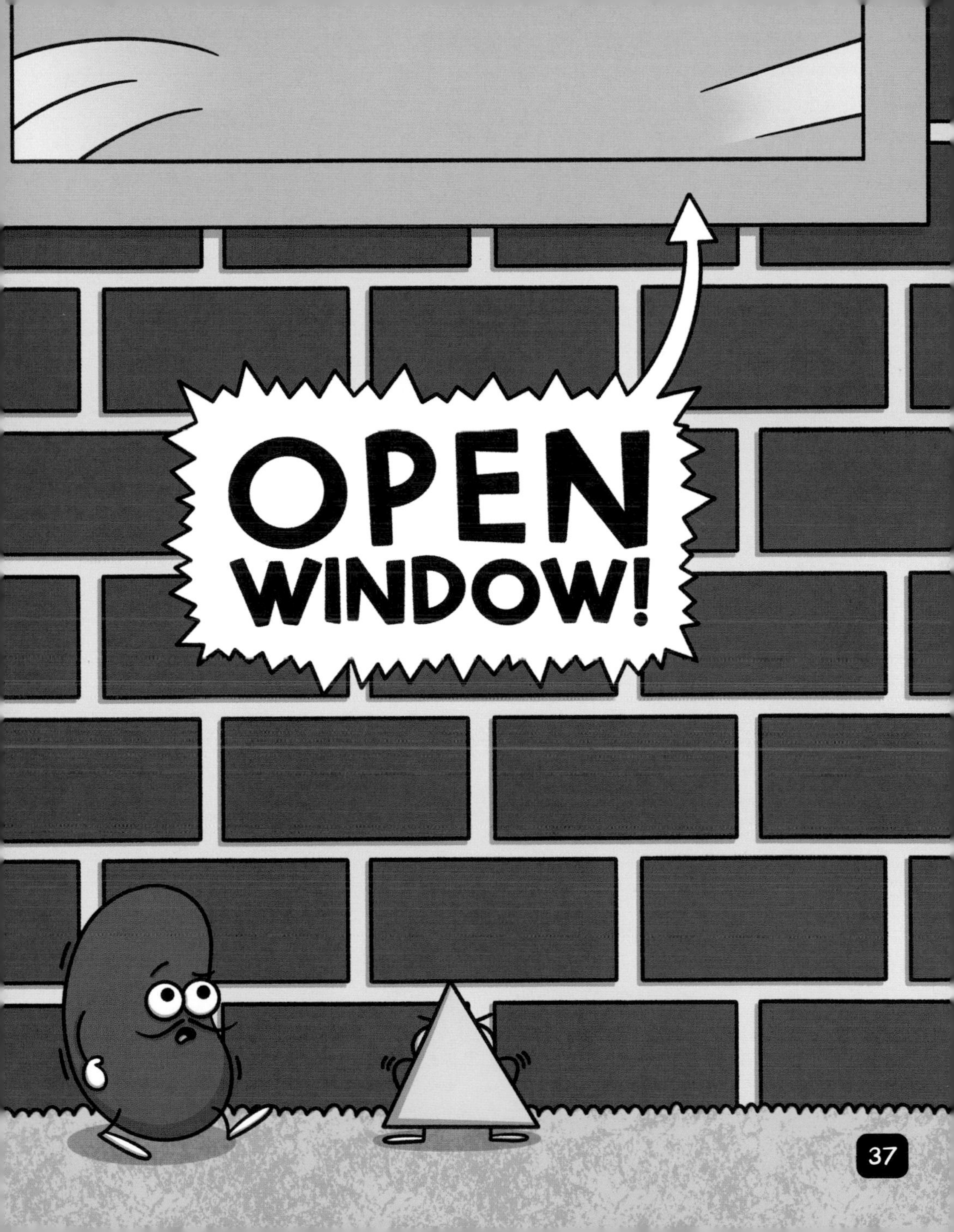
OPEN
WINDOW!

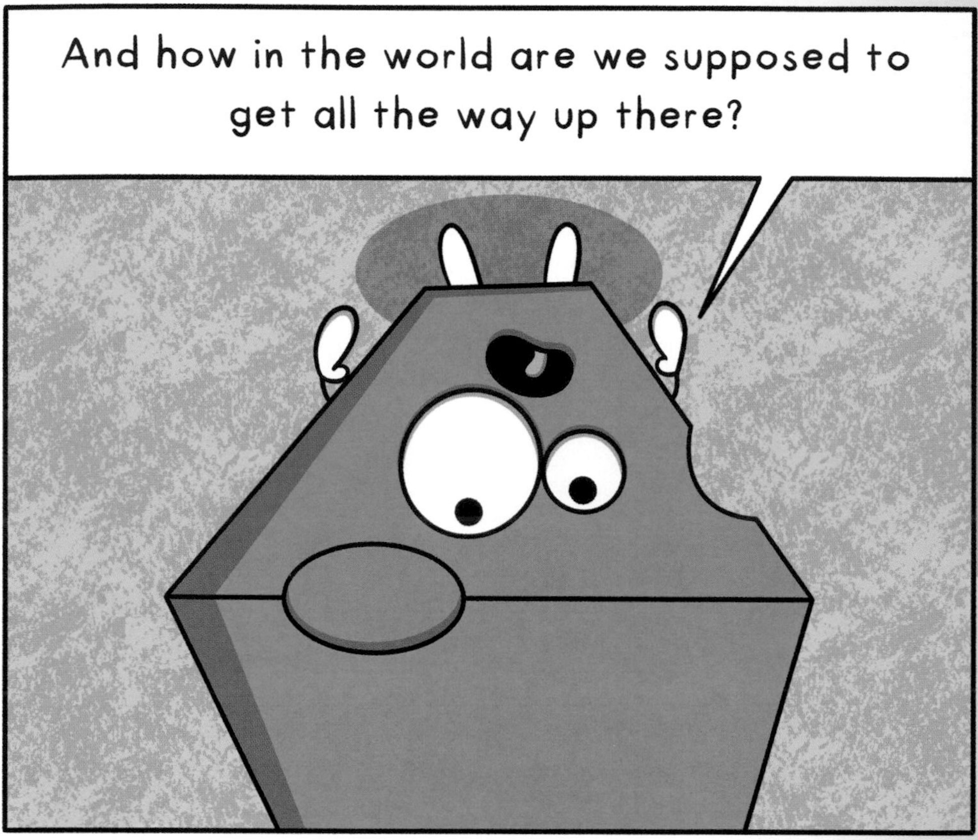
And how in the world are we supposed to get all the way up there?

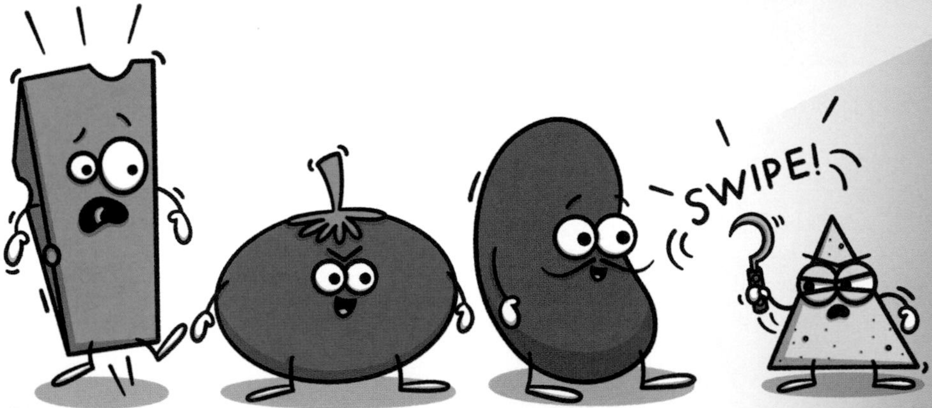
SWIPE!

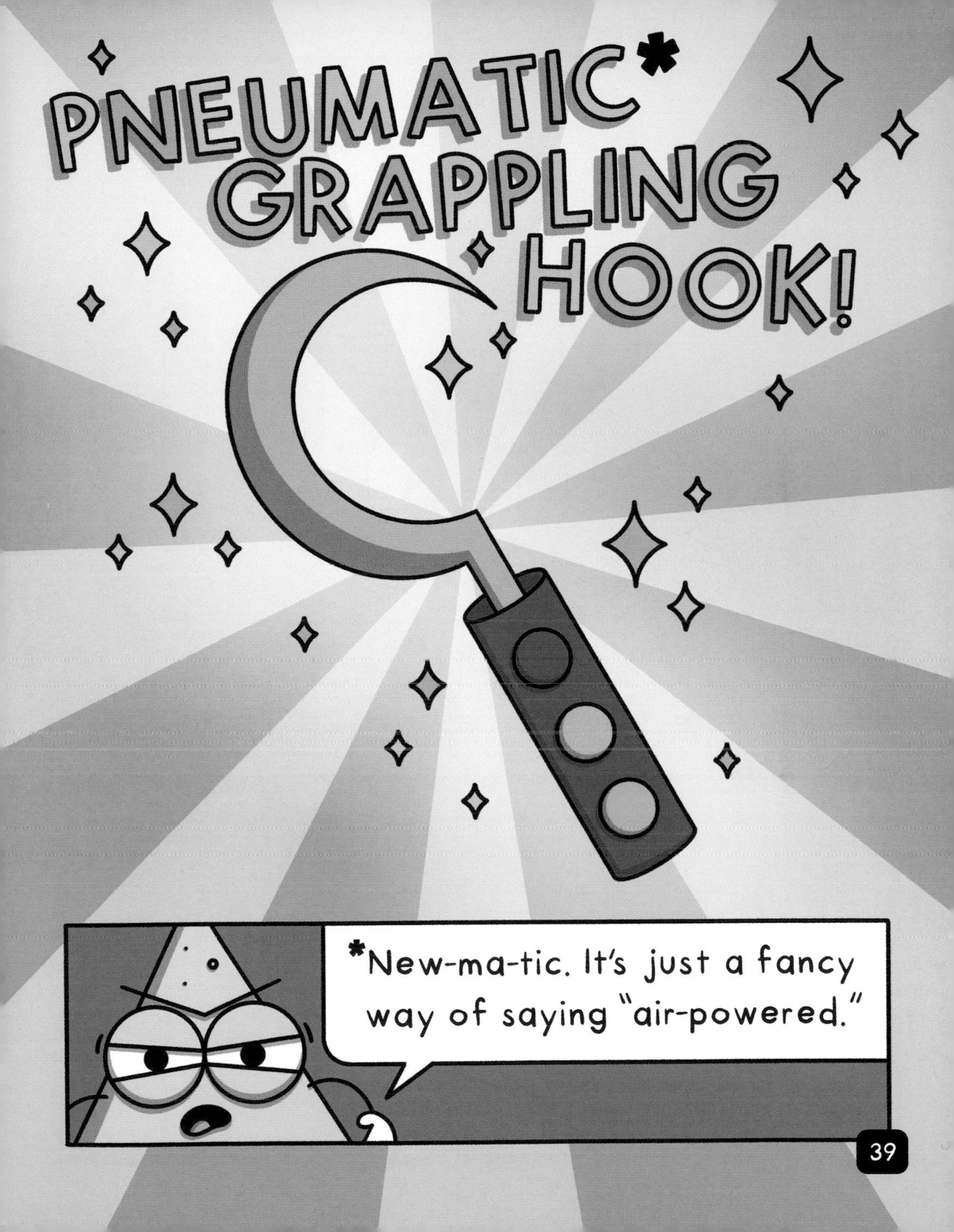
PNEUMATIC* GRAPPLING HOOK!
*New-ma-tic. It's just a fancy way of saying "air-powered."

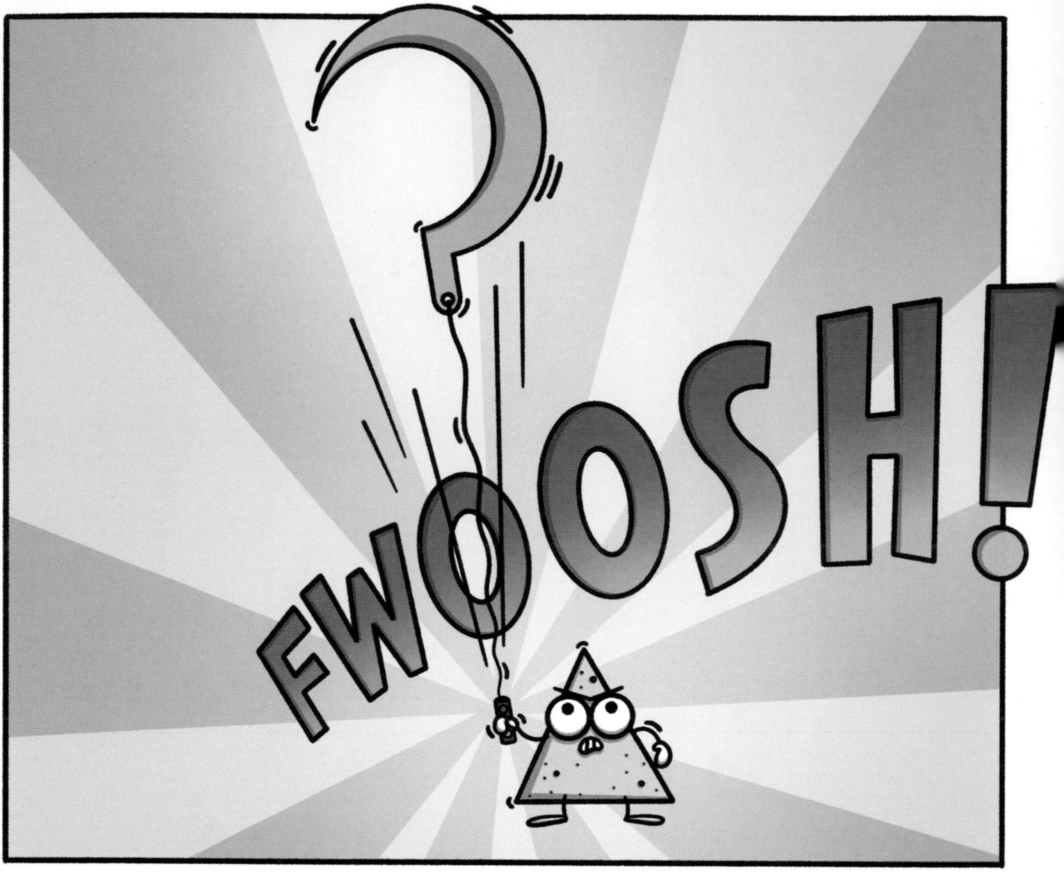
FWOOSH!

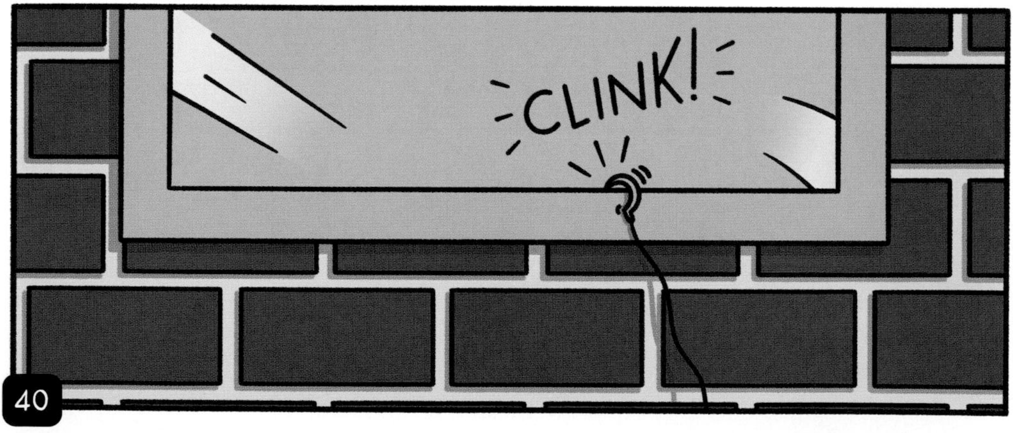
CLINK!

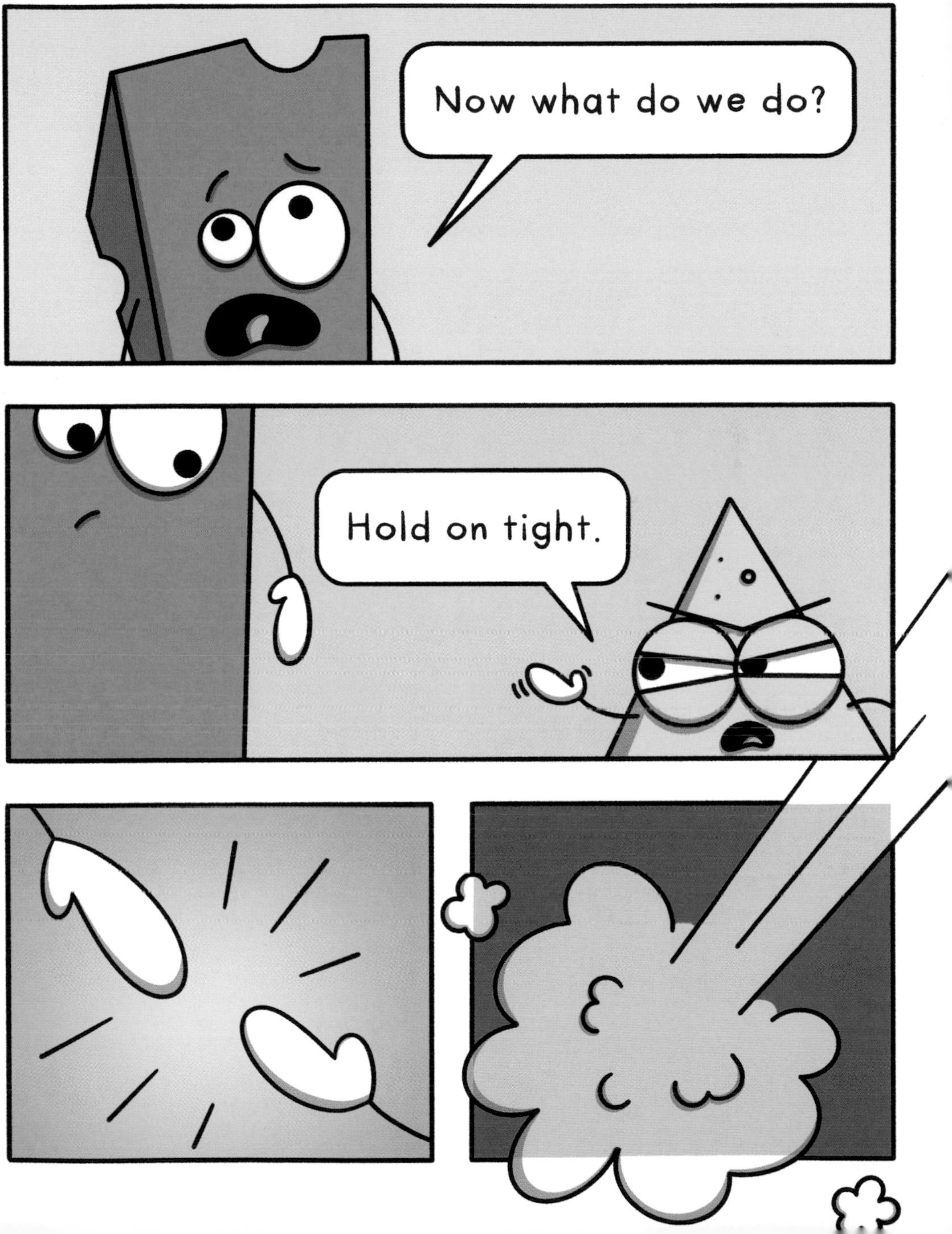
Now what do we do?
Hold on tight.

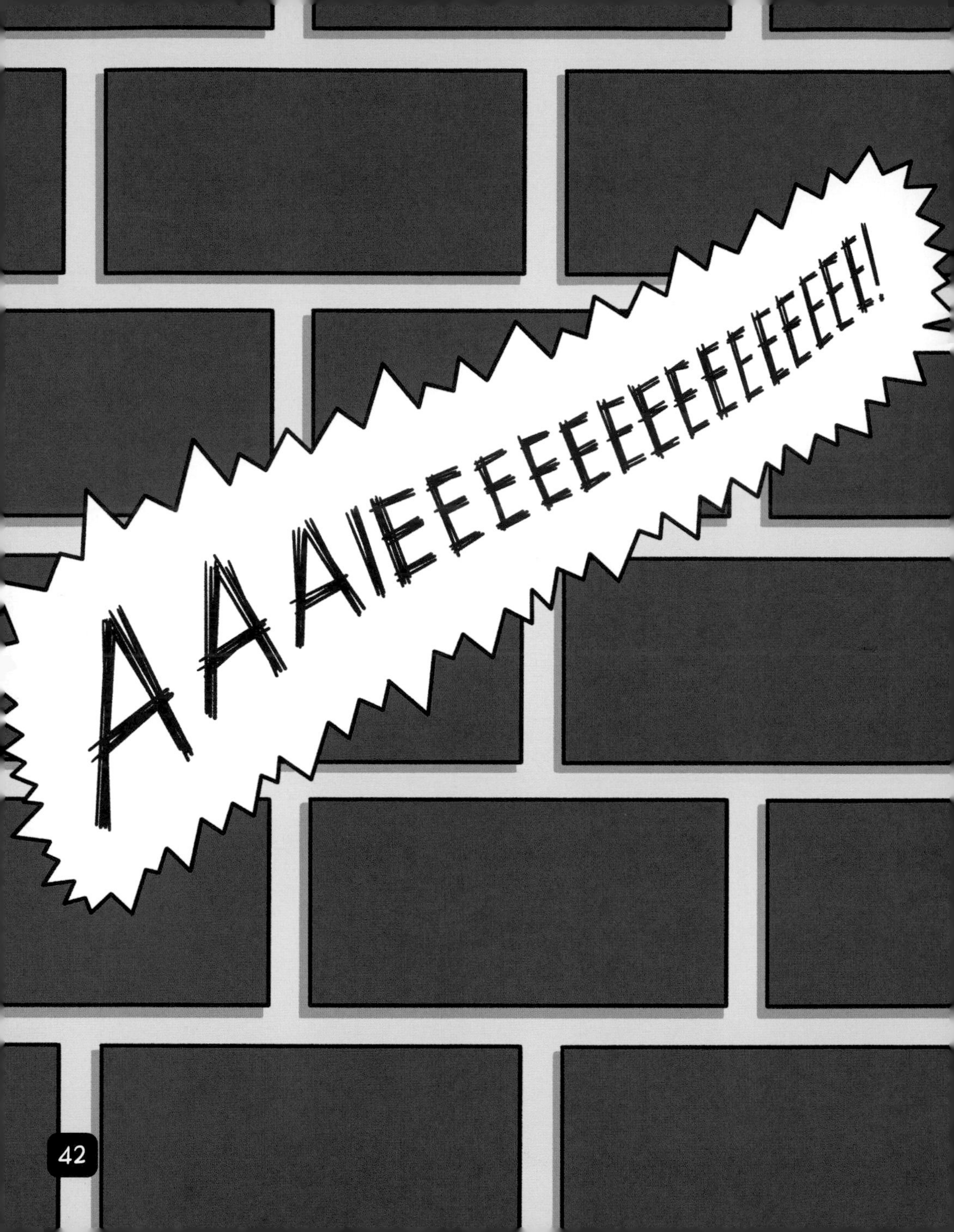
AAAIEEEEEEEEEEEEEE!

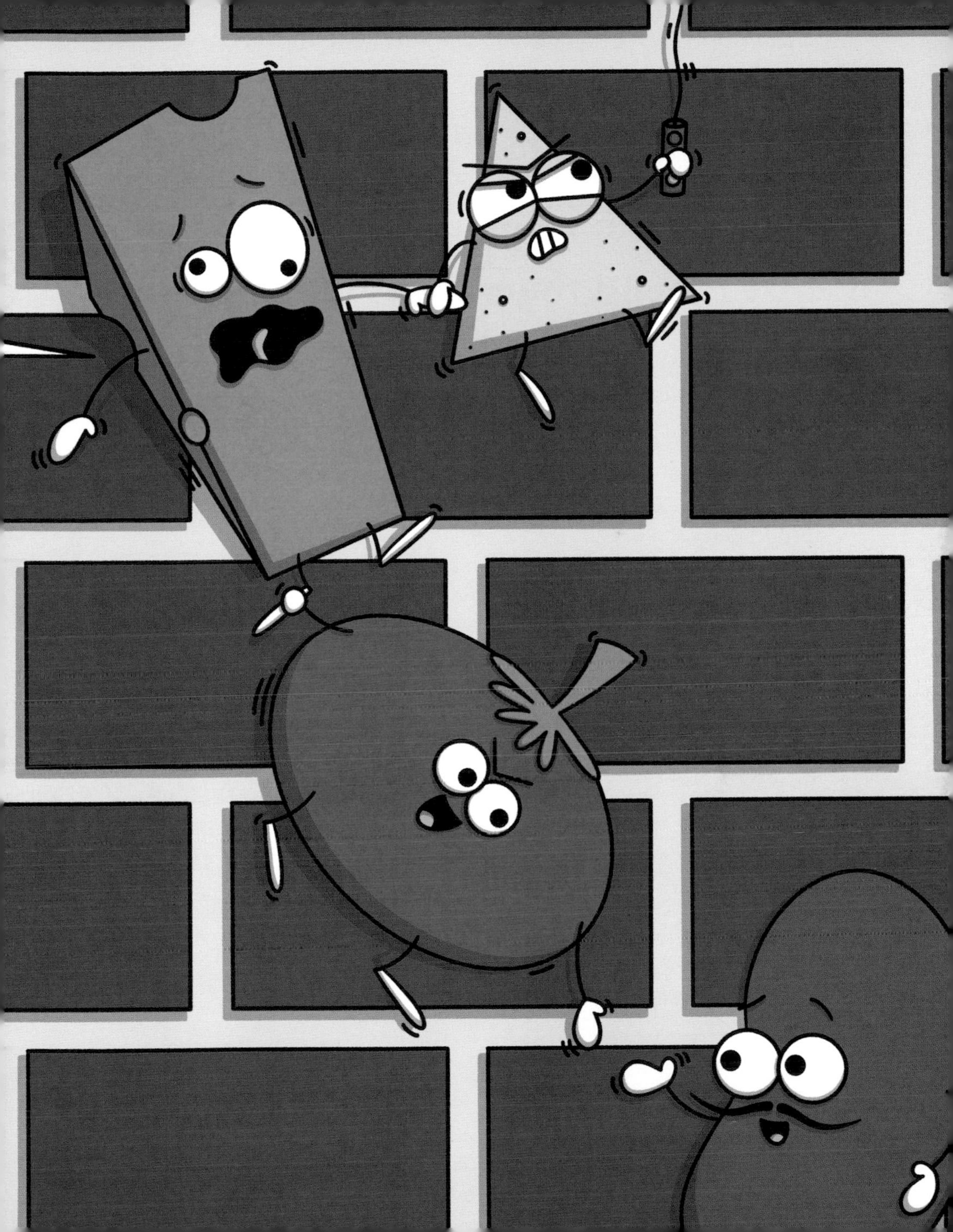

CHAPTER 4

Perched on the windowsill, the Hunger Heroes found themselves looking in on something entirely unexpected.

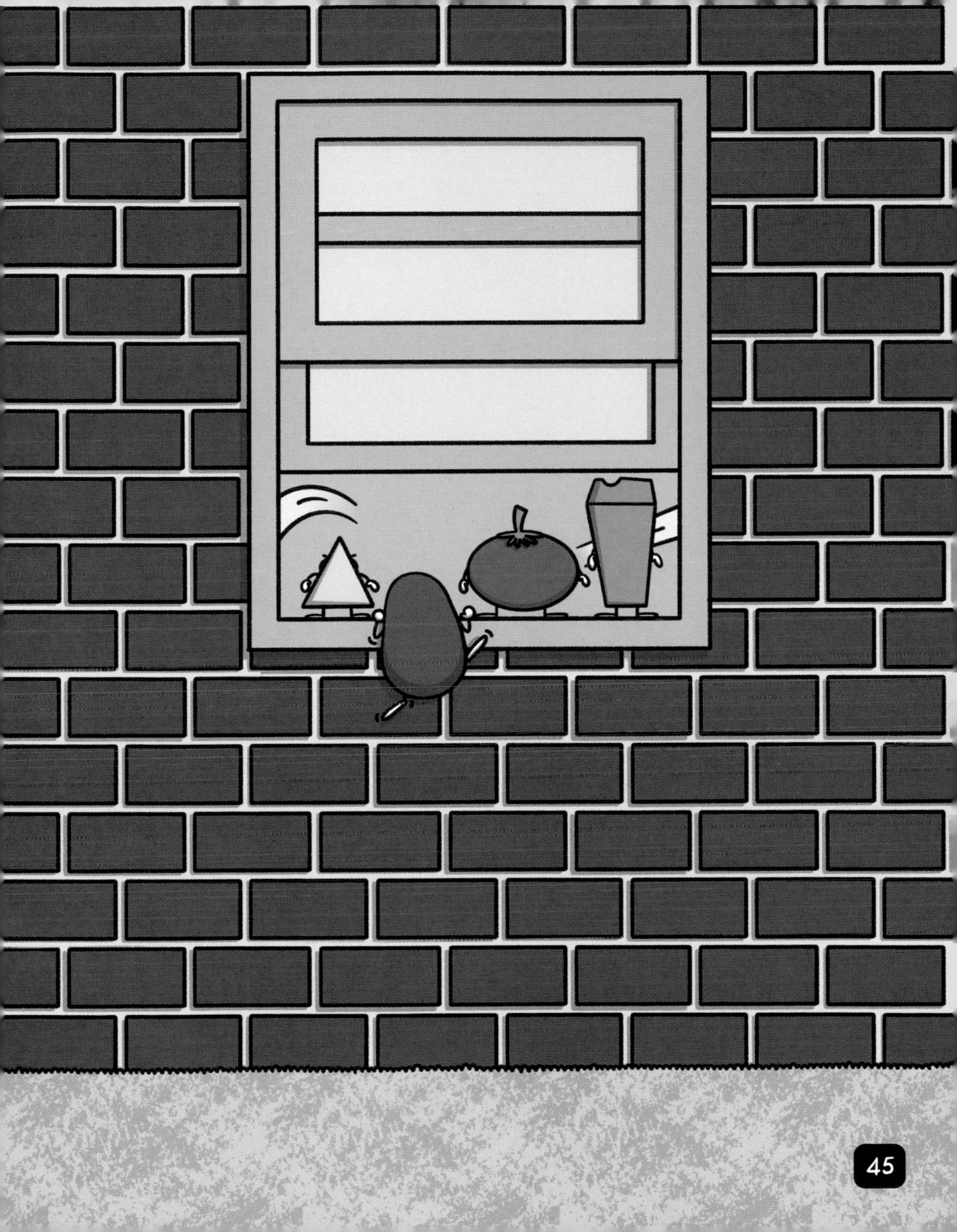

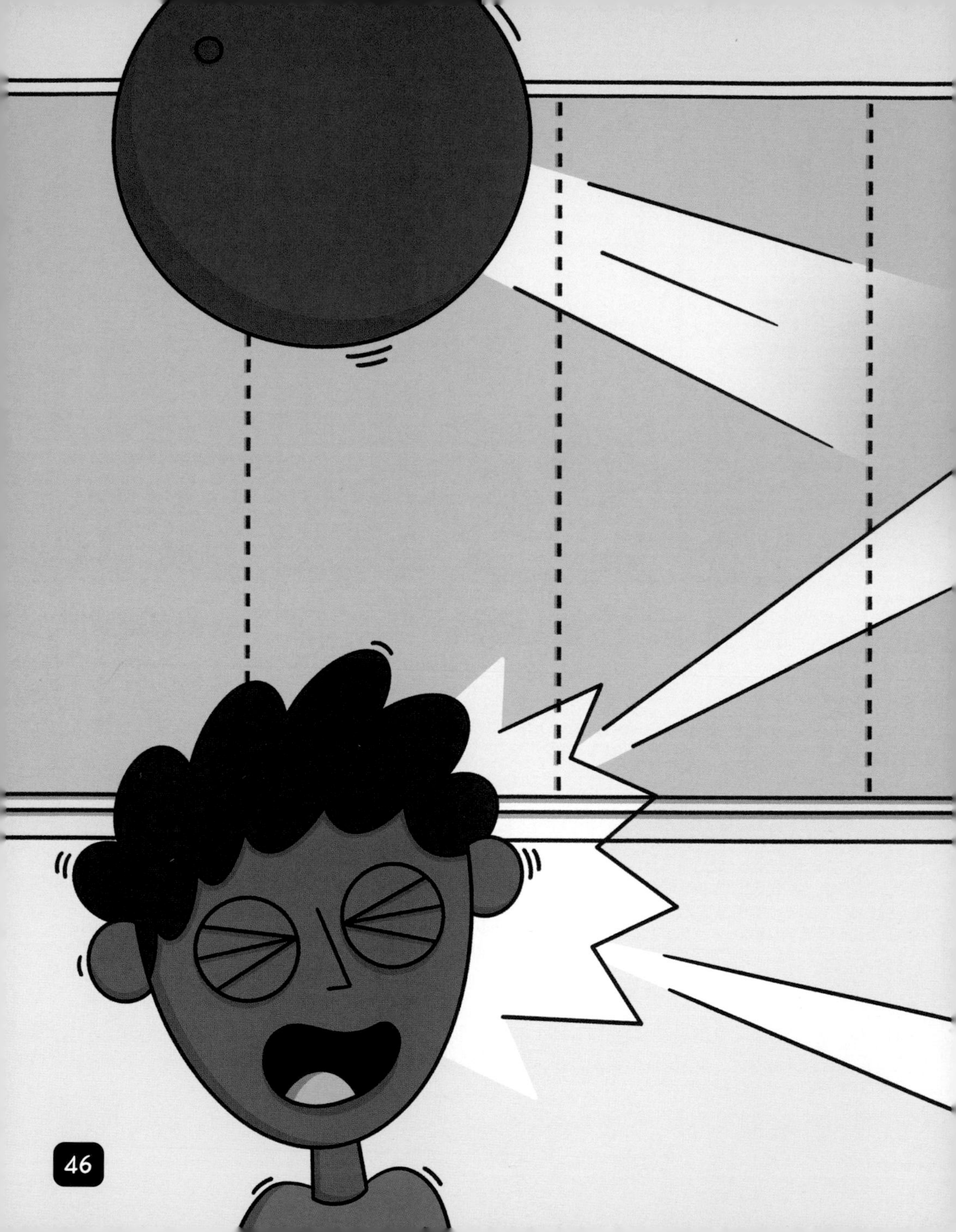

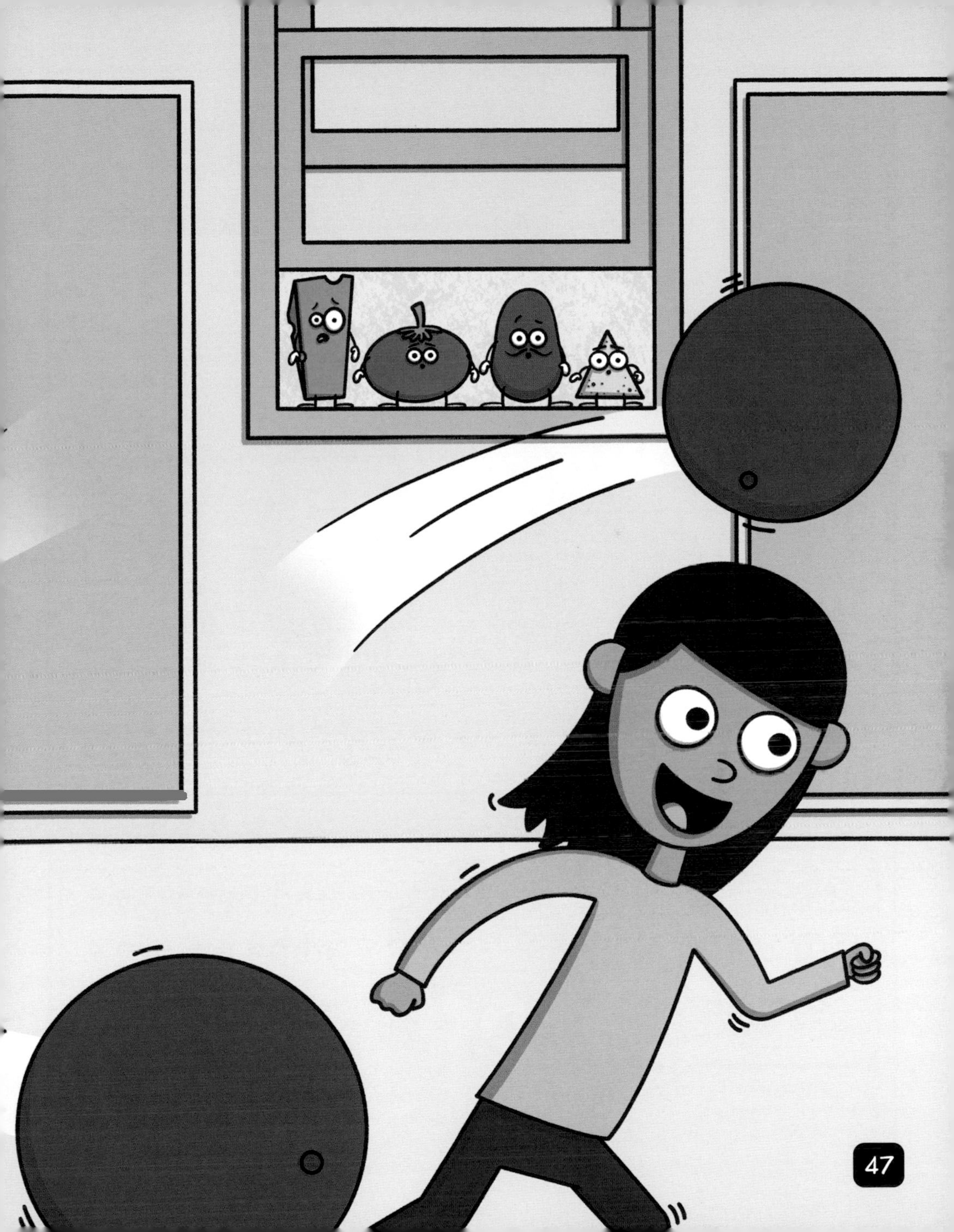

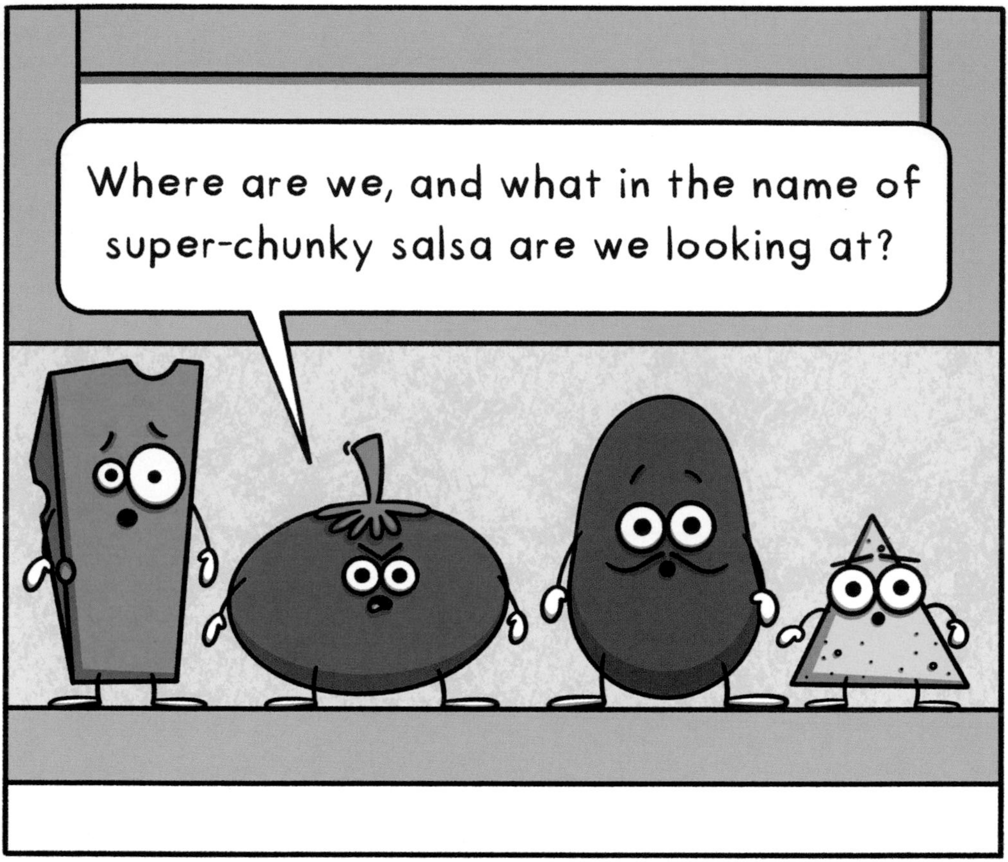
Where are we, and what in the name of super-chunky salsa are we looking at?

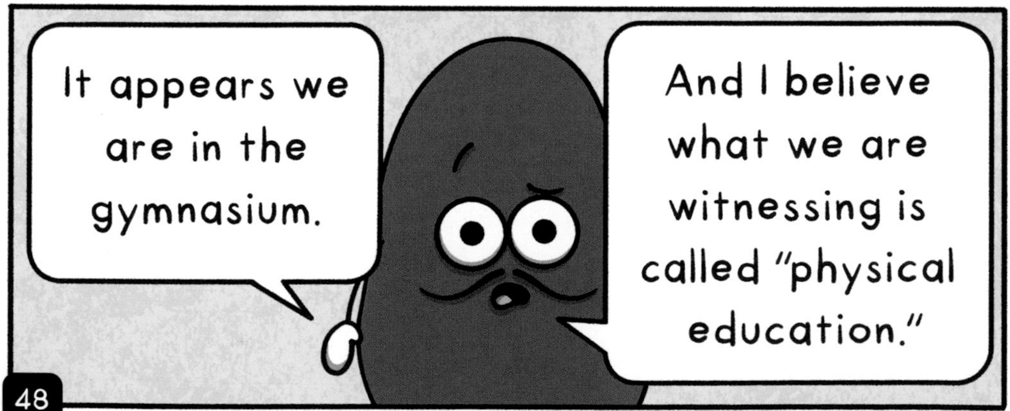
It appears we are in the gymnasium.
And I believe what we are witnessing is called "physical education."

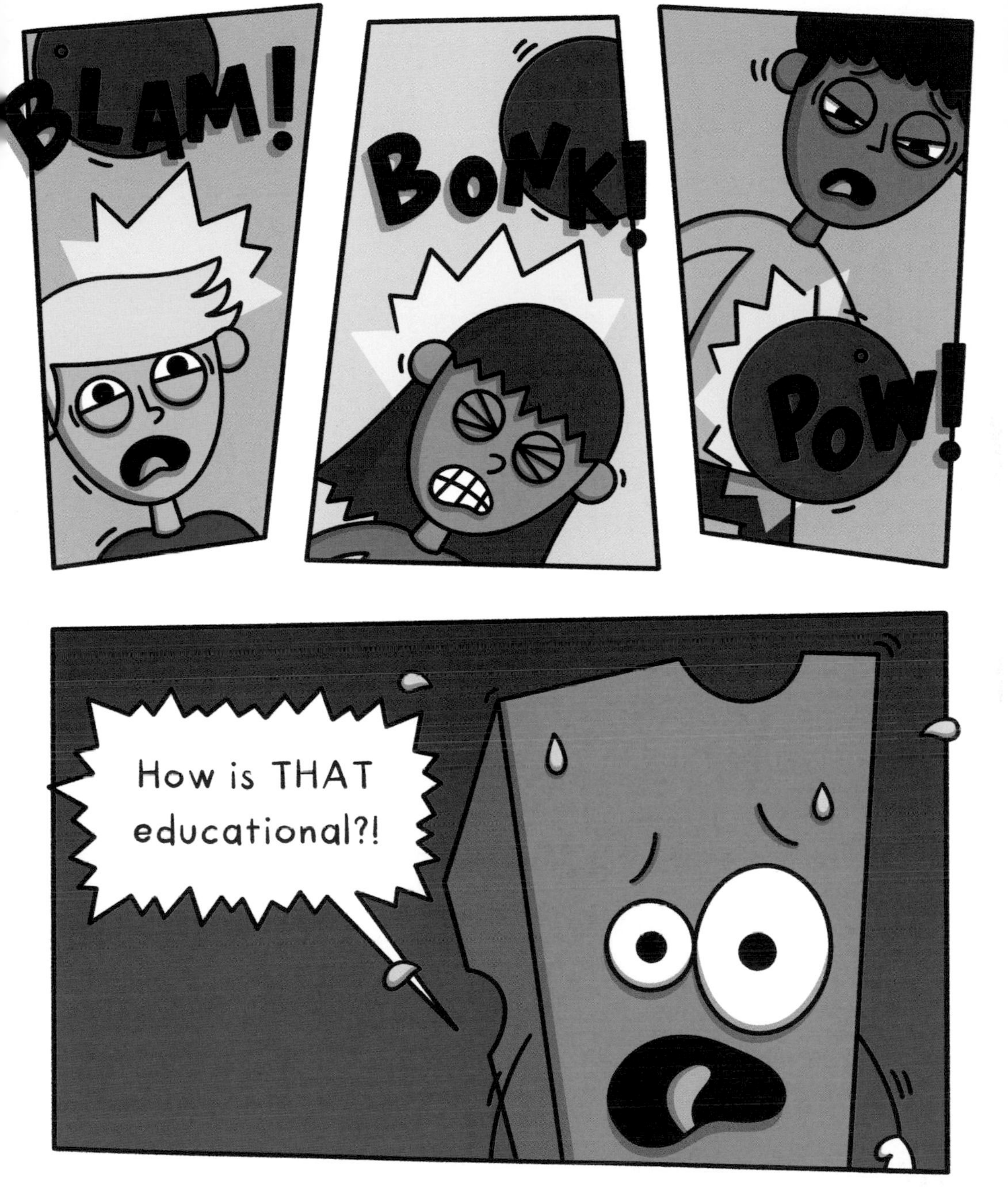
BLAM!
BONK!
POW!
How is THAT educational?!

For the first time in a long time, the Hunger Heroes were baffled about what their next step should be.

"Should we look for a different way into the school?" Tammy asked.

Leonard nodded.

But Chip Ninja nixed that suggestion just a second later.

"There's no time," she said. "Jason needs us NOW."

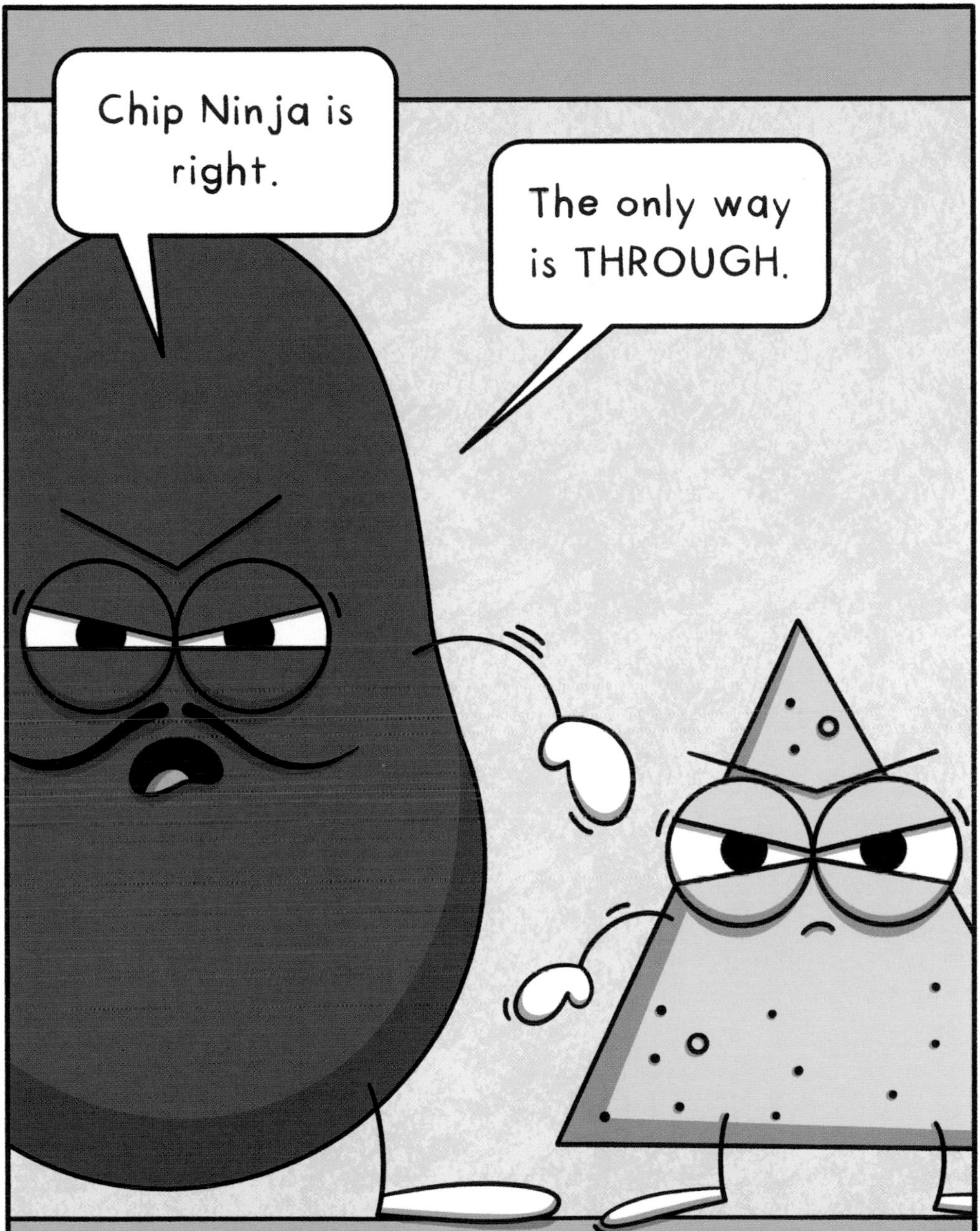
Chip Ninja is right.
The only way is THROUGH.

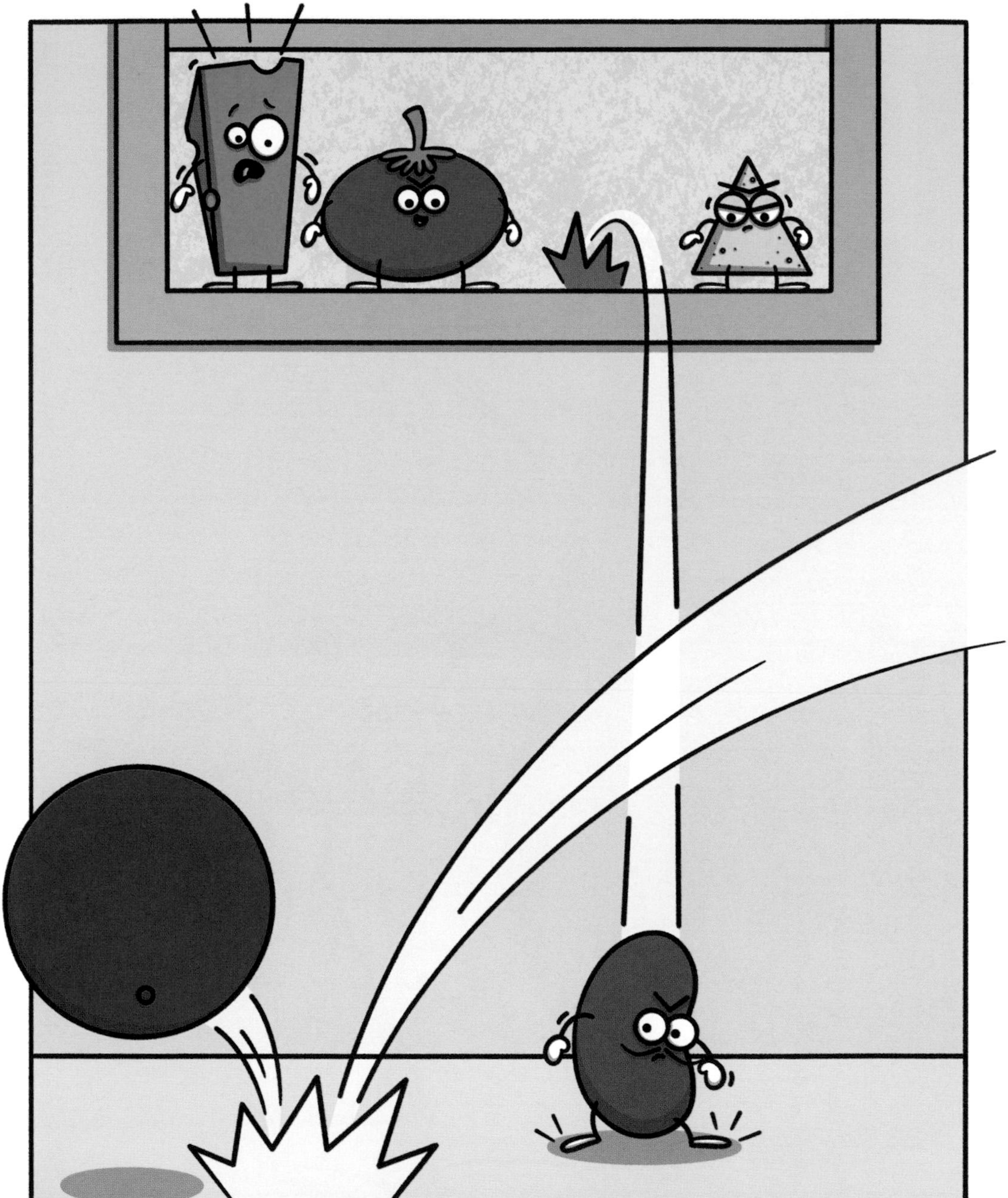

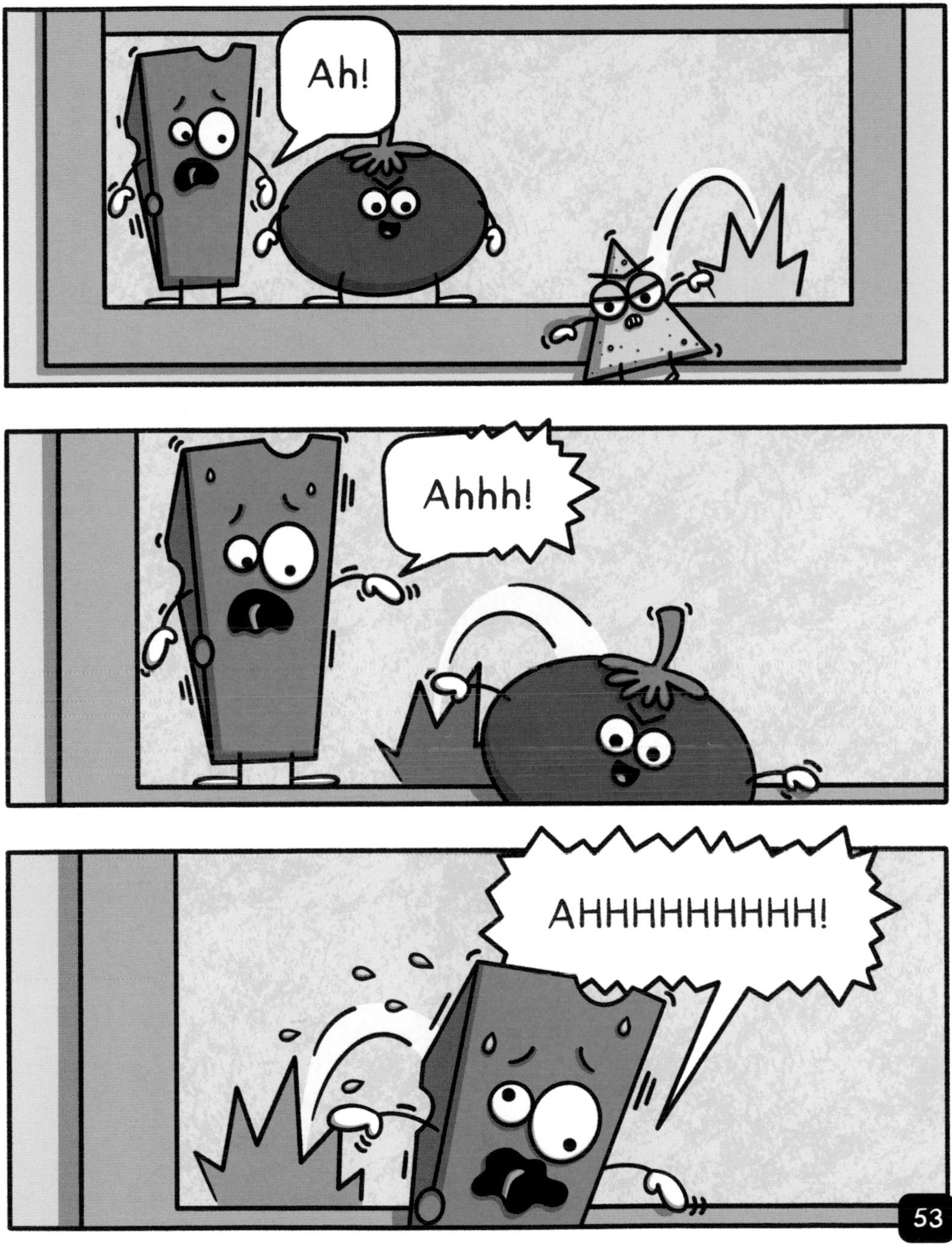
Ah!
Ahhh!
AHHHHHHHHH!

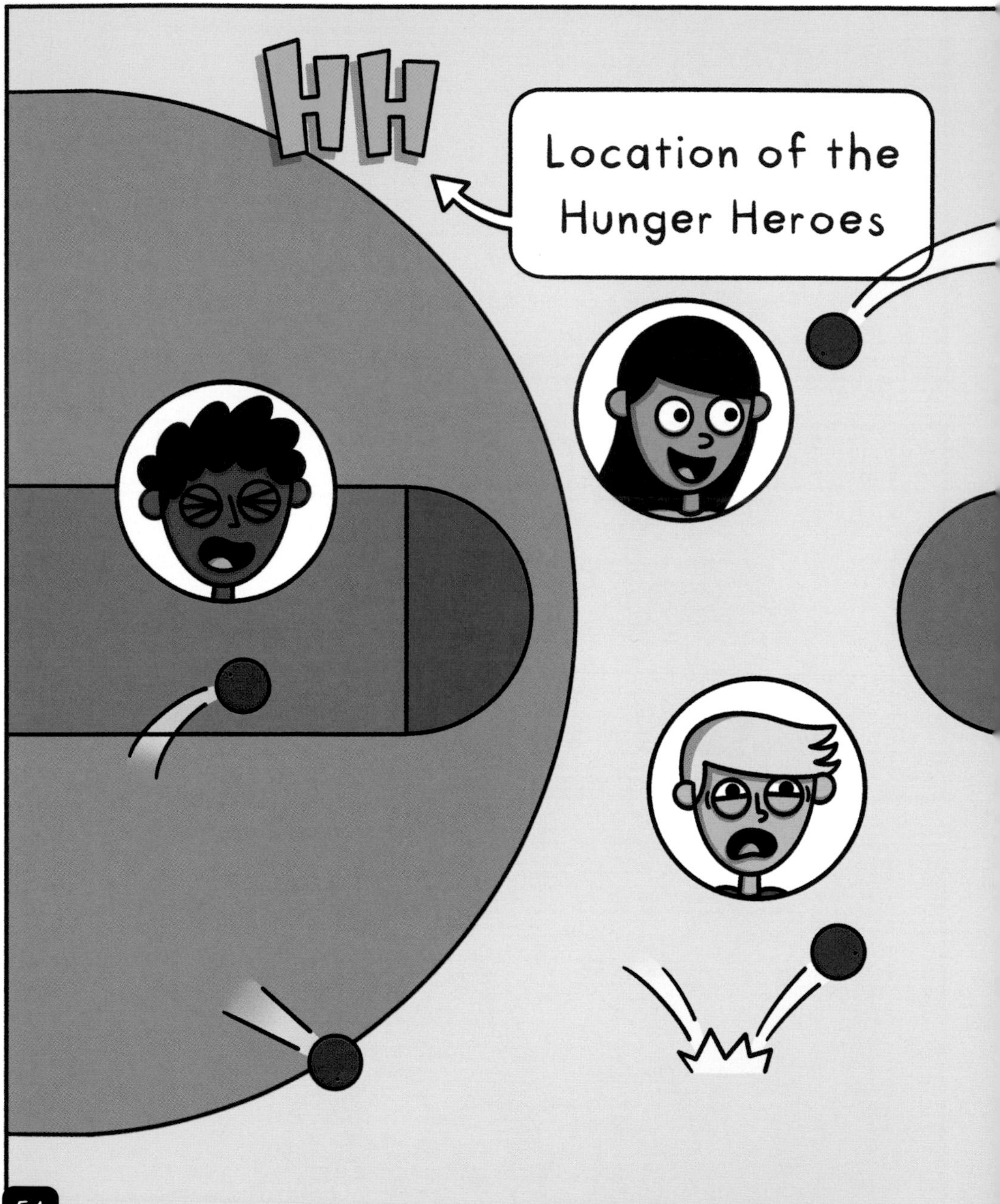
HH
Location of the Hunger Heroes

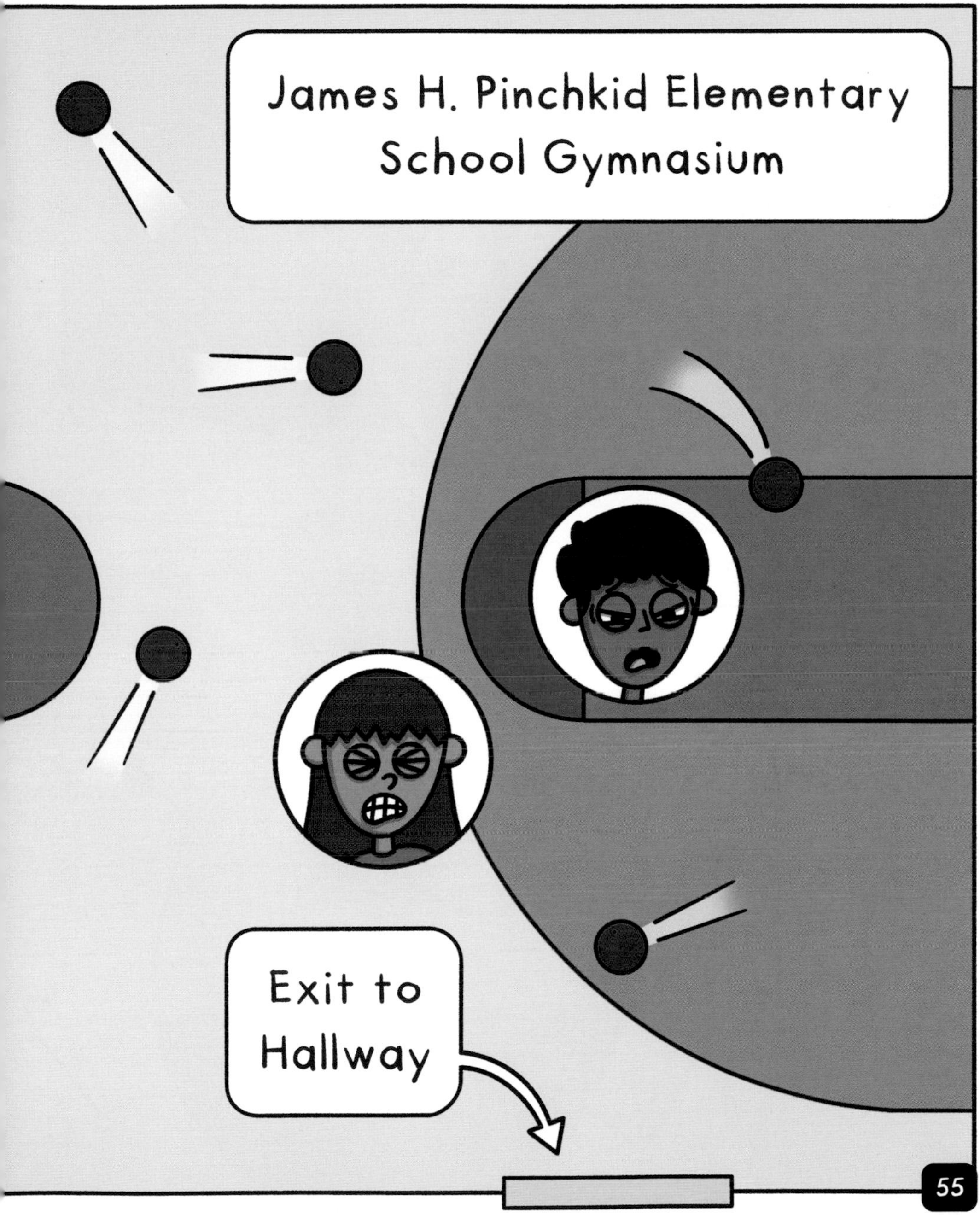
James H. Pinchkid Elementary School Gymnasium
Exit to Hallway

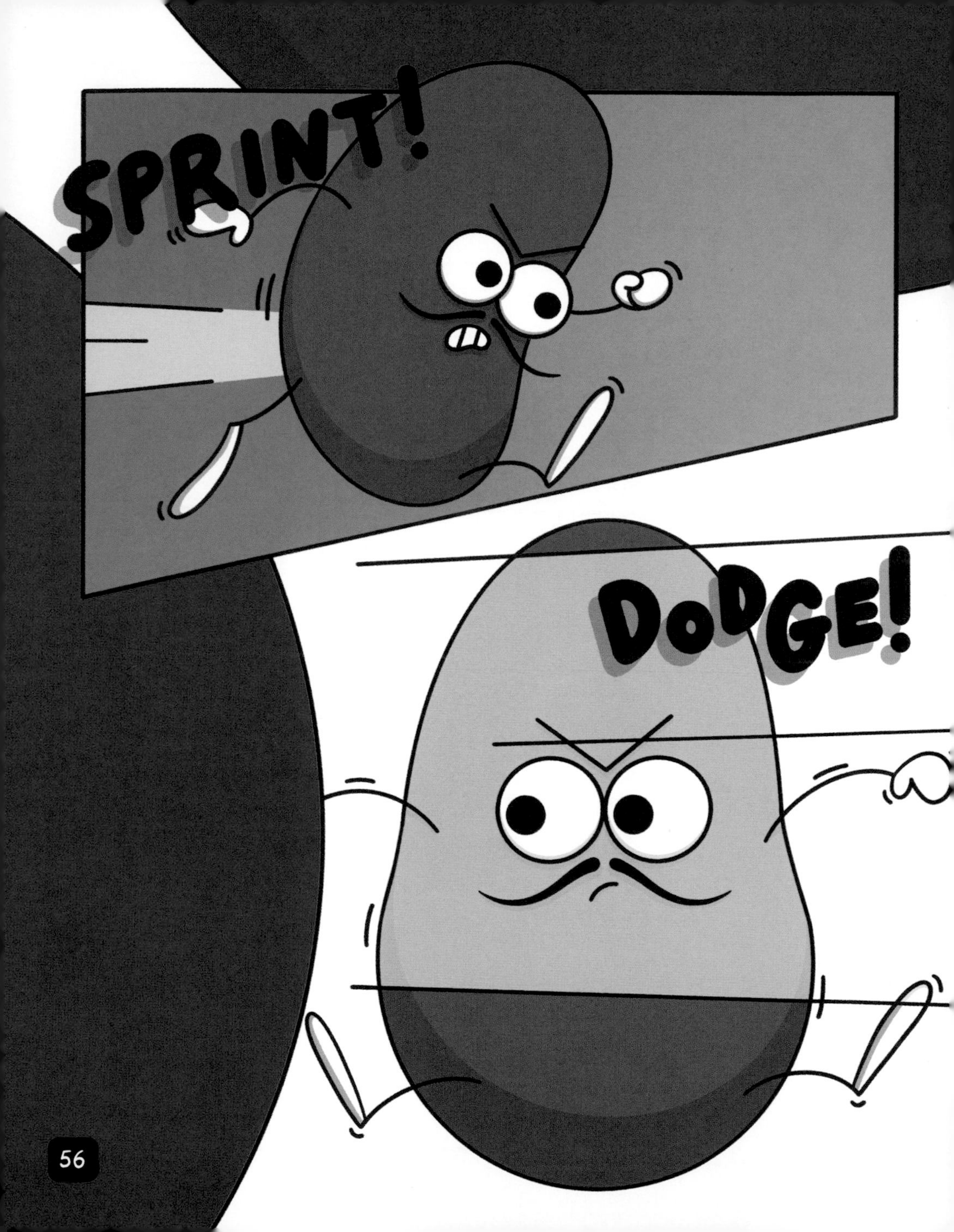
SPRINT!
DODGE!

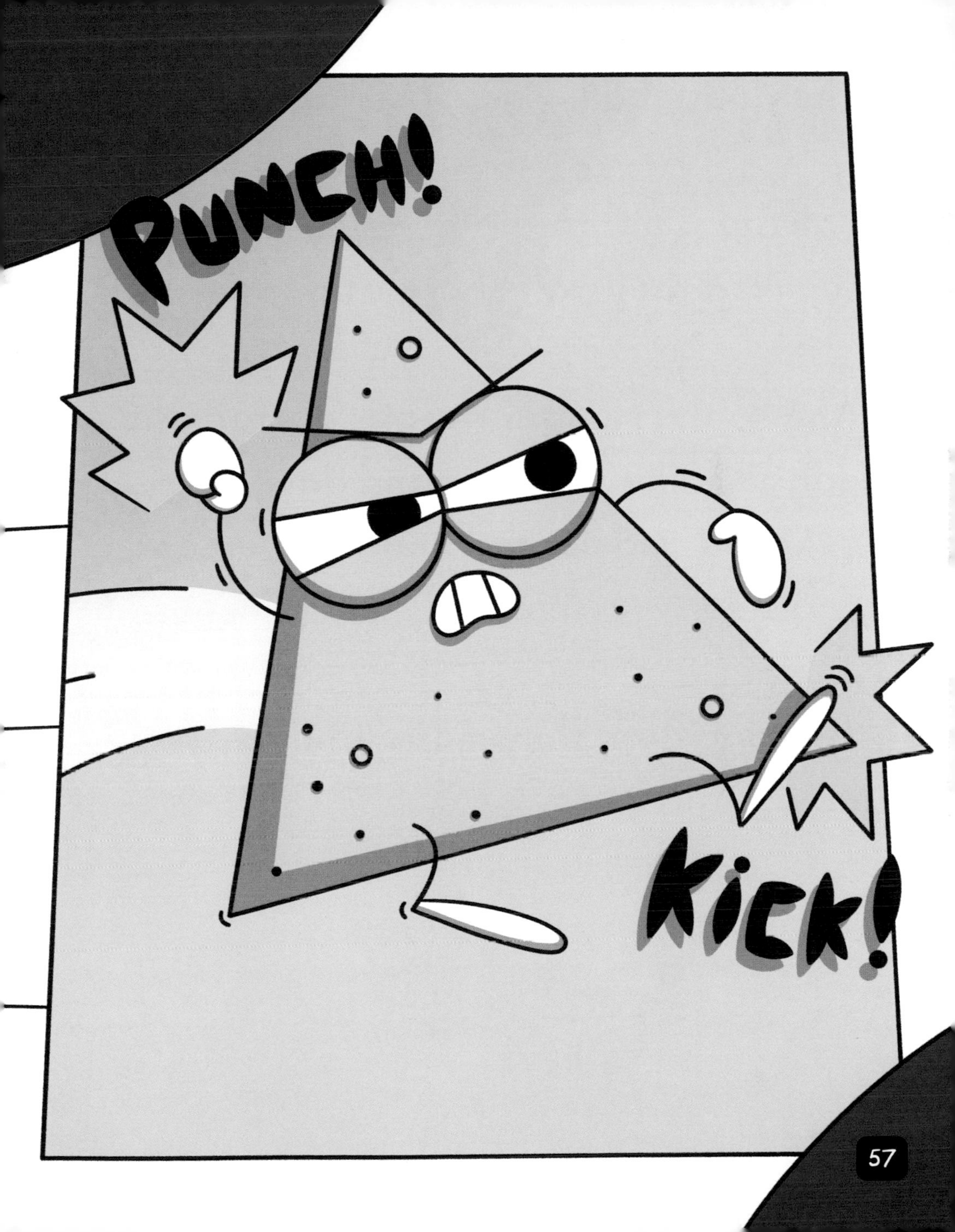
PUNCH!
KICK!

The dodgeballs came fast and furious.

But the superheroic foursome had survived their fair share of danger.

And so the Hunger Heroes darted and dodged. They ducked and dove. They punched and punted and swatted and charged.

Step-by-step, they made their way across the gym.

ROLL!

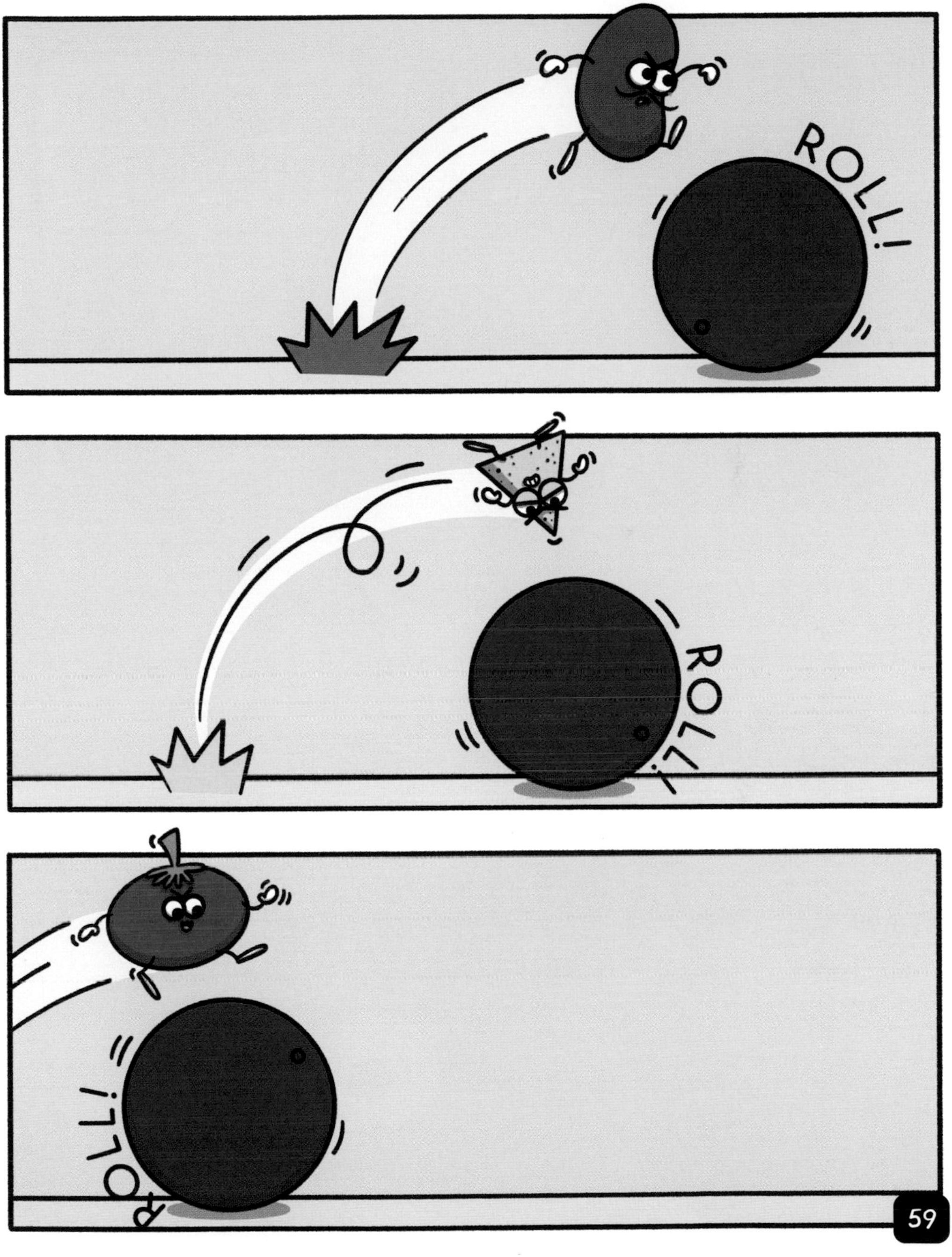
ROLL!
ROLL!
ROLL!

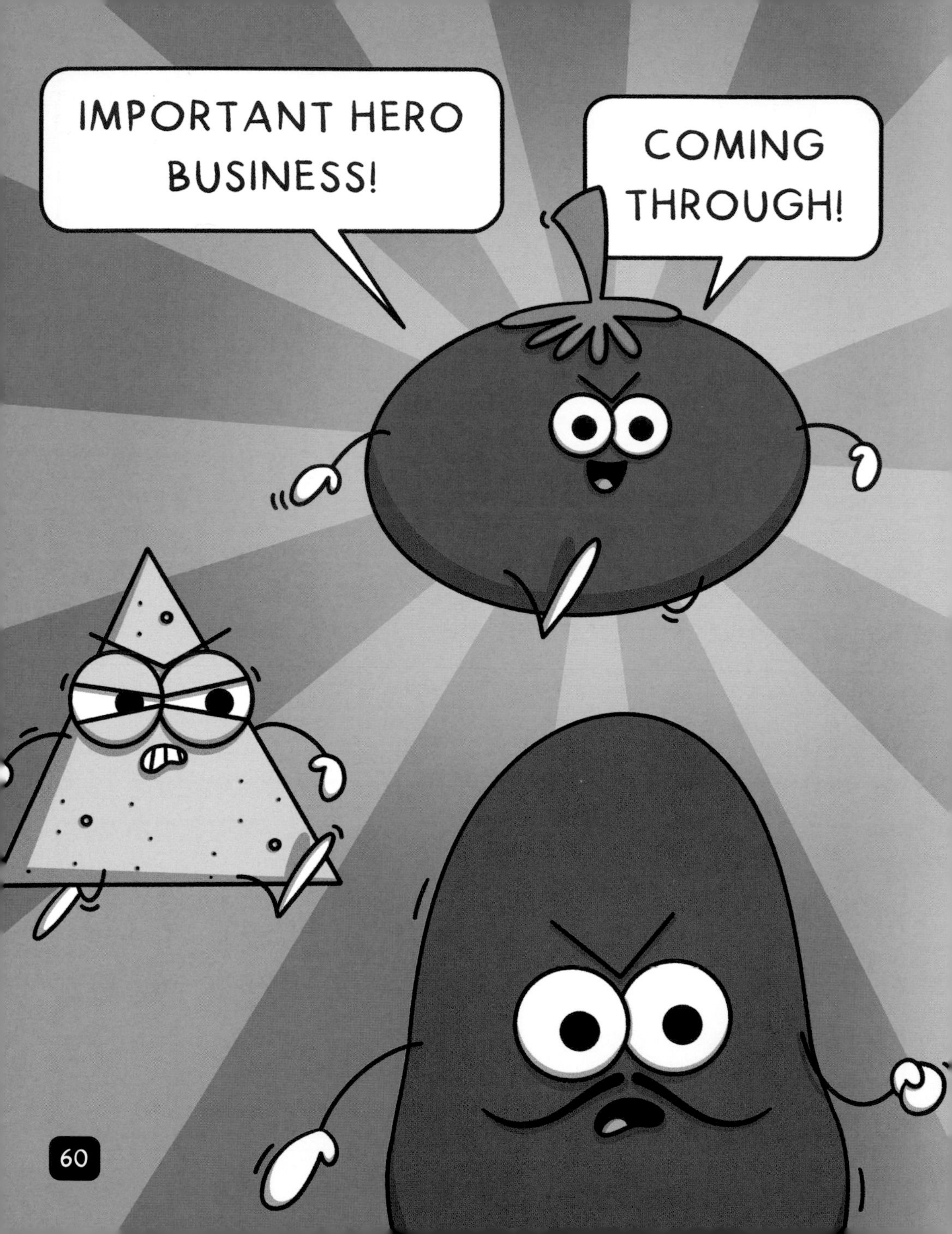
IMPORTANT HERO BUSINESS!
COMING THROUGH!

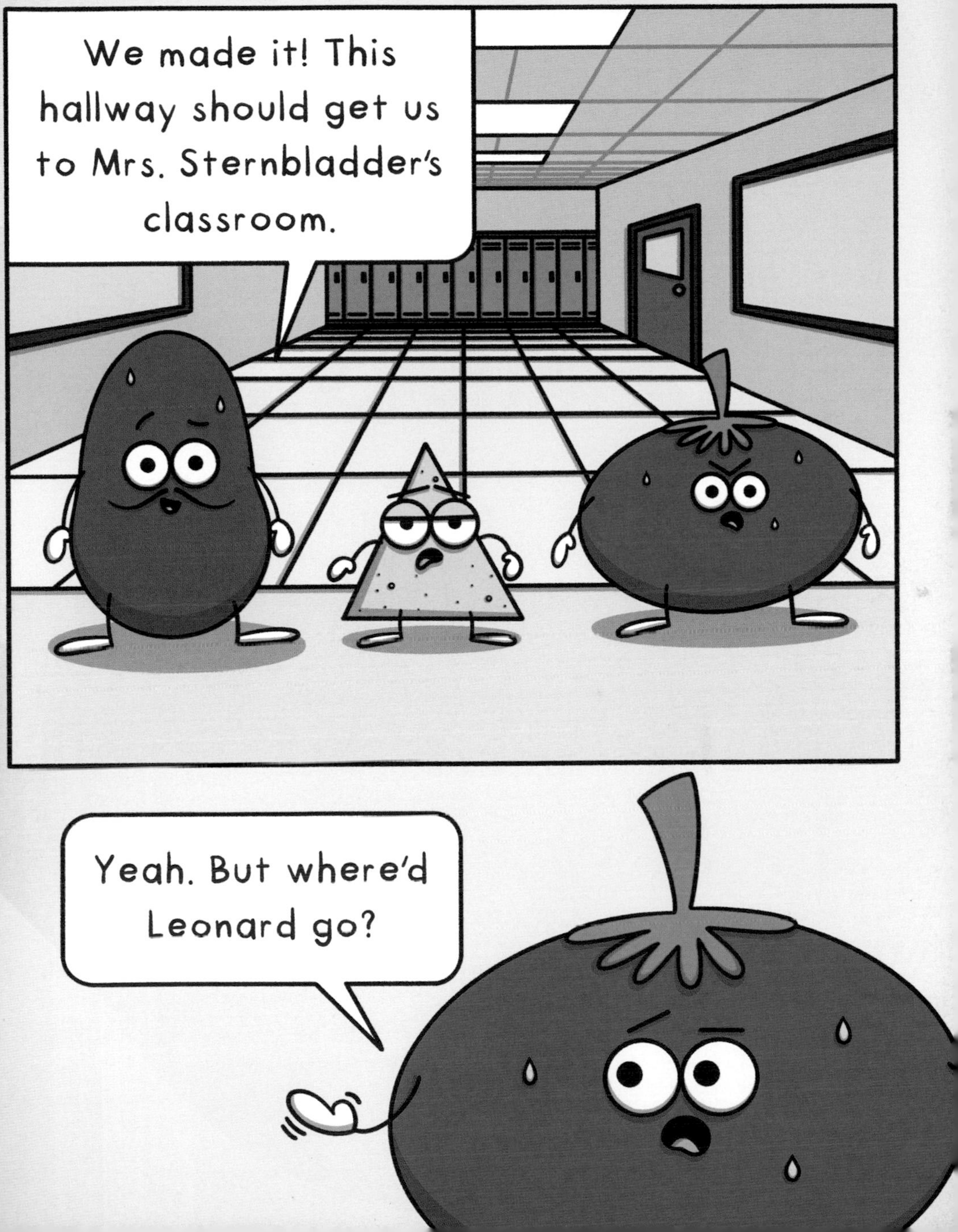
We made it! This hallway should get us to Mrs. Sternbladder's classroom.
Yeah. But where'd Leonard go?

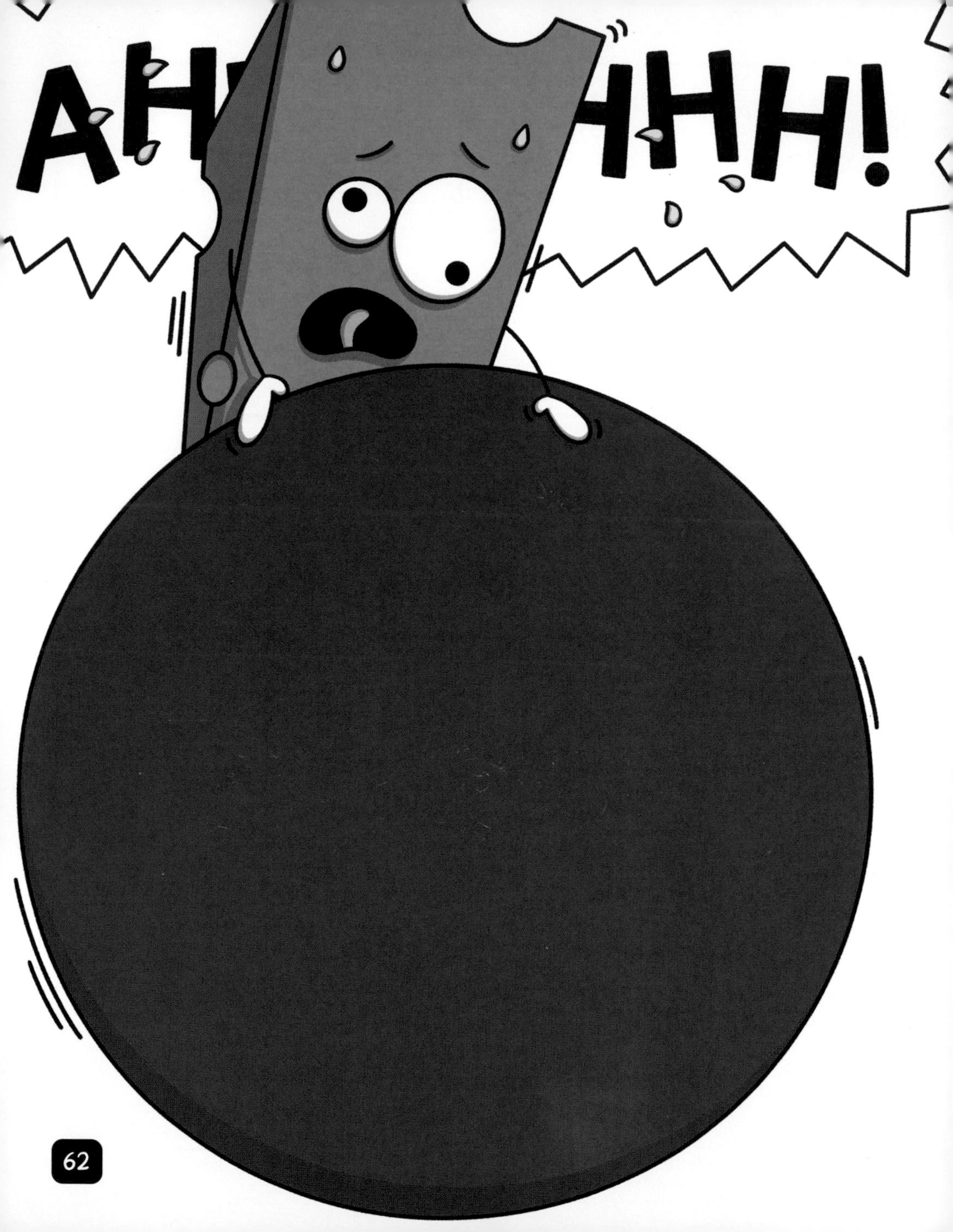
AH HHH!

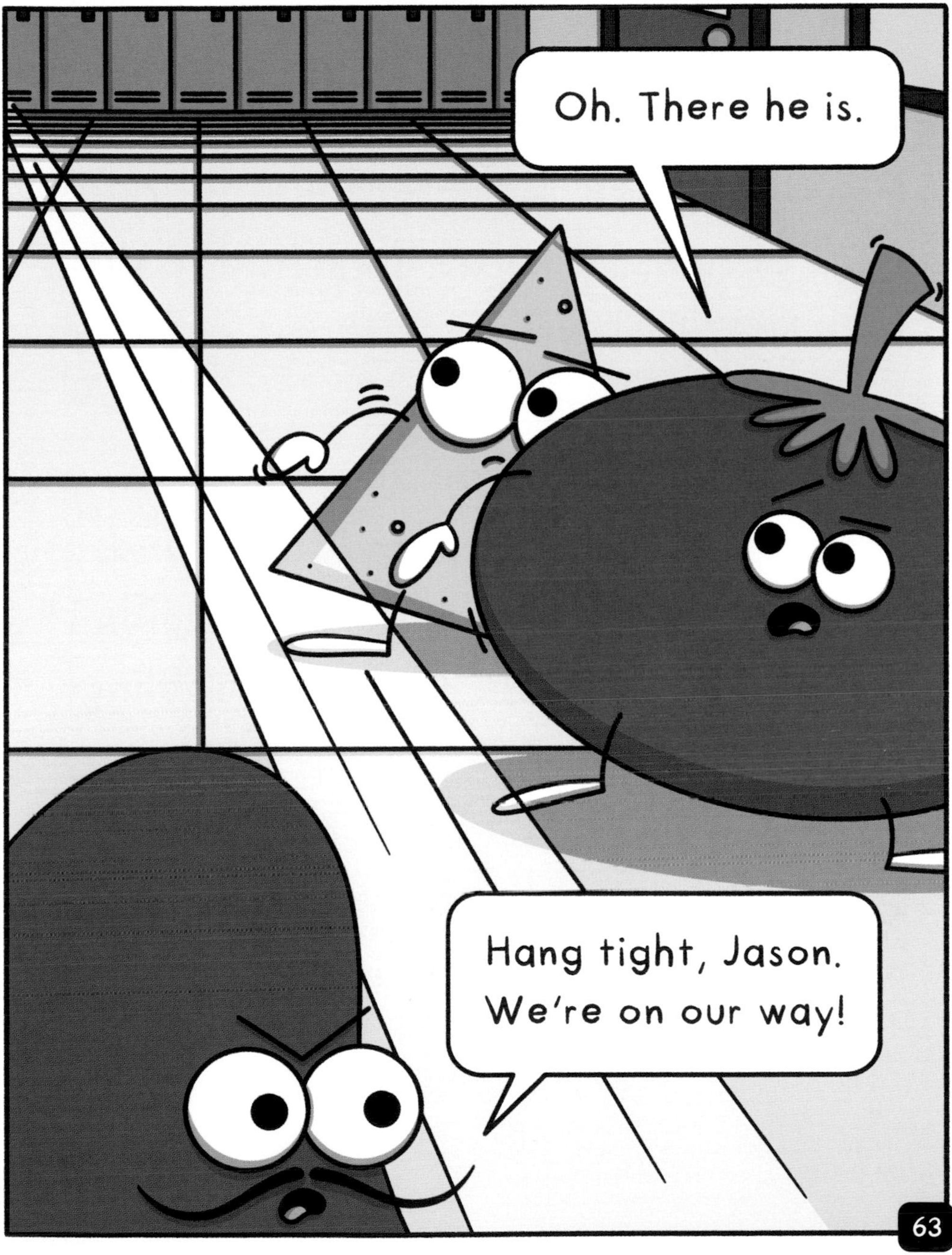
Oh. There he is.
Hang tight, Jason. We're on our way!

CHAPTER 4½

As you can see, Mrs. Sternbladder had a lot of rules. Most of them had to do with NOT EATING.

Mrs. Sternbladder couldn't stand snacks. She couldn't stand the sounds of chewing and munching. She couldn't even stand the little noises of nibbling!

Her room was a NO-SNACK ZONE. And if she caught you creating crumbs...well, LOOK OUT.

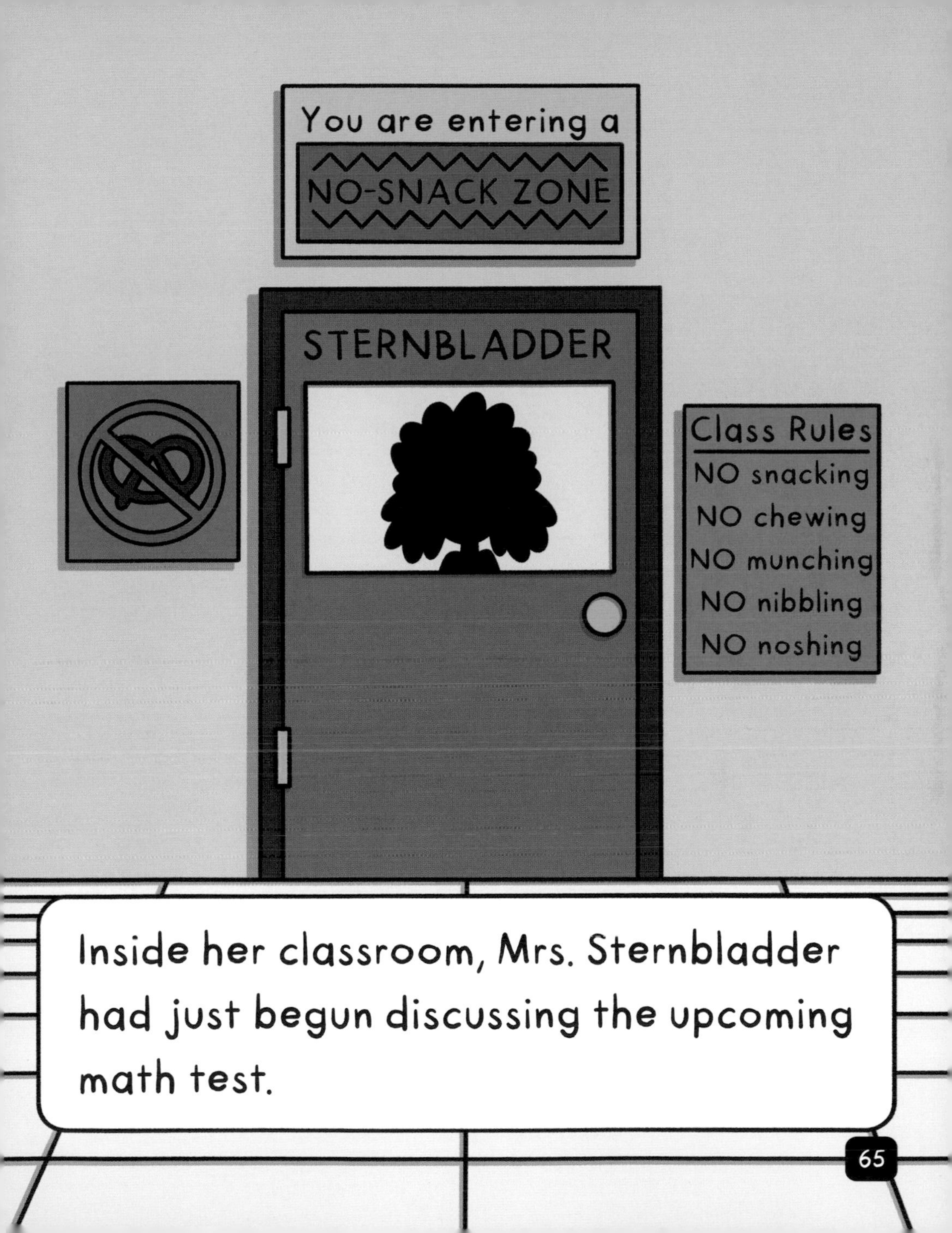
You are entering a
NO-SNACK ZONE
STERNBLADDER
Class Rules
NO snacking
NO chewing
NO munching
NO nibbling
NO noshing

Inside her classroom, Mrs. Sternbladder had just begun discussing the upcoming math test.

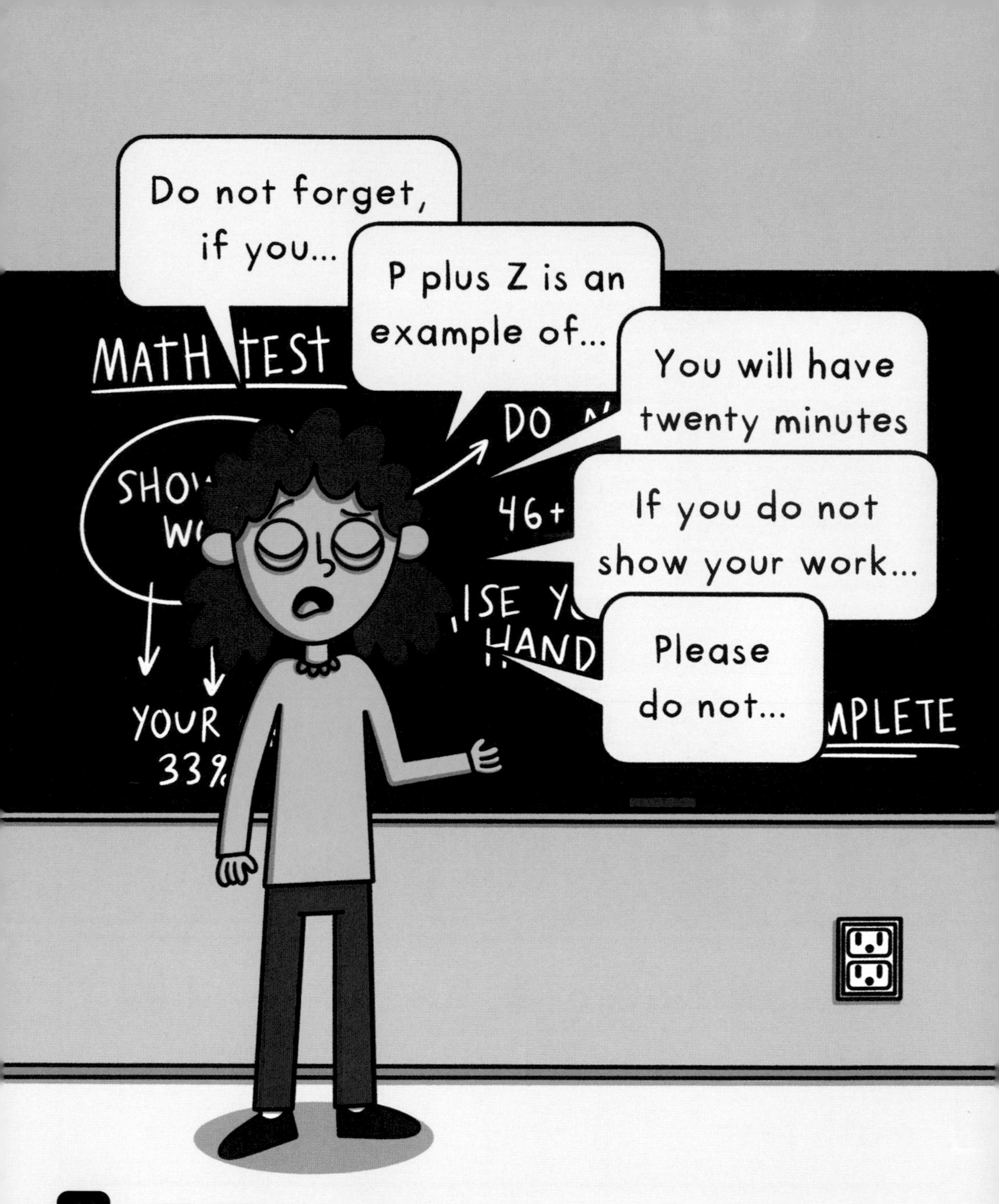
Do not forget, if you...
P plus Z is an example of...
You will have twenty minutes
If you do not show your work...
Please do not...
MATH TEST

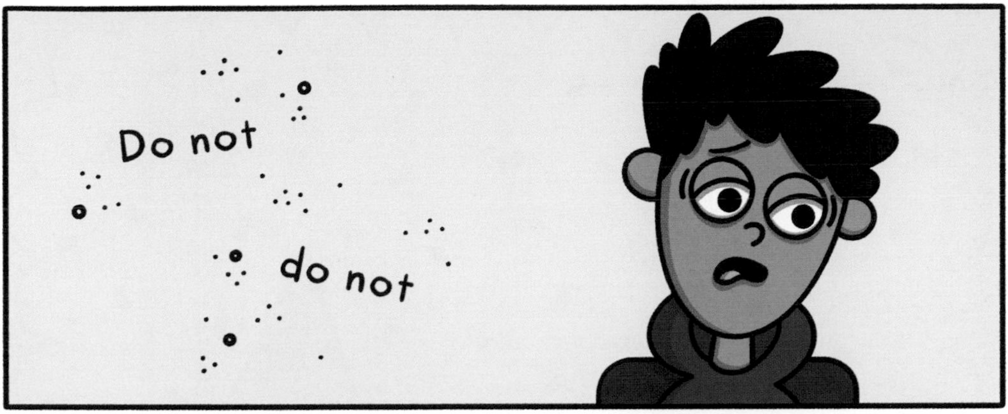
Do not
do not

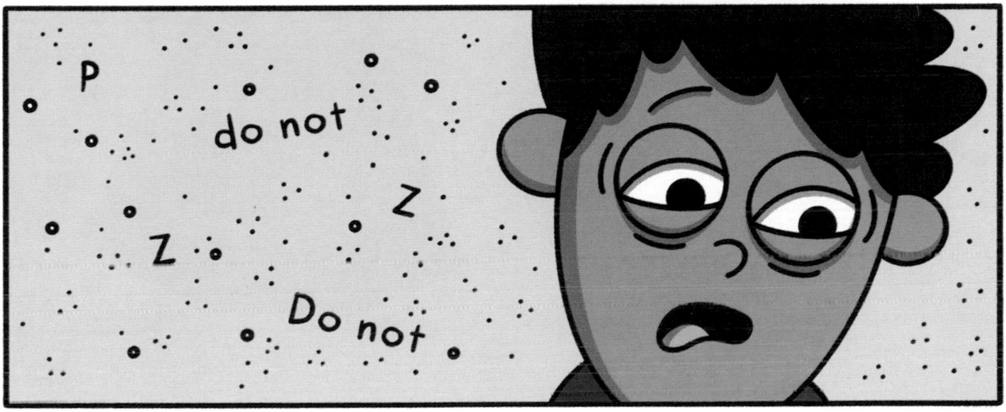
P
do not
Z
Z
Do not

Mrs. Sternbladder's words reached Jason's ears but didn't make it into his brain. As he drifted off, so did his thoughts....

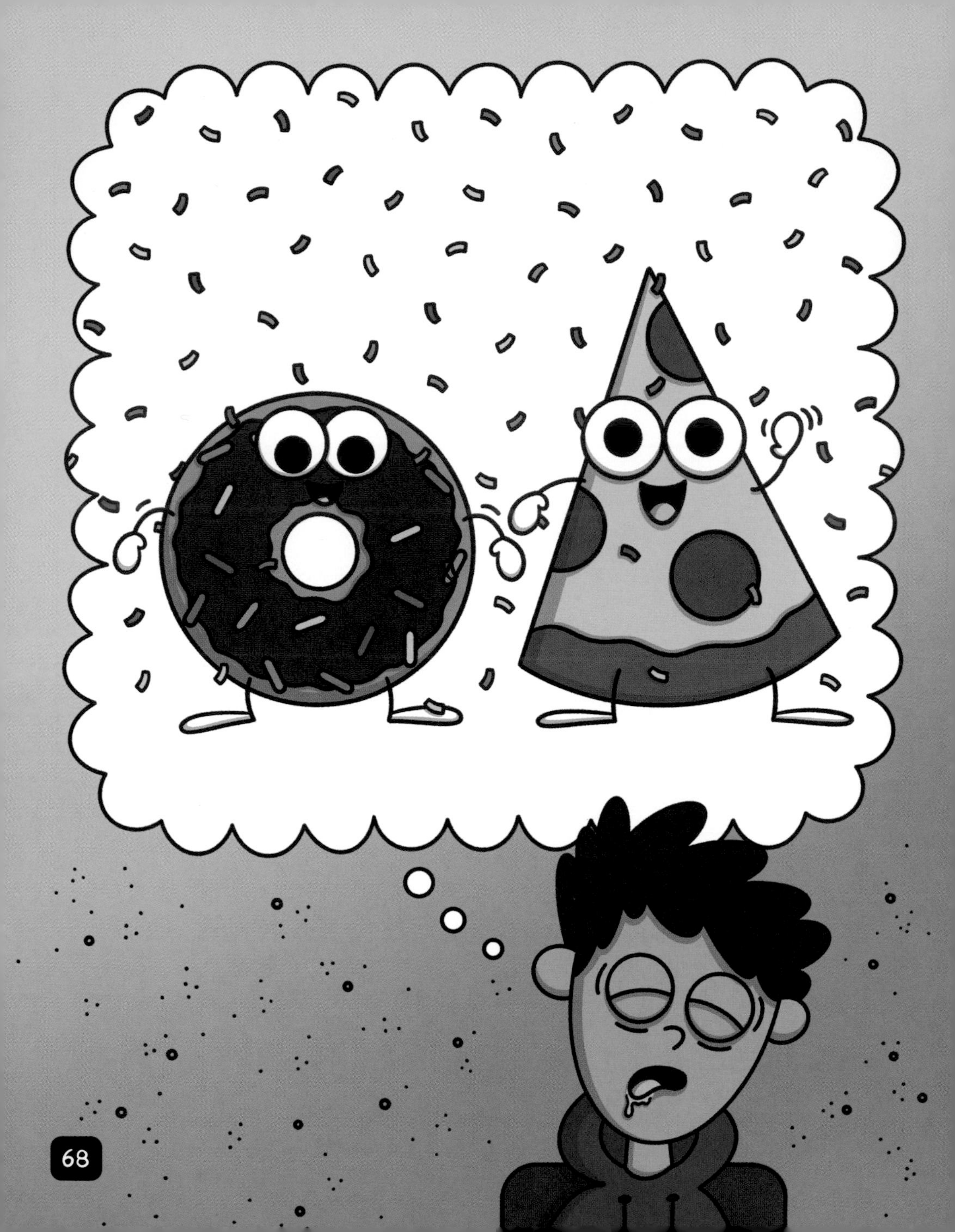

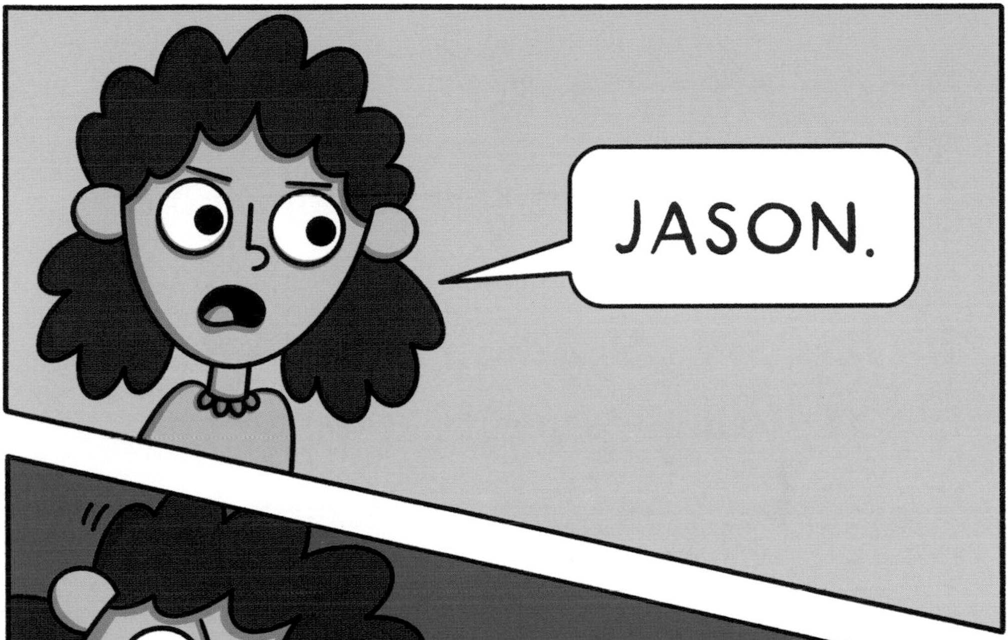
JASON.

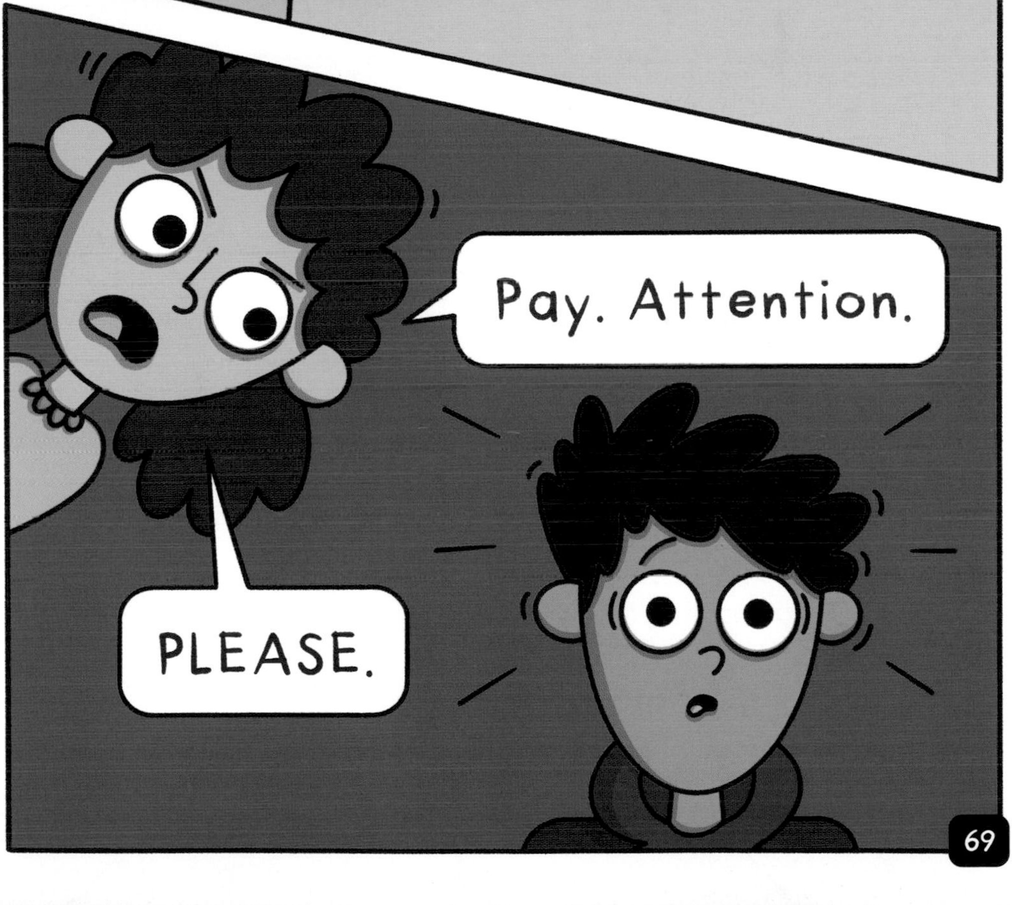
Pay. Attention.
PLEASE.

CHAPTER 5

The Hunger Heroes roamed up and down the halls of the school, searching for Mrs. Sternbladder's classroom. But it was proving very difficult to find.

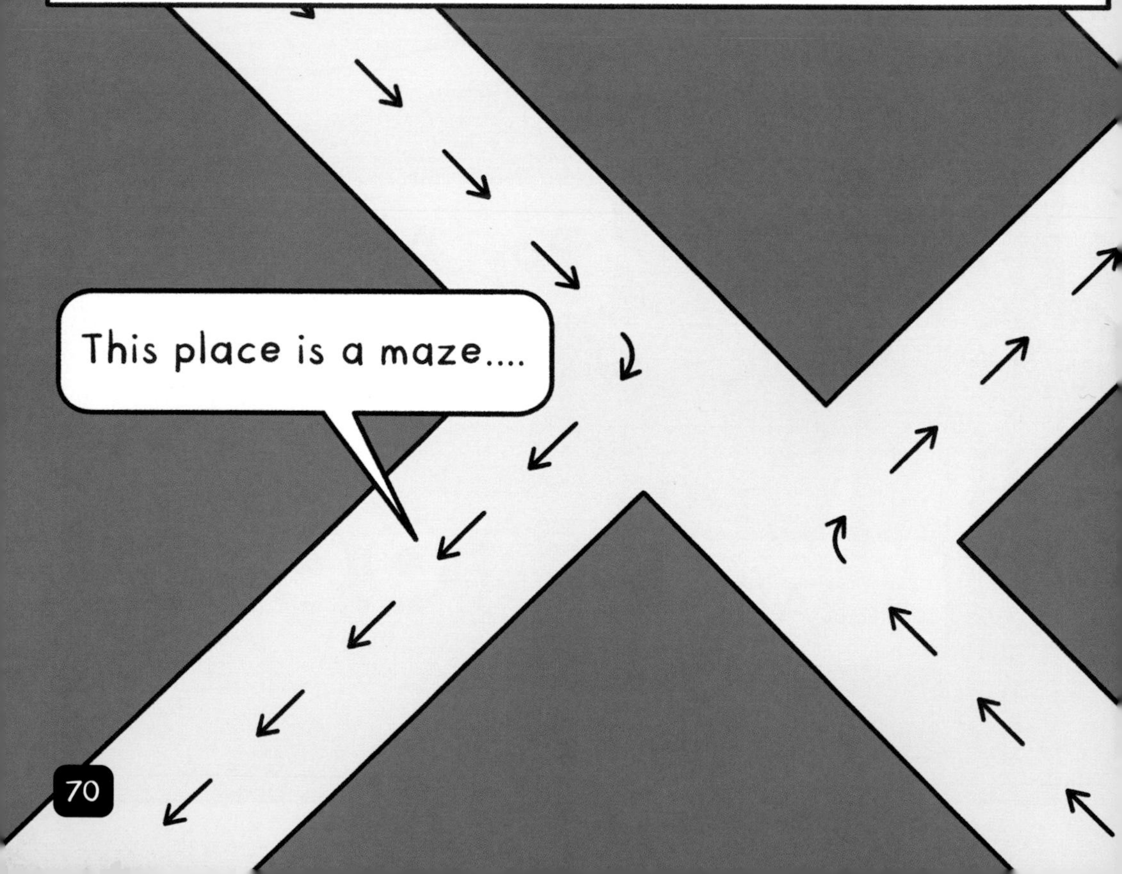
This place is a maze....

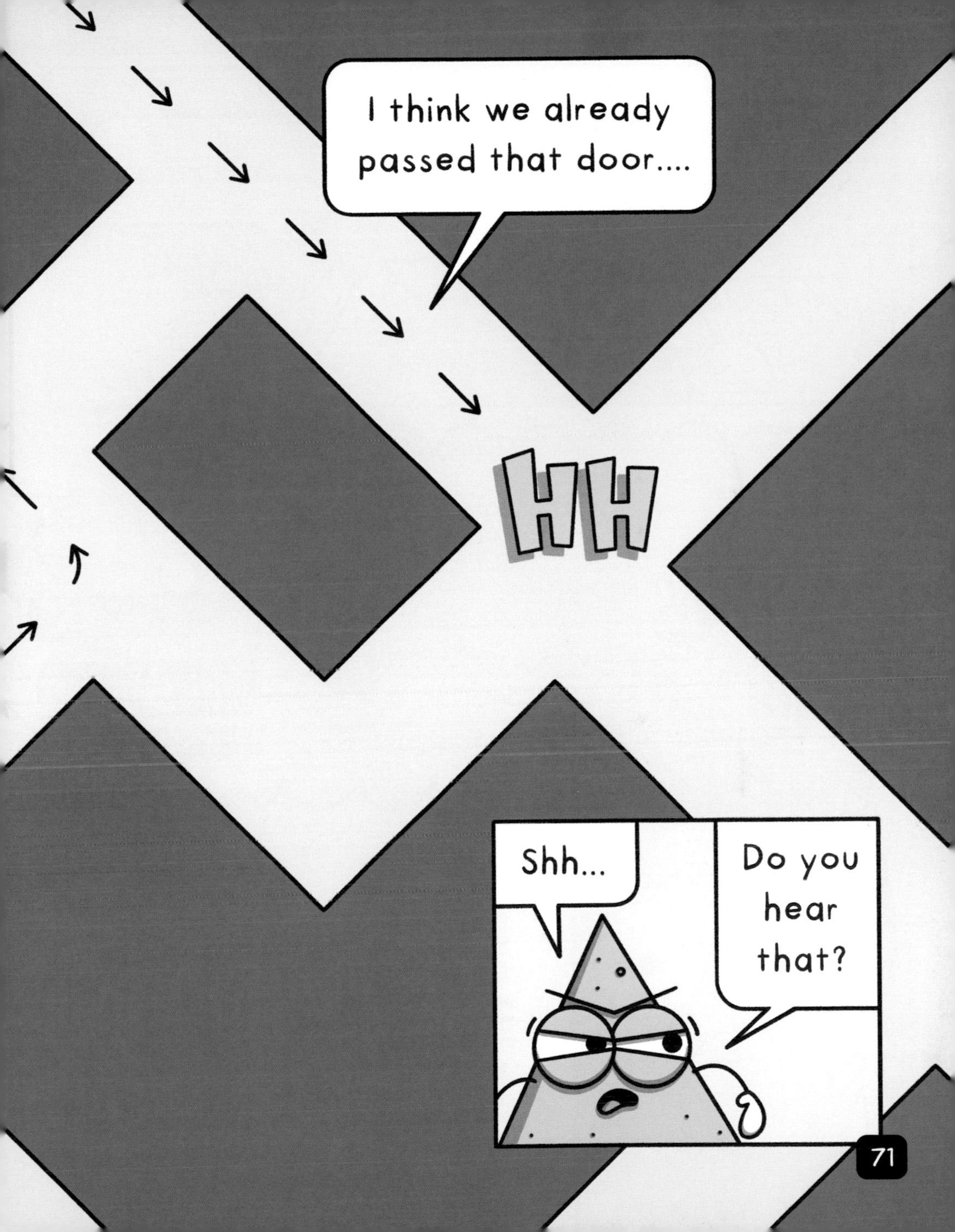
I think we already passed that door....
HH
Shh...
Do you hear that?

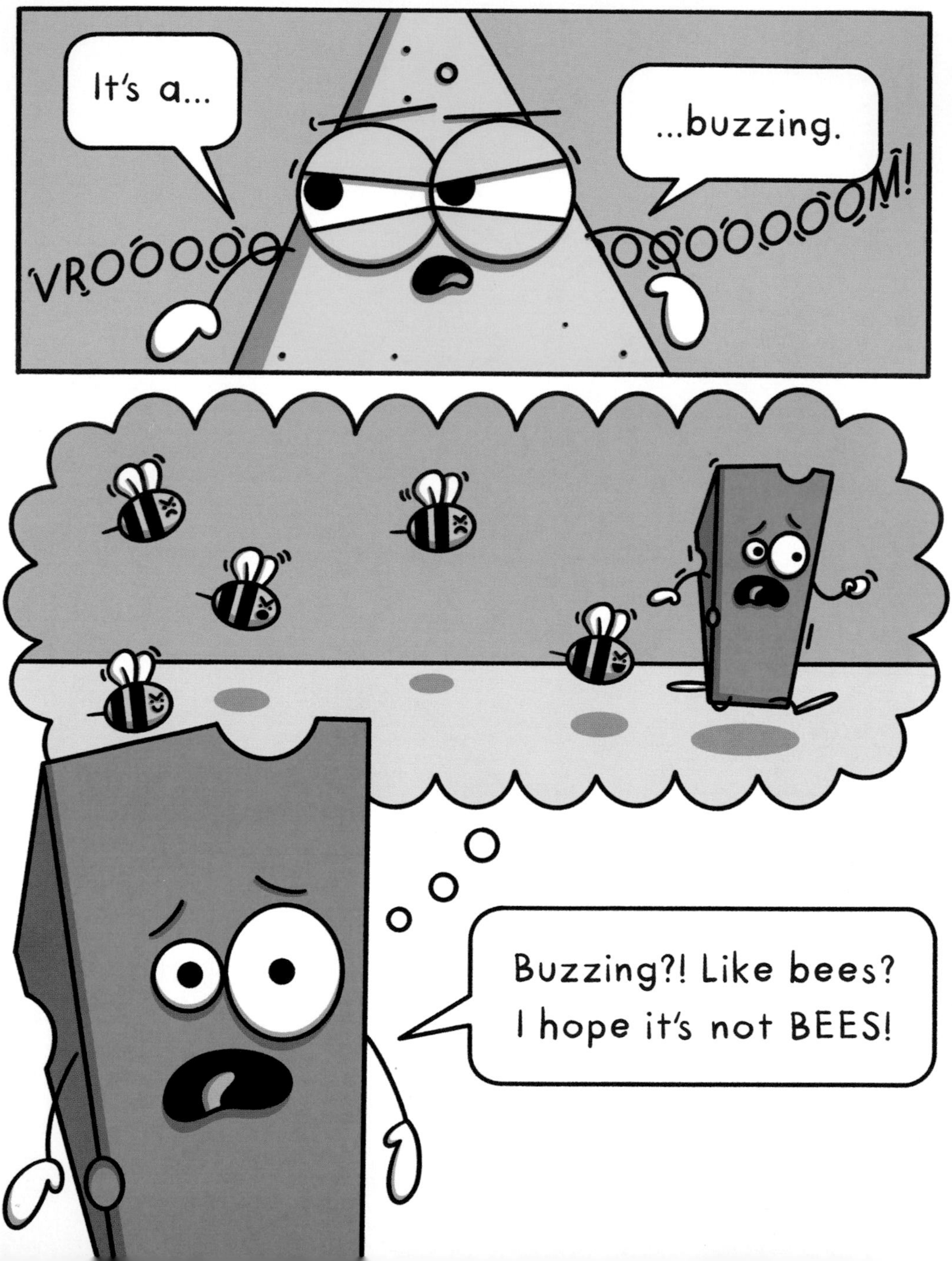
It's a...
VROOOOOOOOOOOOOOOOOM!
...buzzing.
Buzzing?! Like bees? I hope it's not BEES!

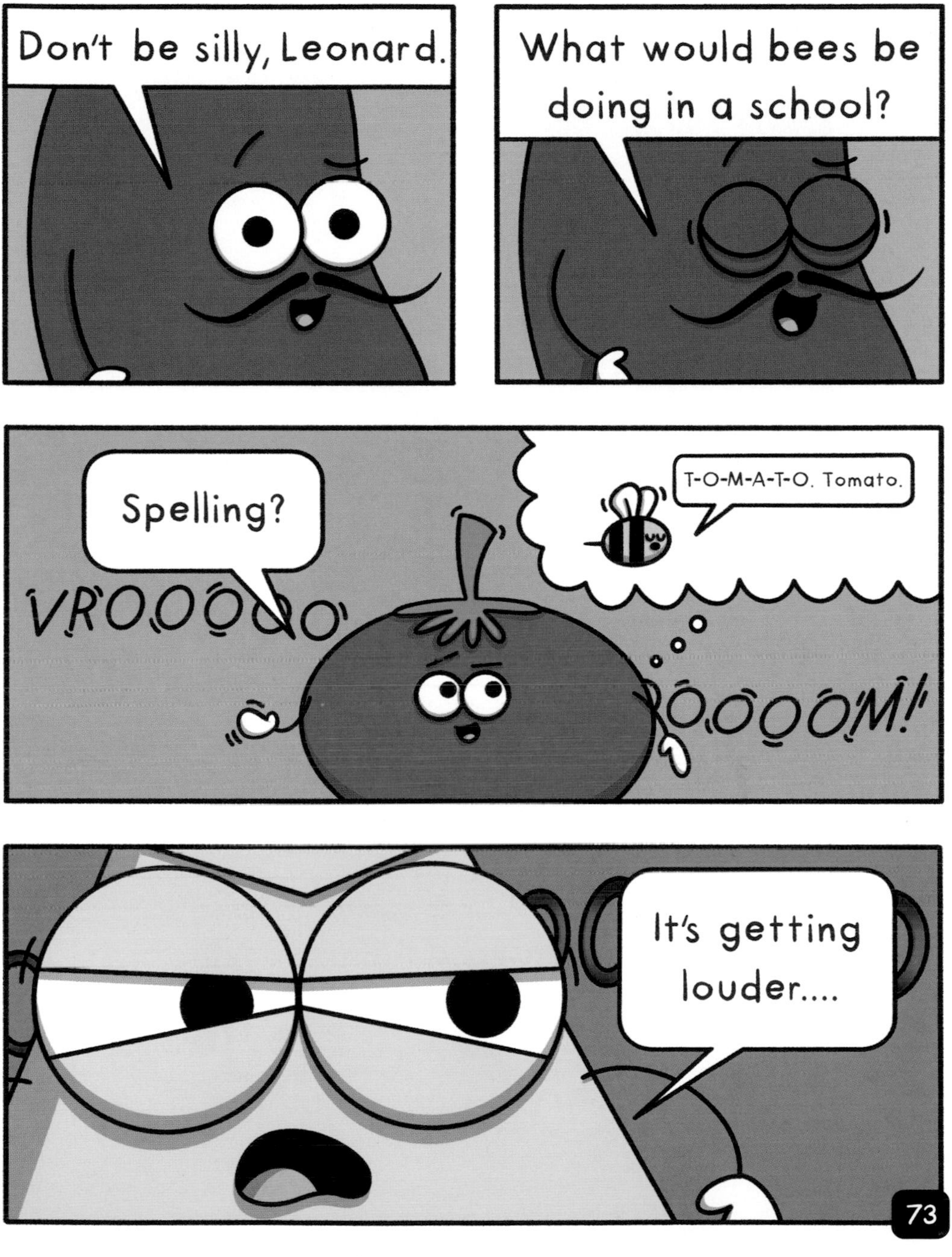
Don't be silly, Leonard.
What would bees be doing in a school?
Spelling?
T-O-M-A-T-O. Tomato.
VROOOOO
OOOOM!
It's getting louder....

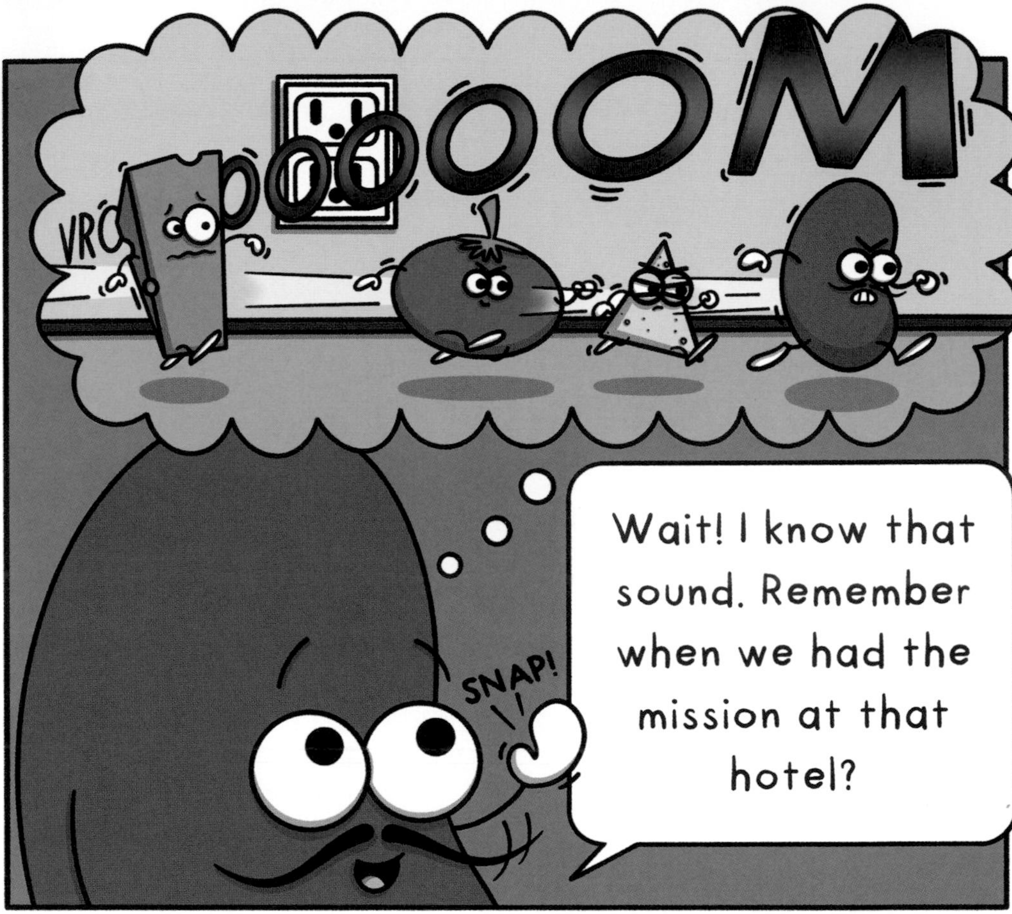
VROOOOOOM
SNAP!
Wait! I know that sound. Remember when we had the mission at that hotel?

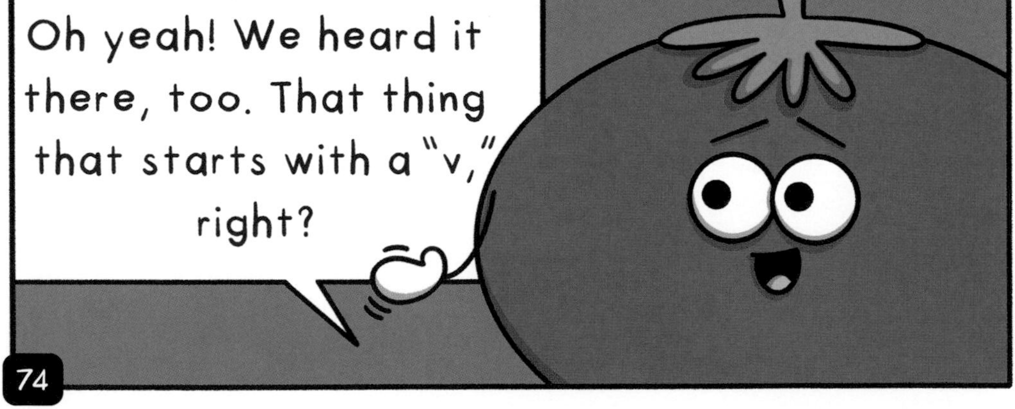
Oh yeah! We heard it there, too. That thing that starts with a "v," right?

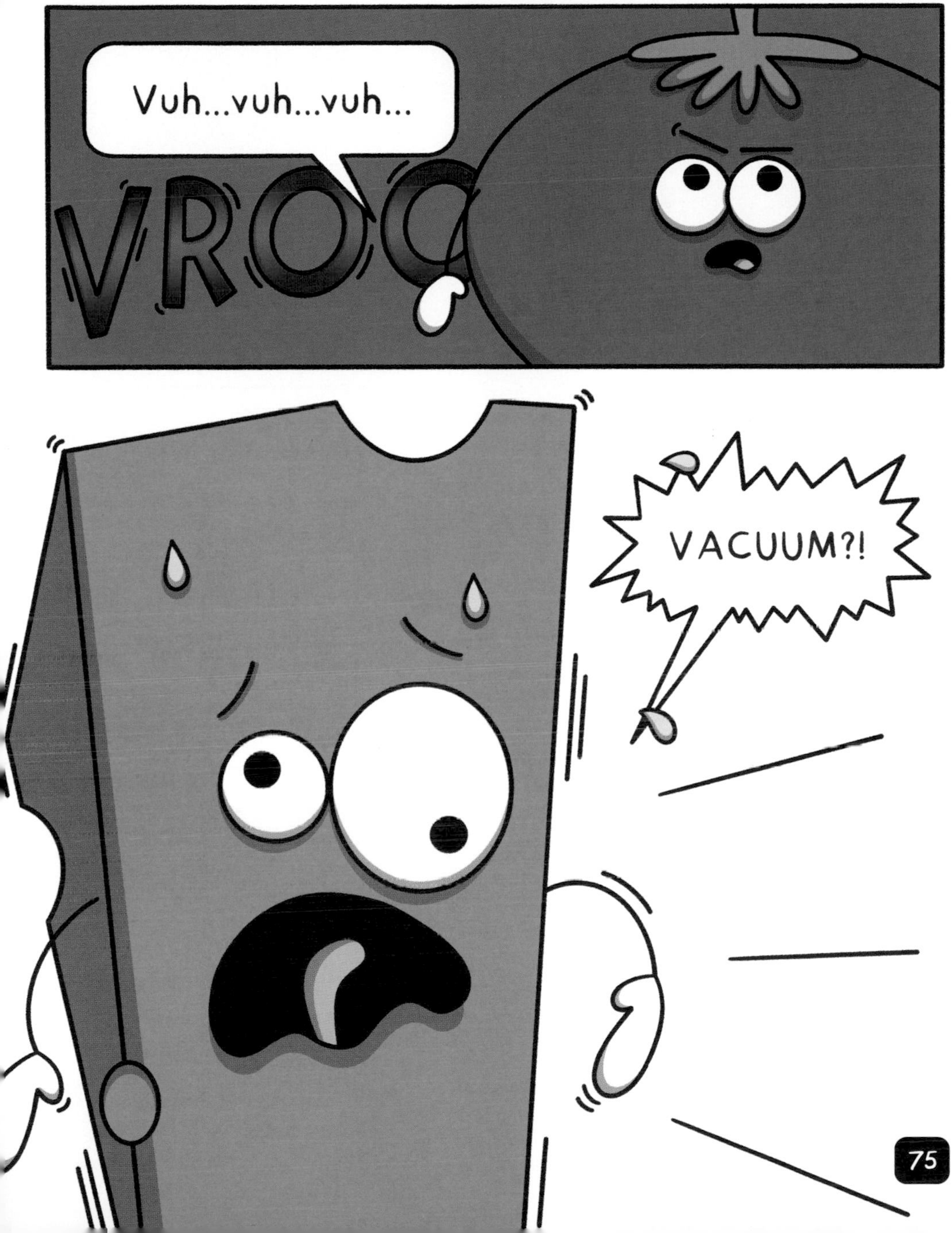
Vuh...vuh...vuh...
VROO
VACUUM?!

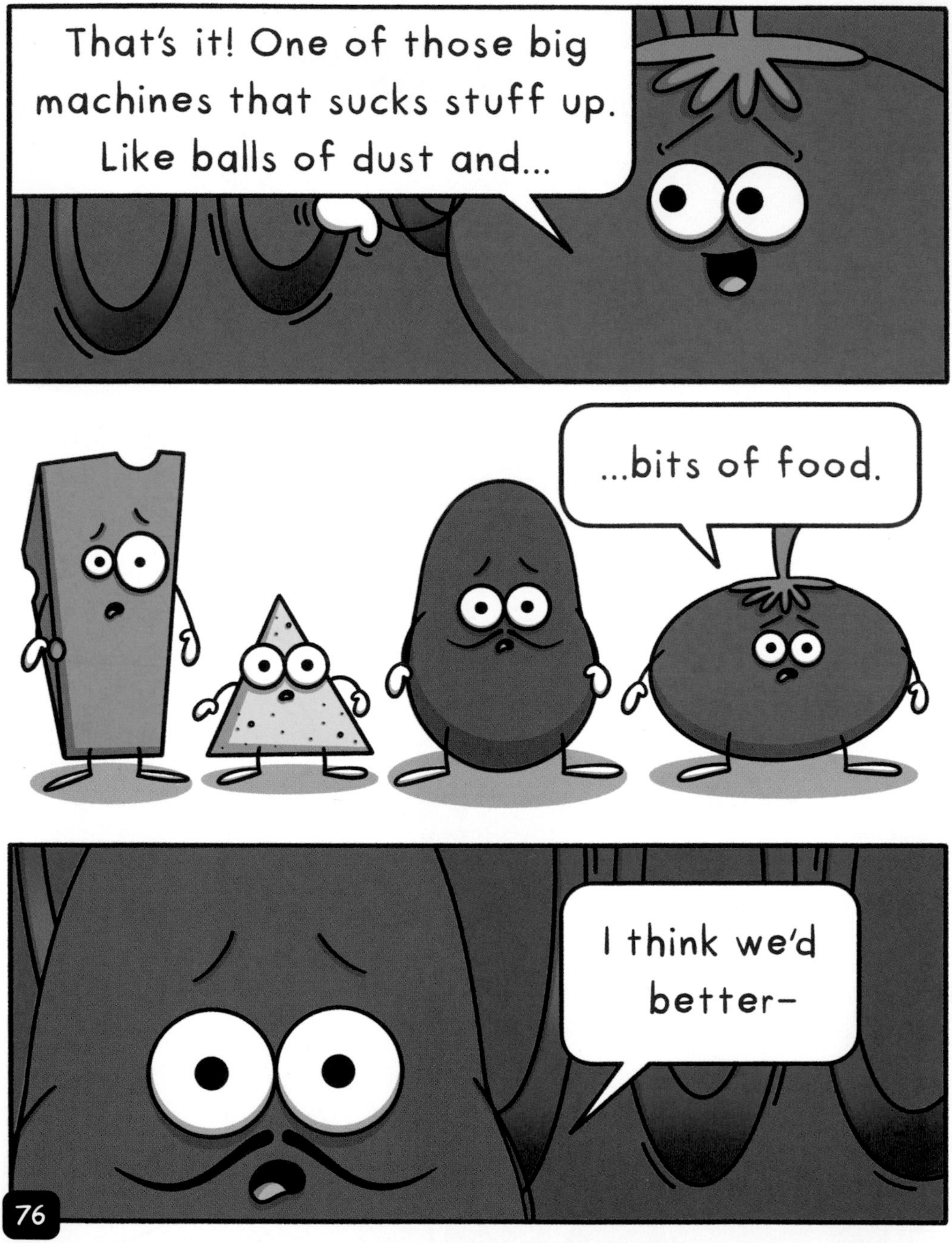
That's it! One of those big machines that sucks stuff up. Like balls of dust and...
...bits of food.
I think we'd better-

RUN!

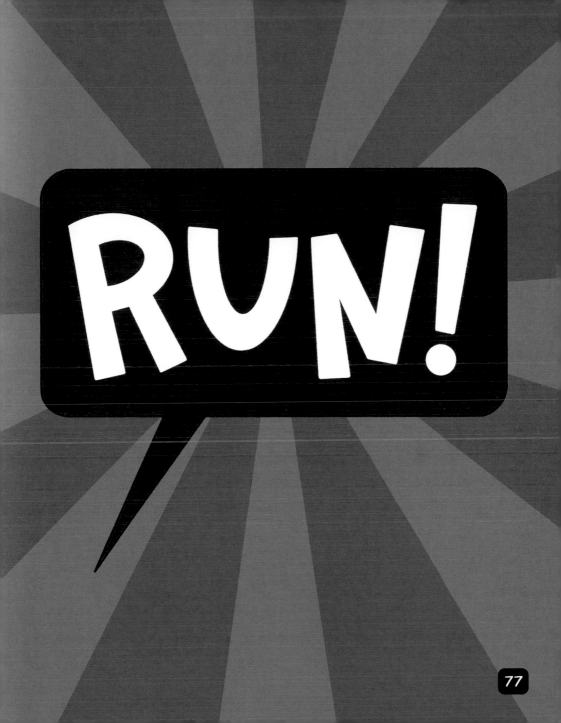

CHAPTER 6

The Hunger Heroes ran as fast as they could, but they couldn't seem to escape the angry buzz of the vacuum cleaner.

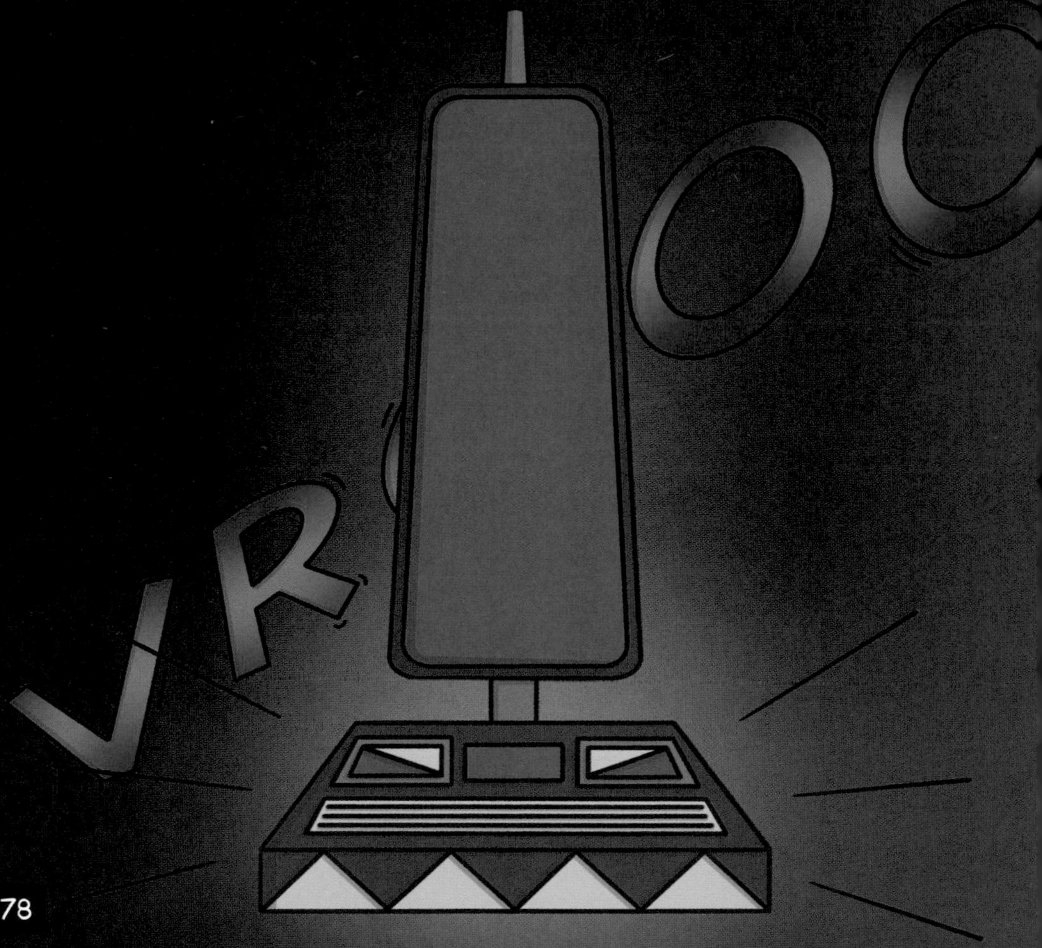
VROOO

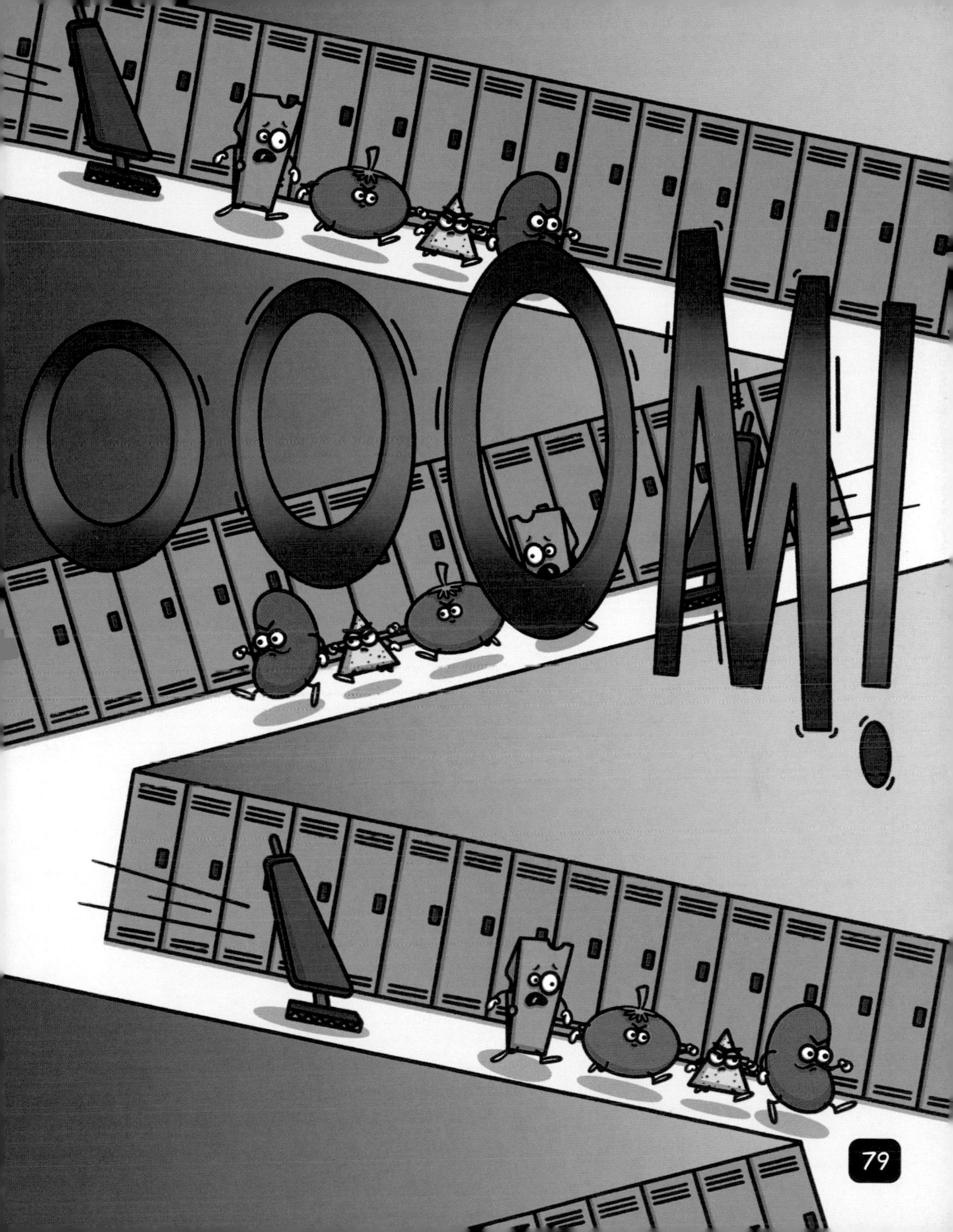
OOOM!

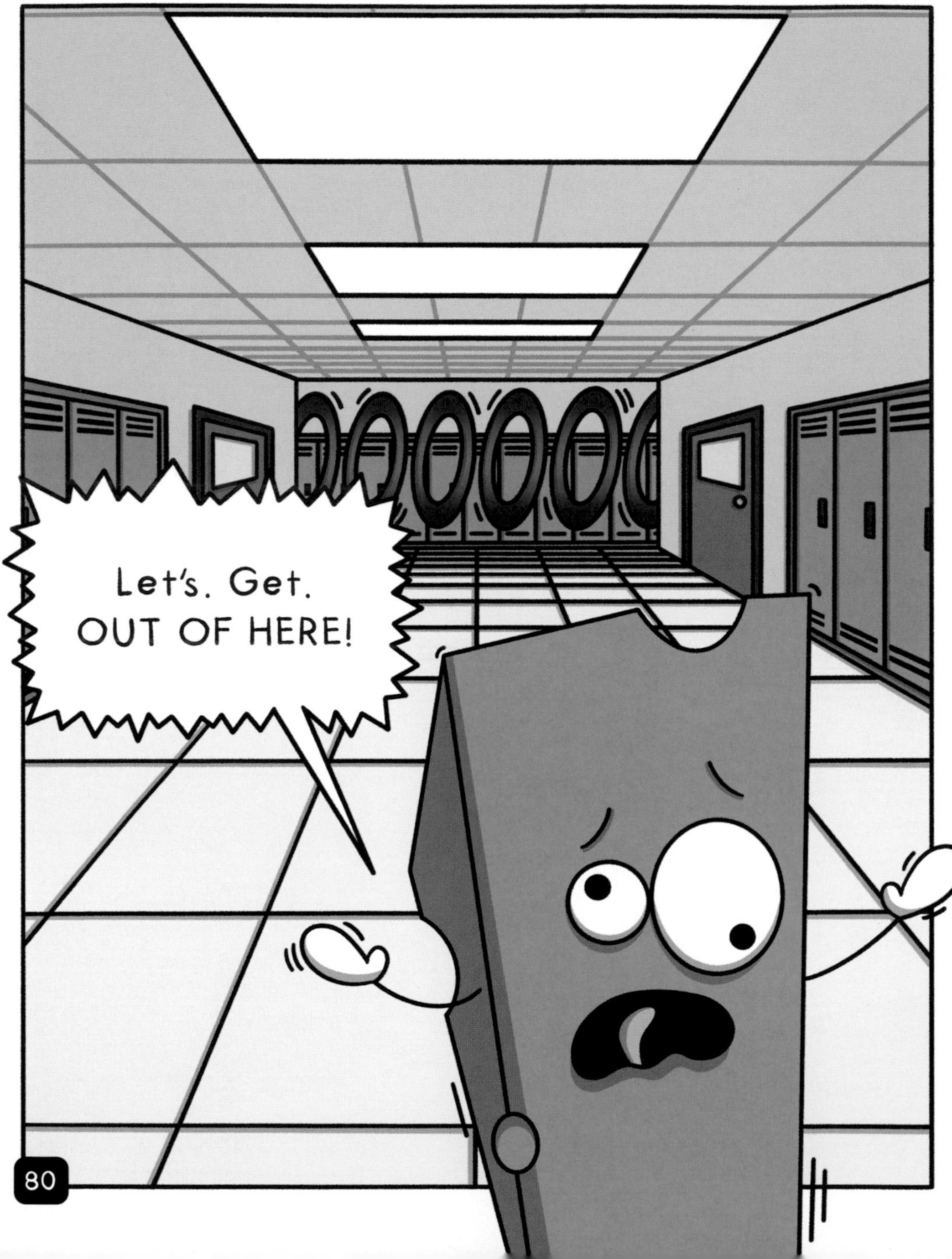
Let's. Get. OUT OF HERE!

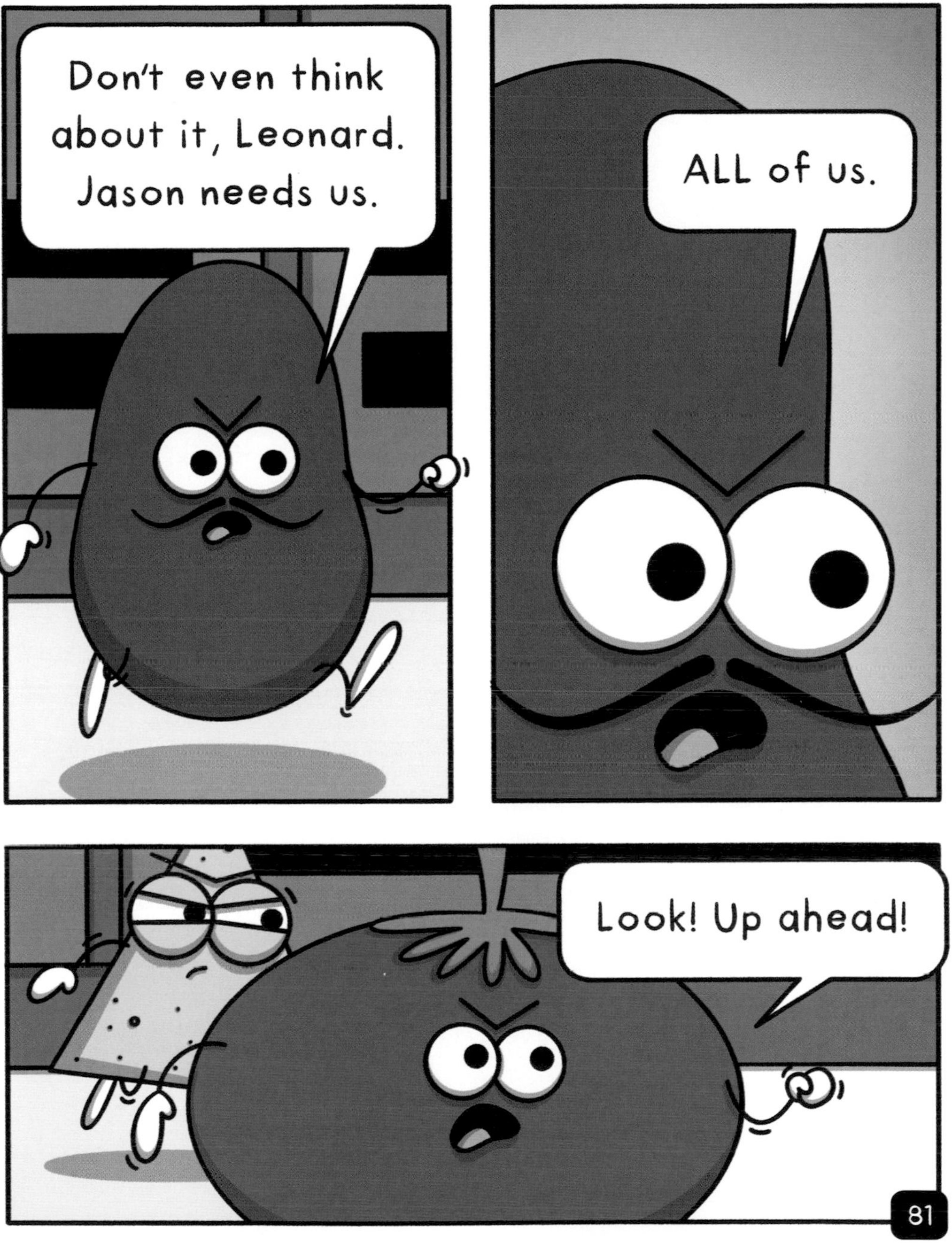

Don't even think about it, Leonard. Jason needs us.
ALL of us.
Look! Up ahead!

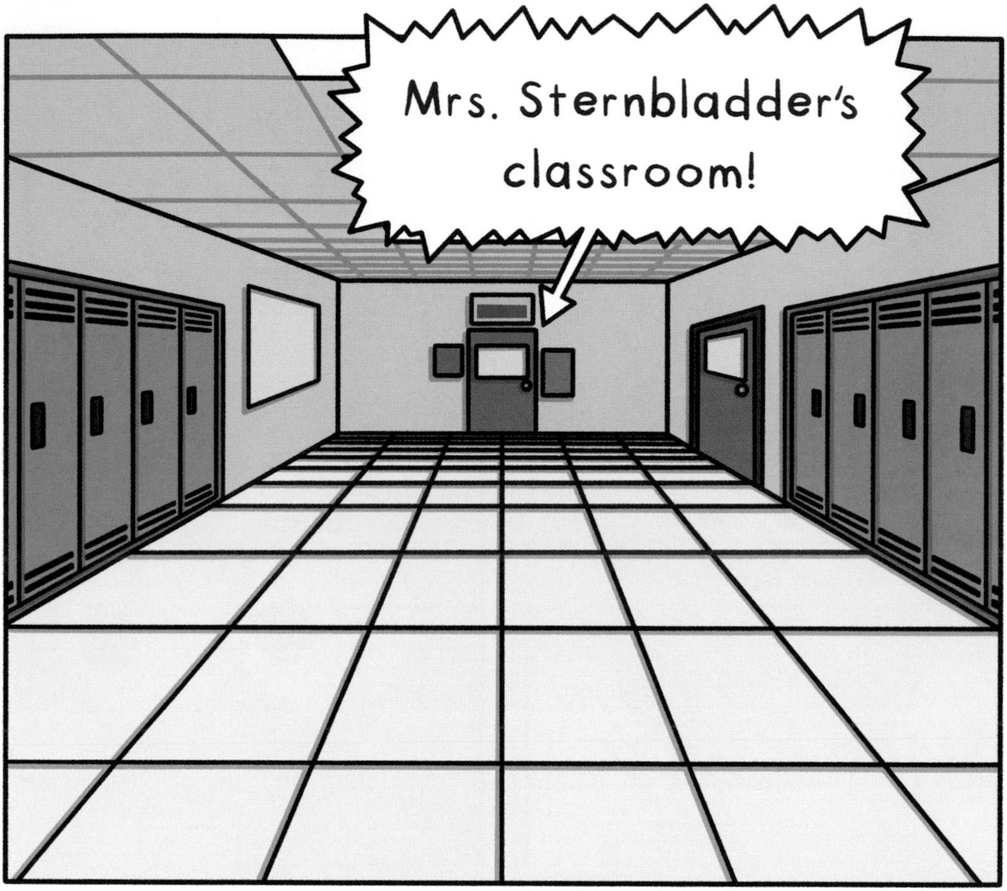
Mrs. Sternbladder's classroom!

Mr. Toots slowed to a stop. Then, as the rest of the Hunger Heroes caught up, he quickly reviewed the steps of the Ol' Razzle-Dazzle.

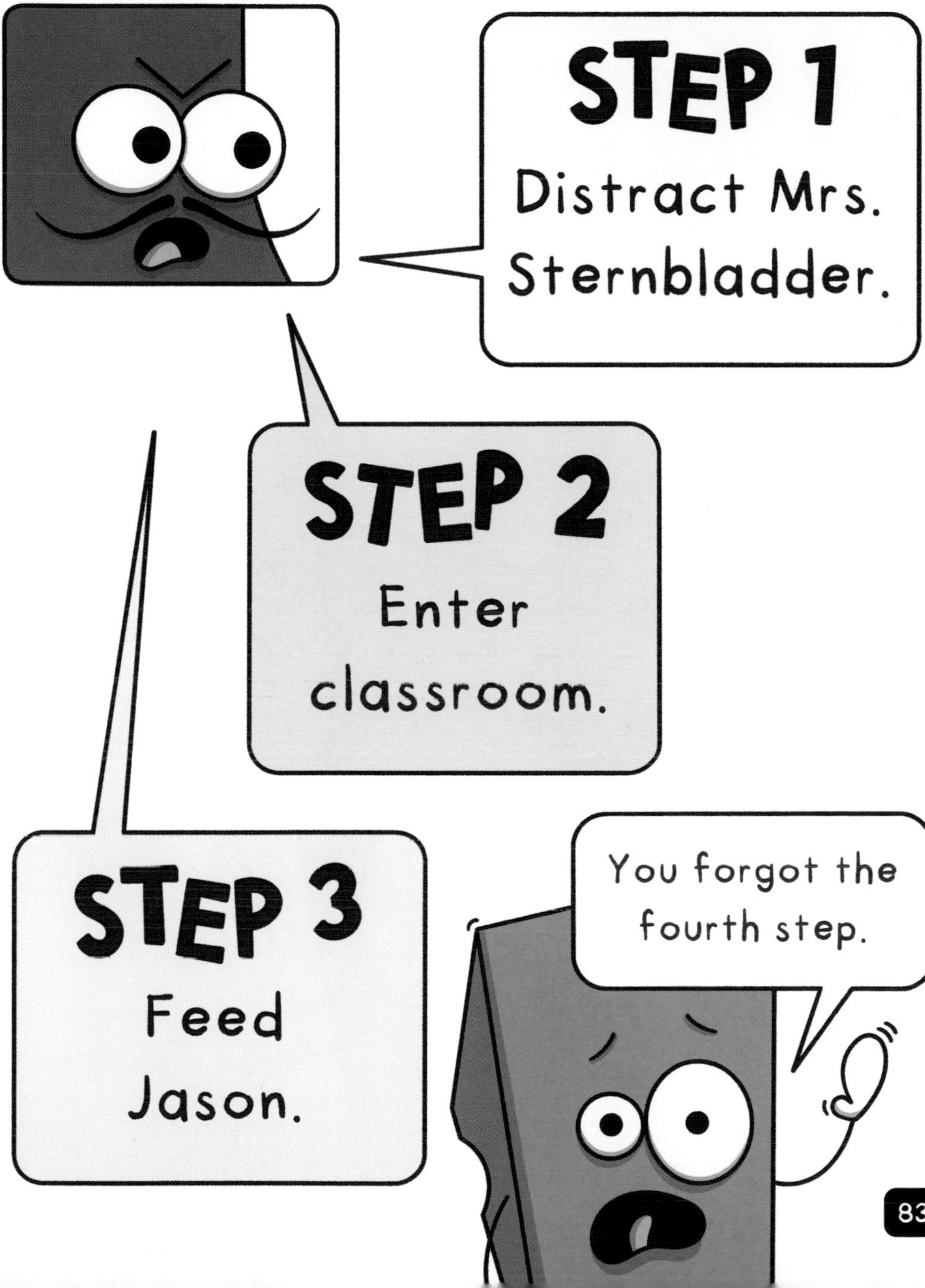
STEP 1
Distract Mrs. Sternbladder.
STEP 2
Enter classroom.
STEP 3
Feed Jason.
You forgot the fourth step.

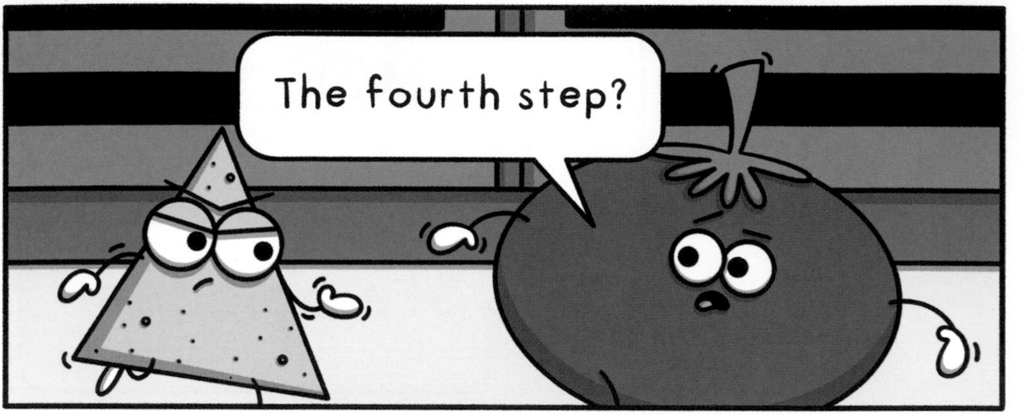
The fourth step?

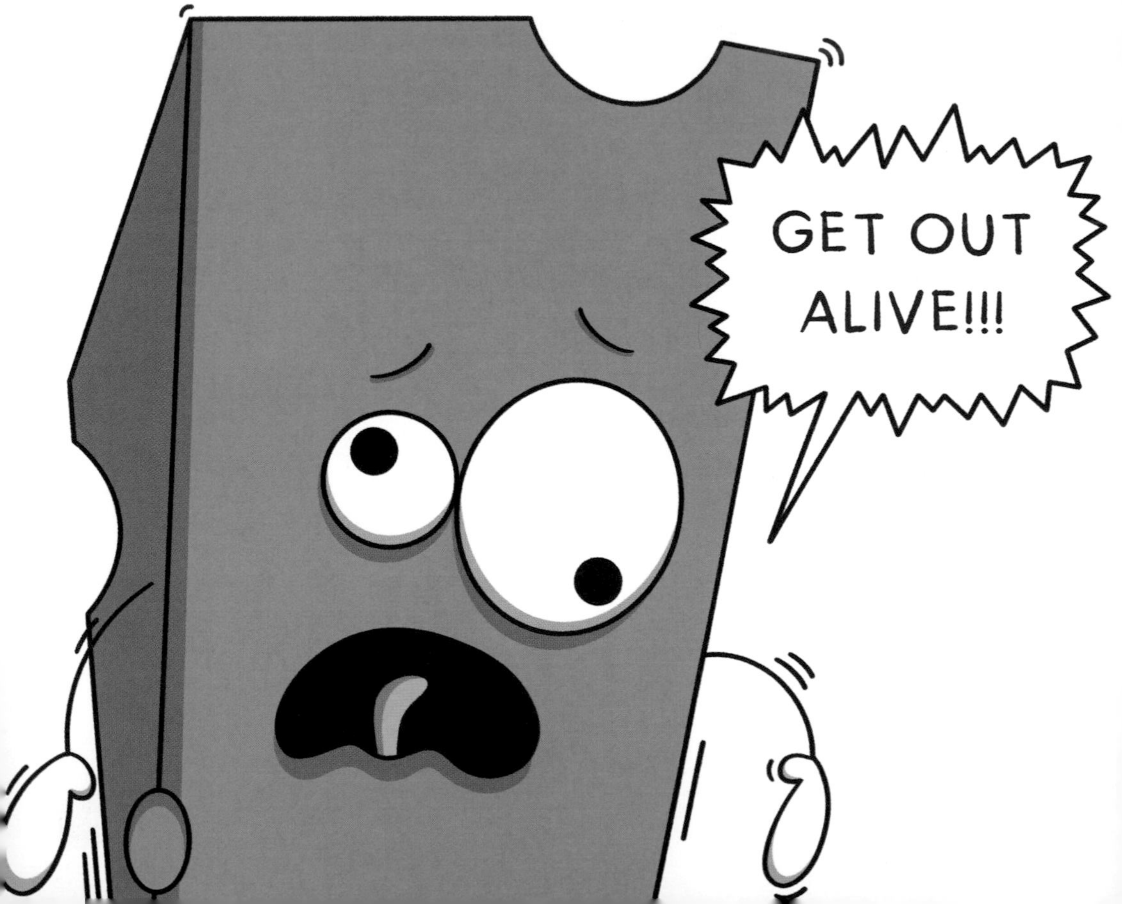
GET OUT
ALIVE!!!

There, there, Leonard. No one's going to the Great Taco Shop in the Sky. Not today. Not on my watch.

"We just need a distraction," Chip Ninja said. "Something to get Mrs. Sternbladder out of her classroom so we can get Jason an Emergency Snack."

The Hunger Heroes looked around the hallway.

"You want a distraction?" said Tammy. "I'll give you a distraction!"

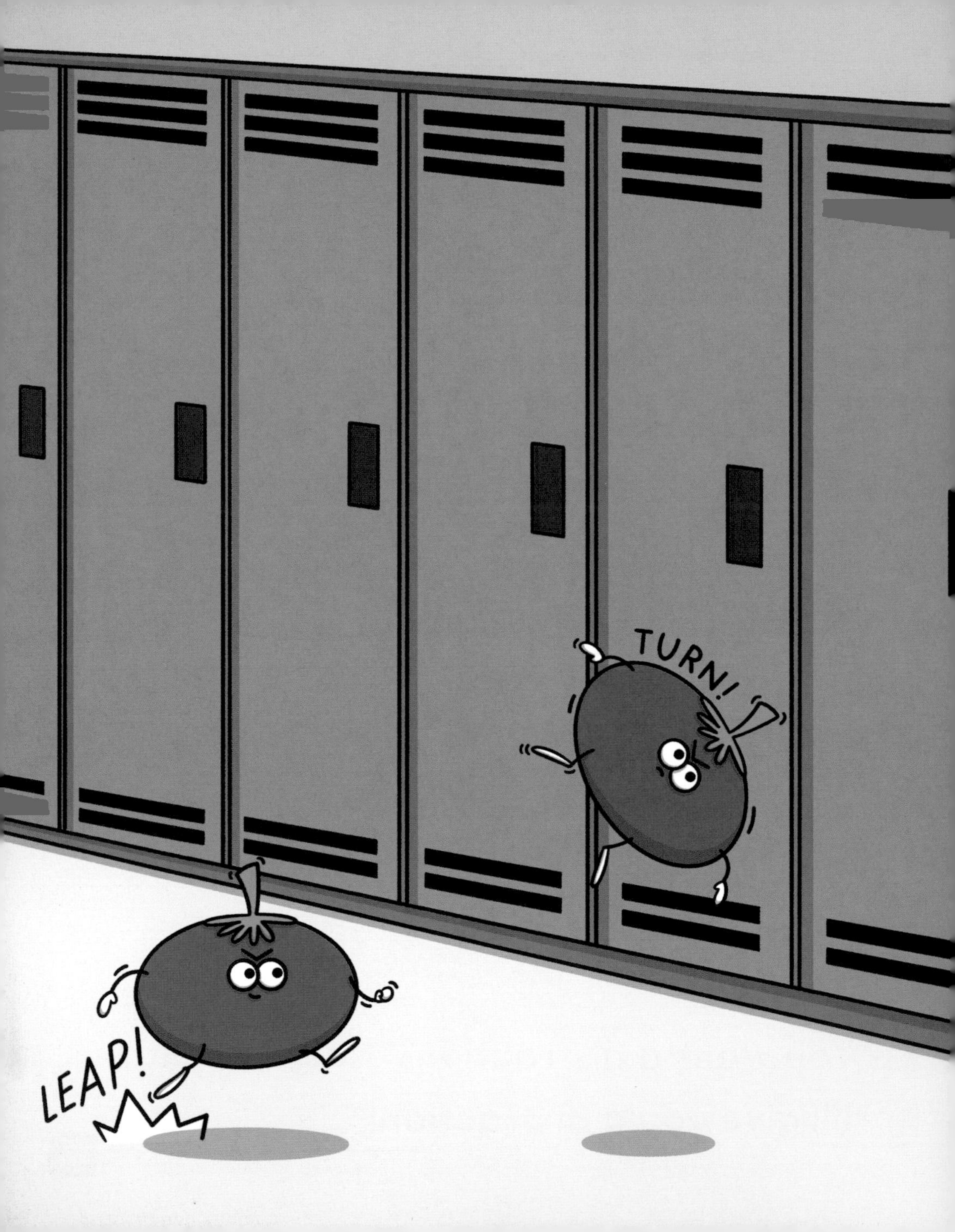
TURN!
LEAP!

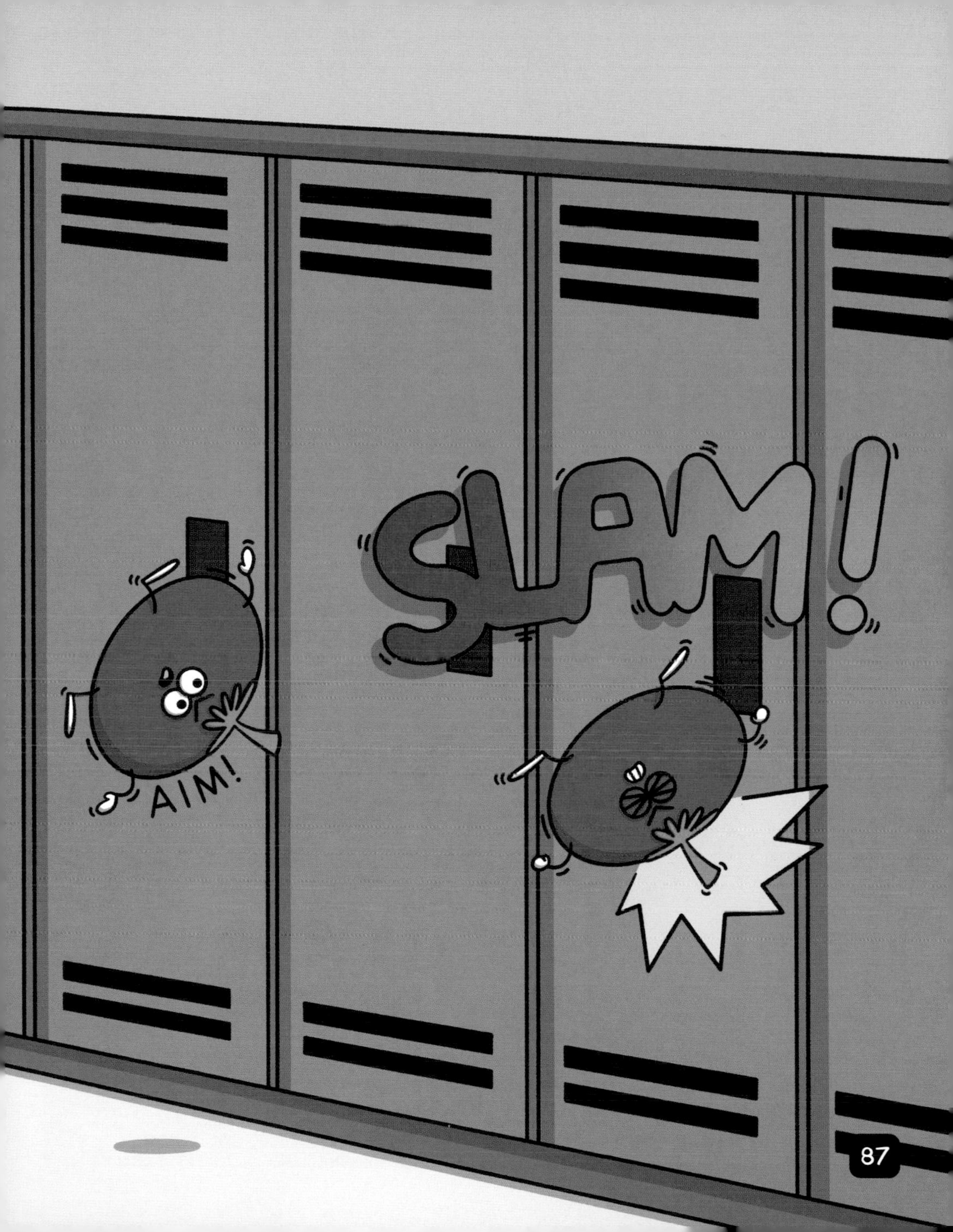
AIM!
SLAM!

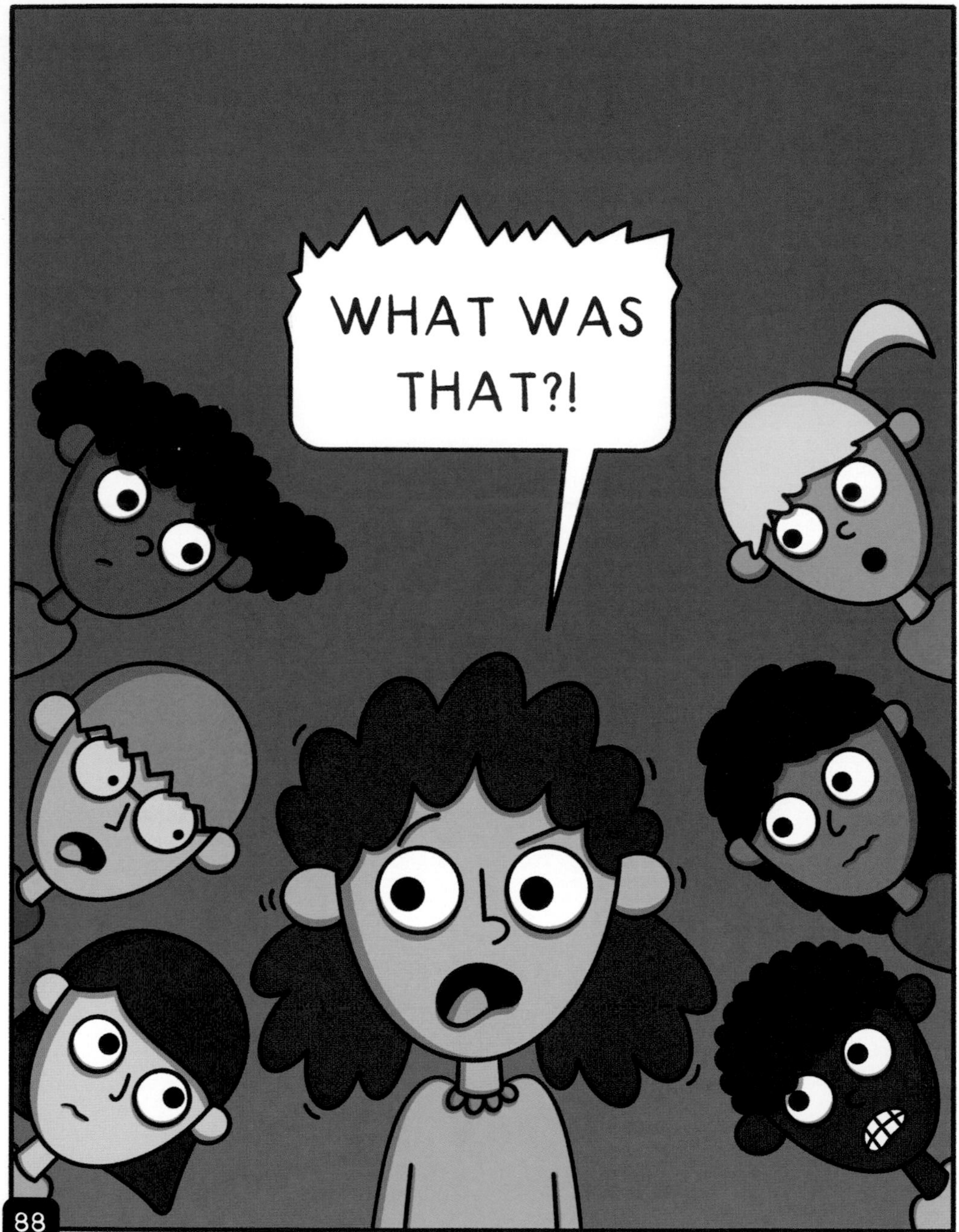
WHAT WAS THAT?!

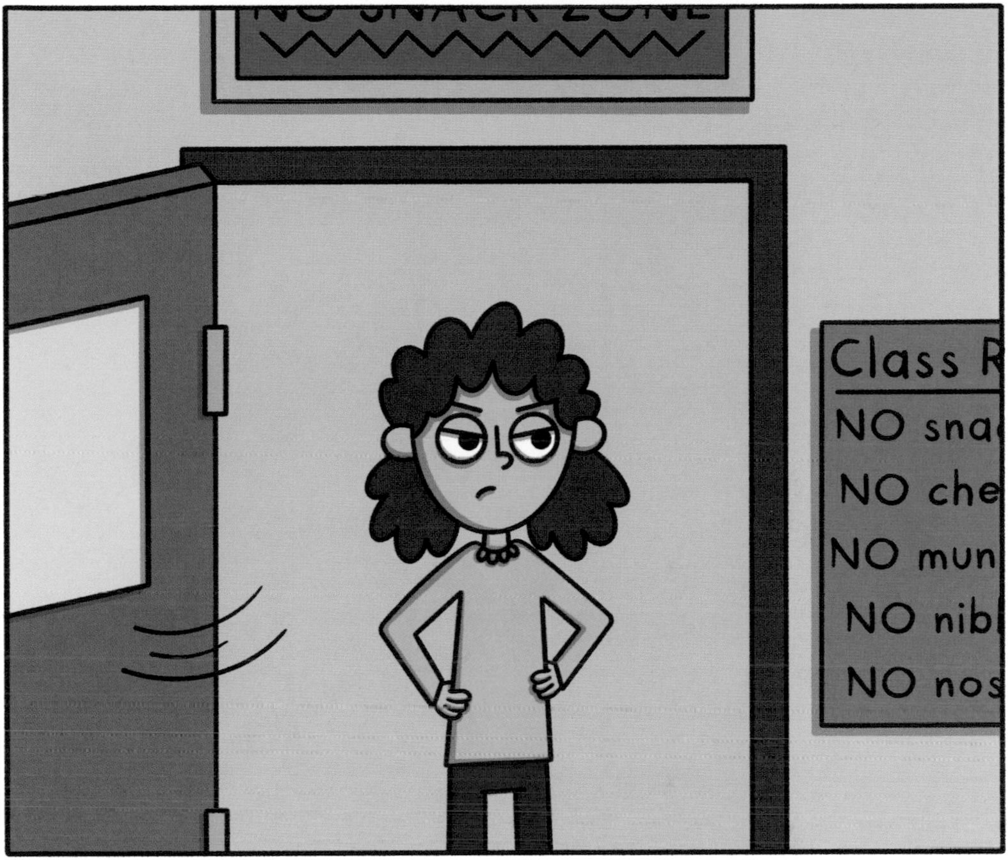
Class R
NO sna
NO che
NO mun
NO nib
NO nos

Mrs. Sternbladder didn't see anything odd right outside her classroom, so she headed down the hall.

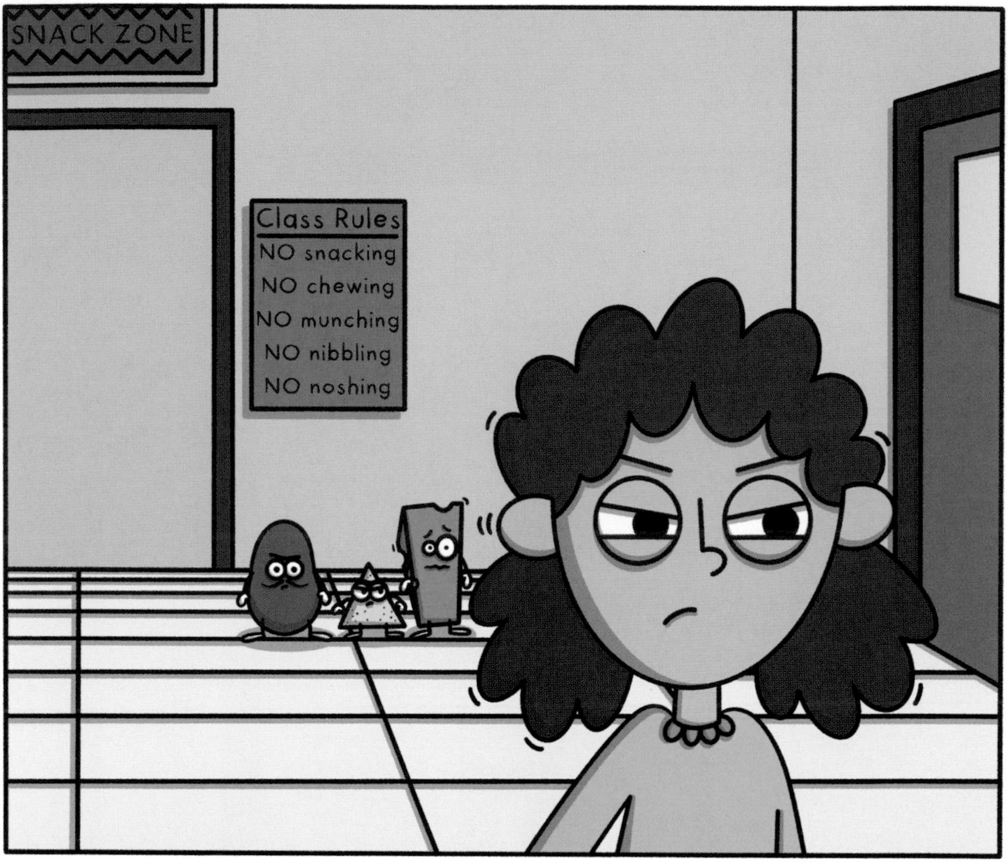
SNACK ZONE
Class Rules
NO snacking
NO chewing
NO munching
NO nibbling
NO noshing

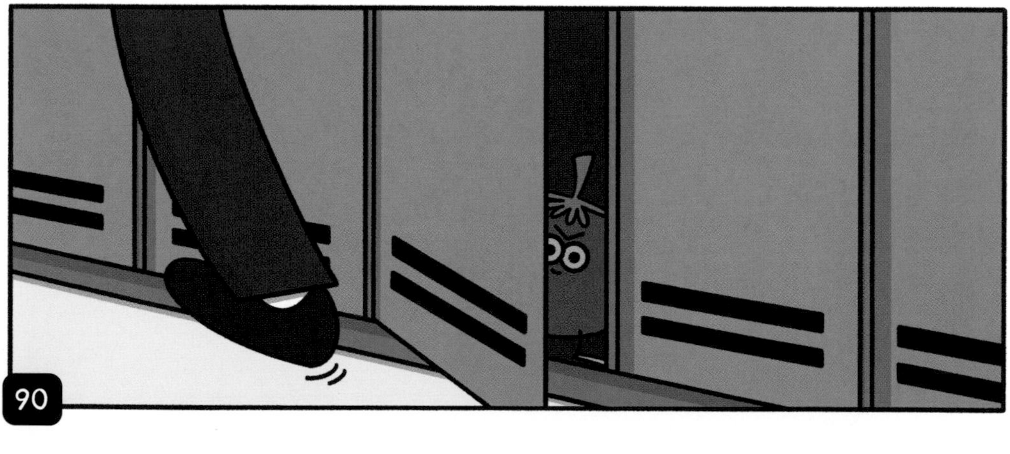

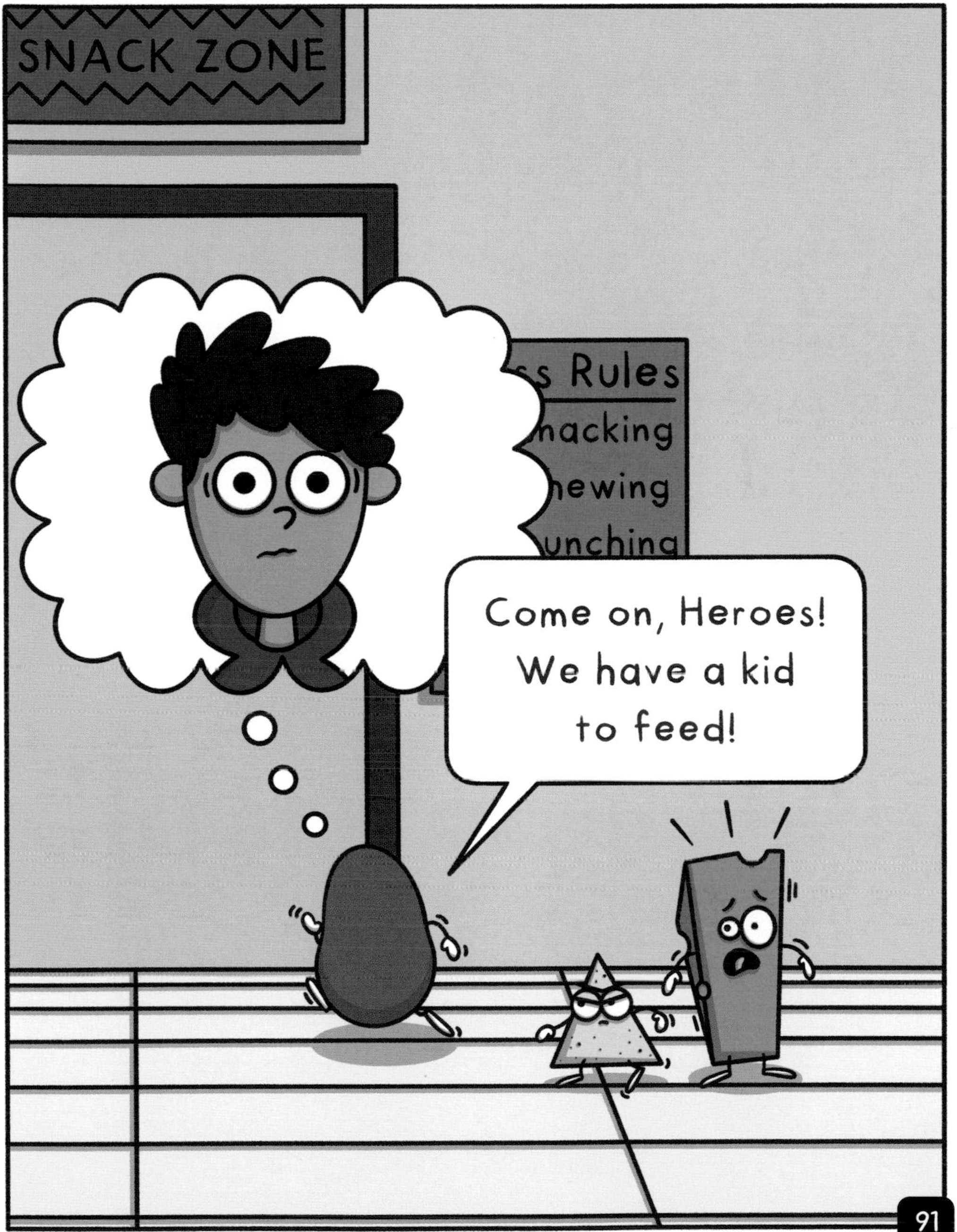
SNACK ZONE
Rules
Come on, Heroes! We have a kid to feed!

CHAPTER 7

The Hunger Heroes stood at the front
of the classroom and searched the sea
of faces before them.

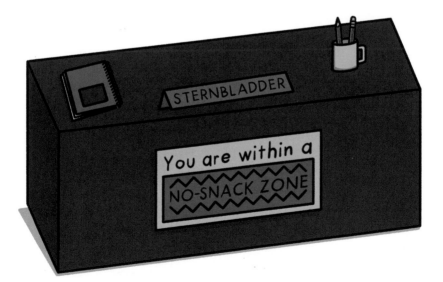

STERNBLADDER

You are within a
NO-SNACK ZONE

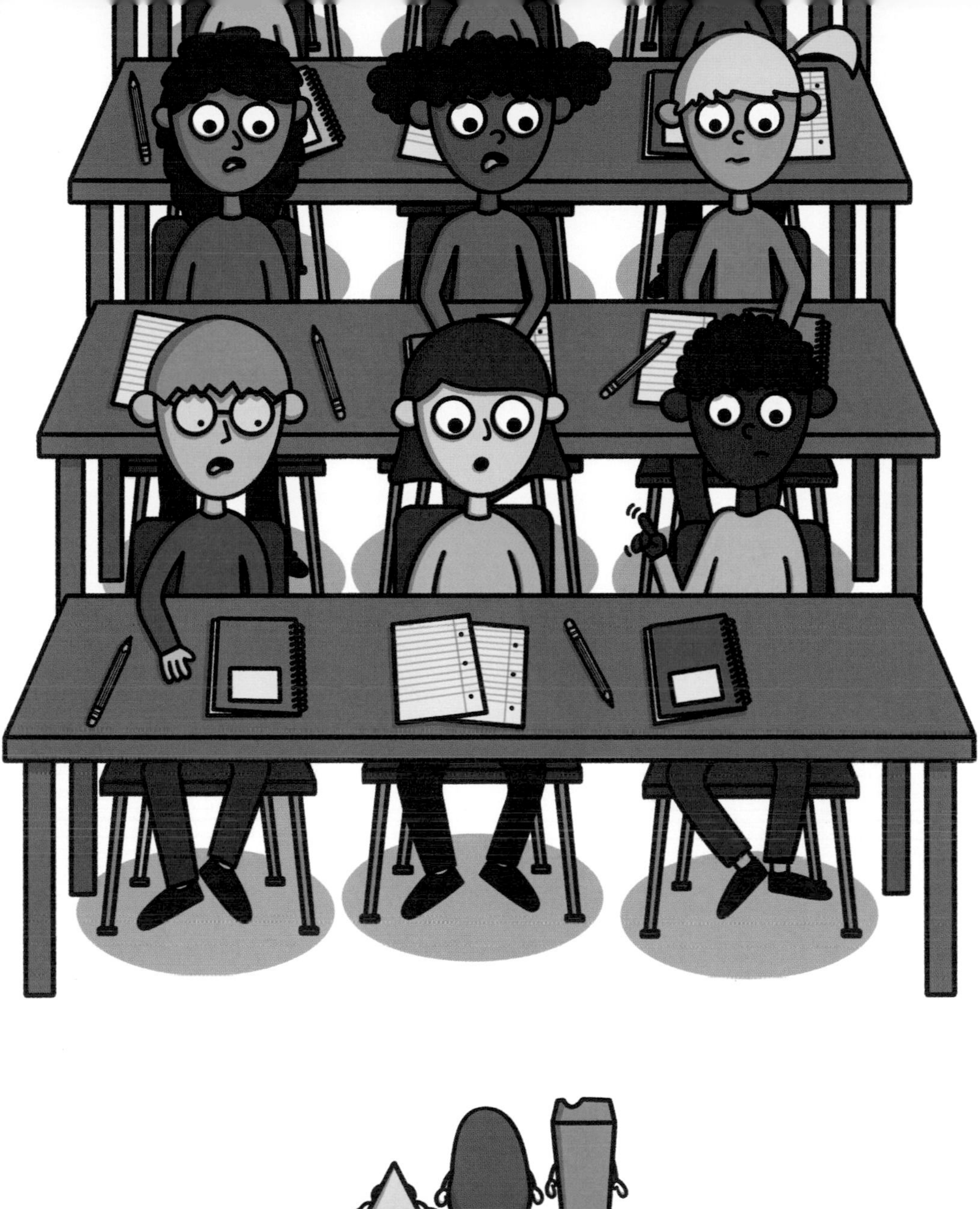

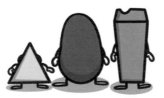

At last, Mr. Toots spotted Jason.

He was all the way at the back of the room, and looking worse than ever.

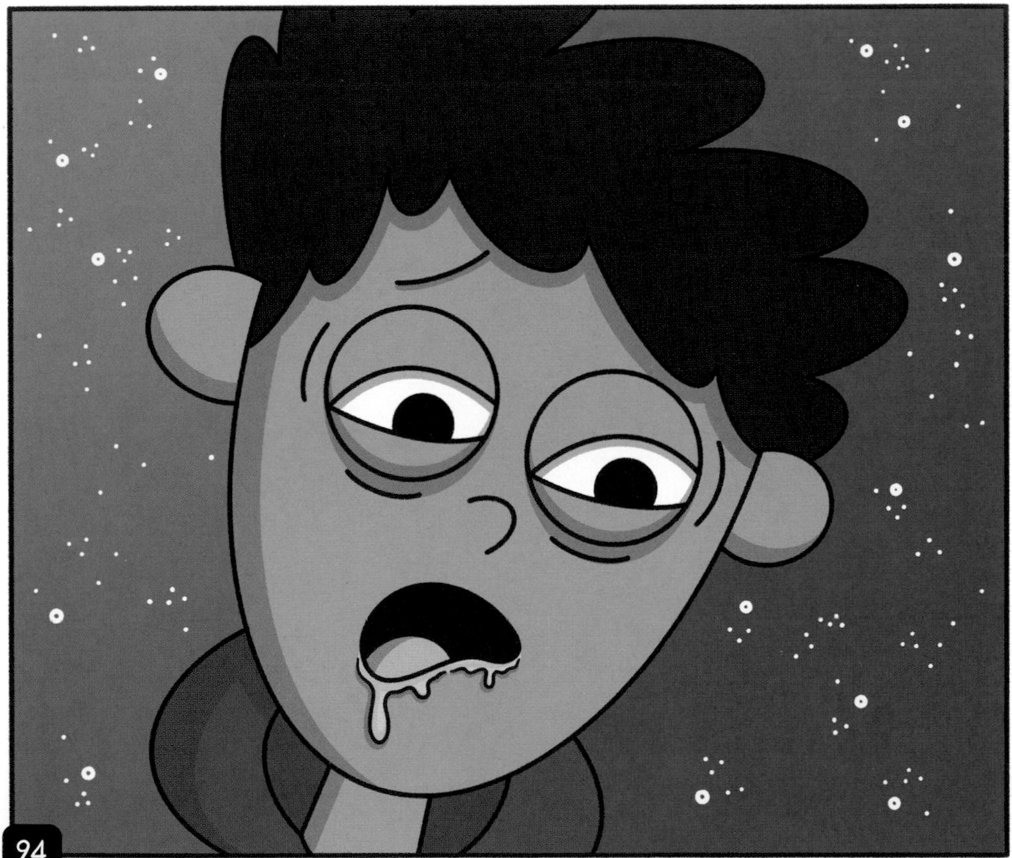

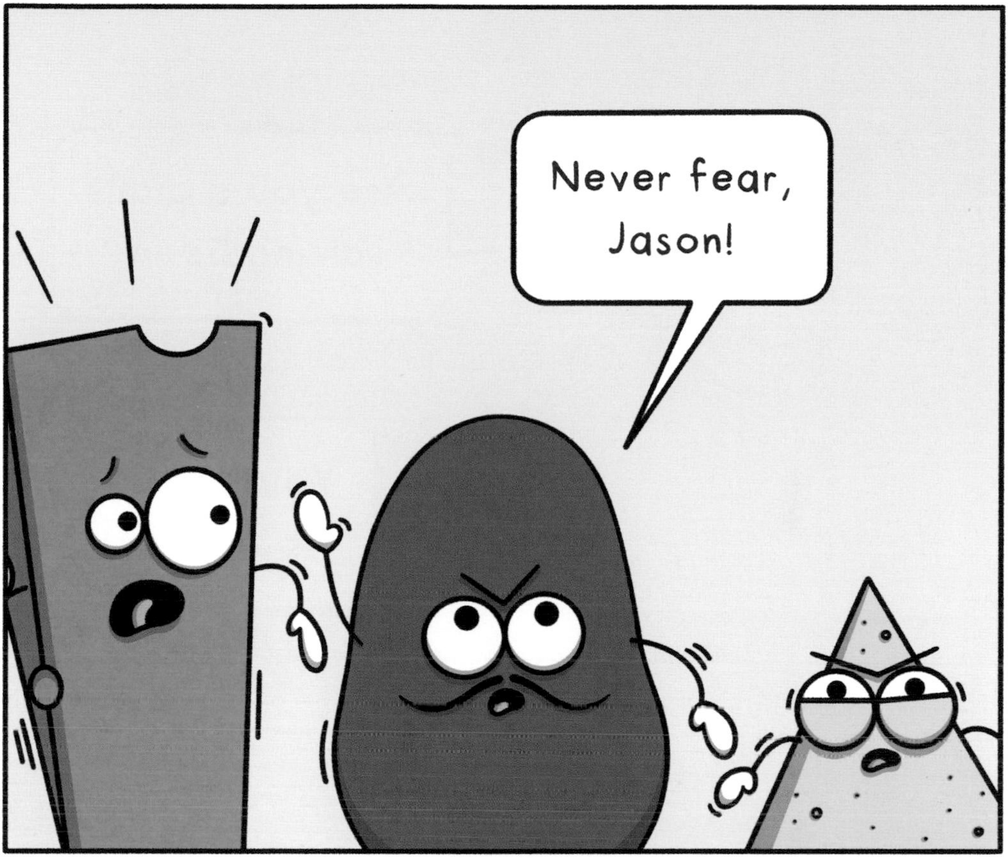
Never fear,
Jason!

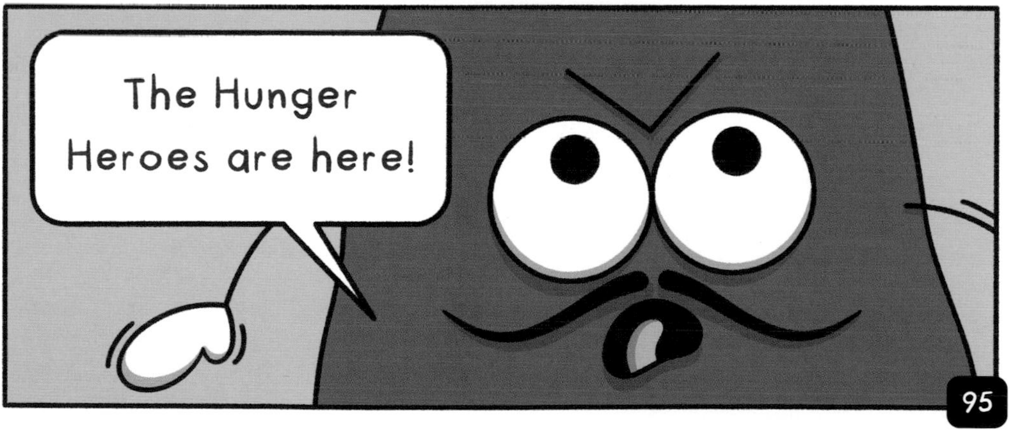
The Hunger
Heroes are here!

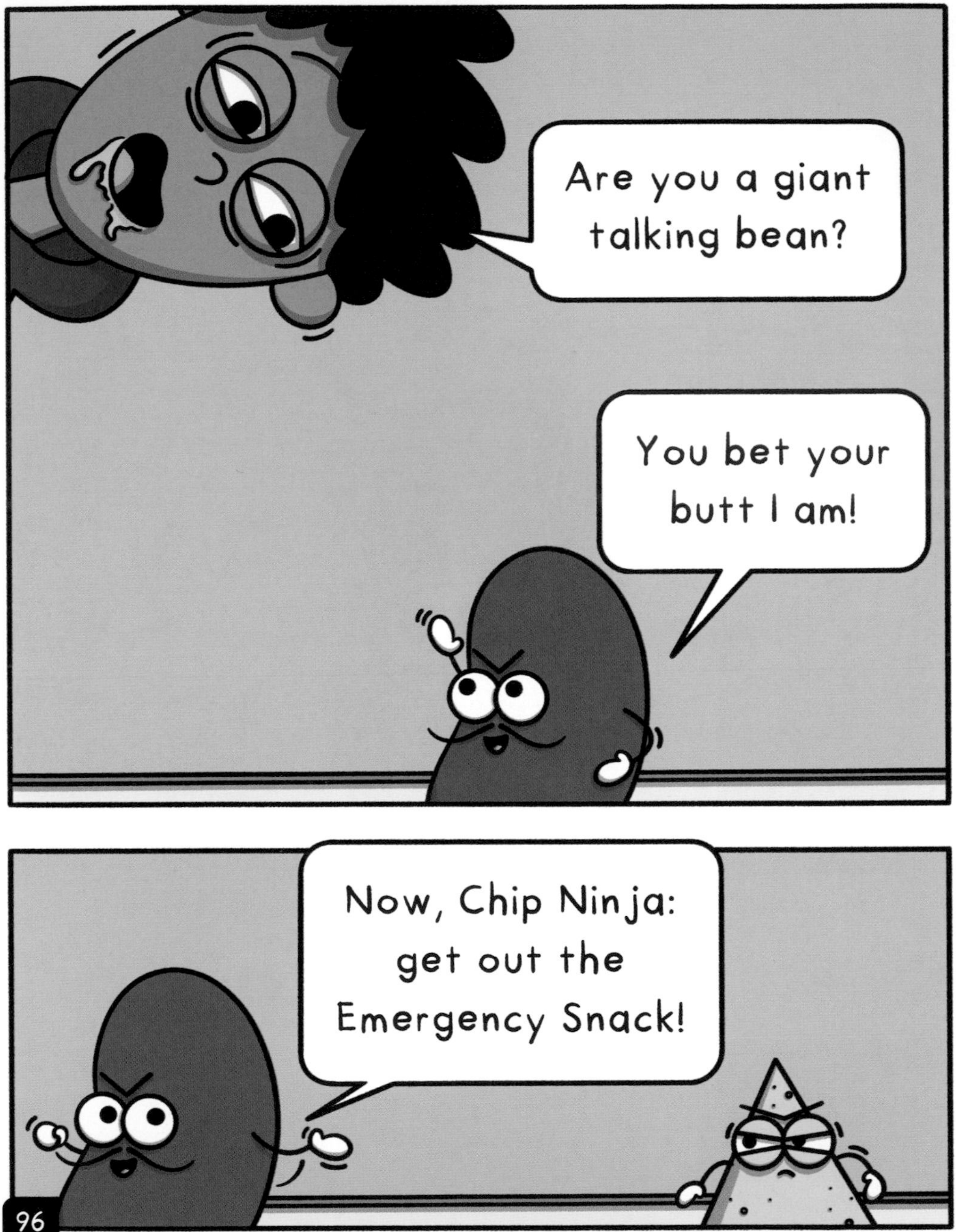
Are you a giant talking bean?
You bet your butt I am!
Now, Chip Ninja: get out the Emergency Snack!

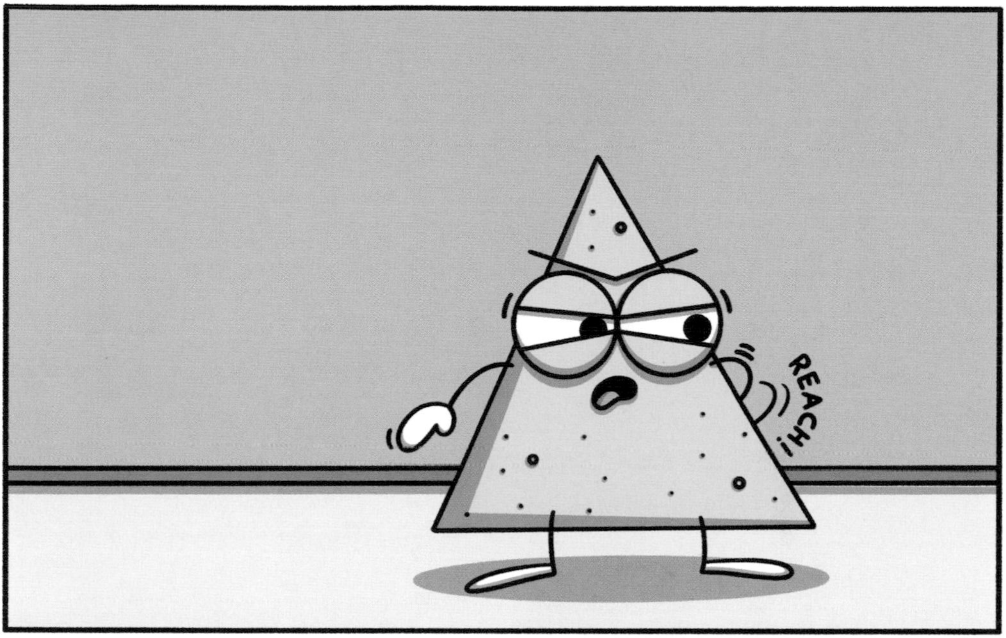
REACH!!

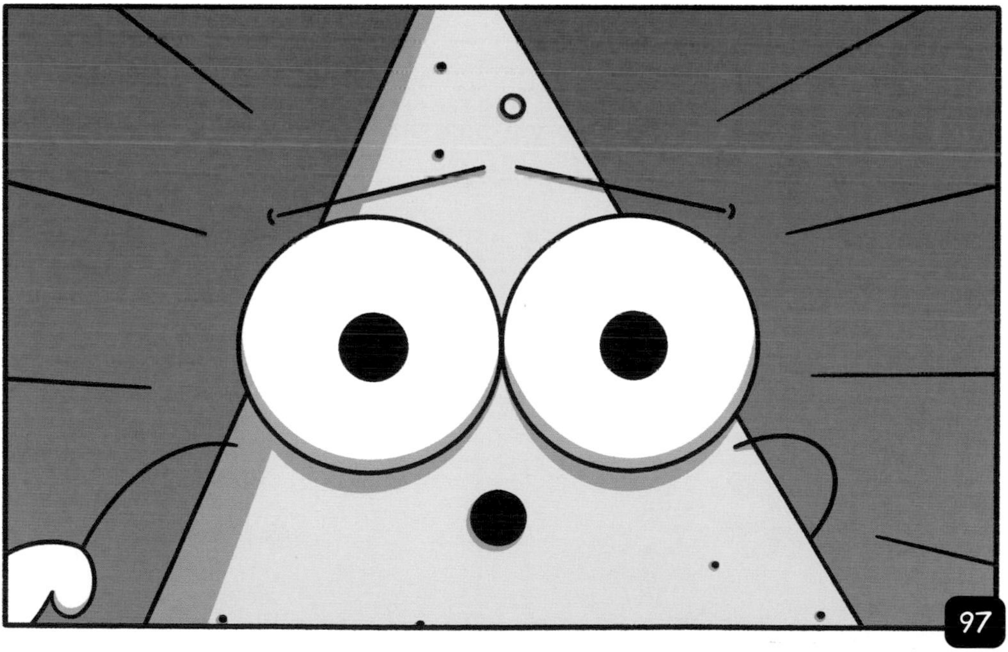

It was a moment the Hunger Heroes would never forget.

Chip Ninja, unprepared? Impossible!

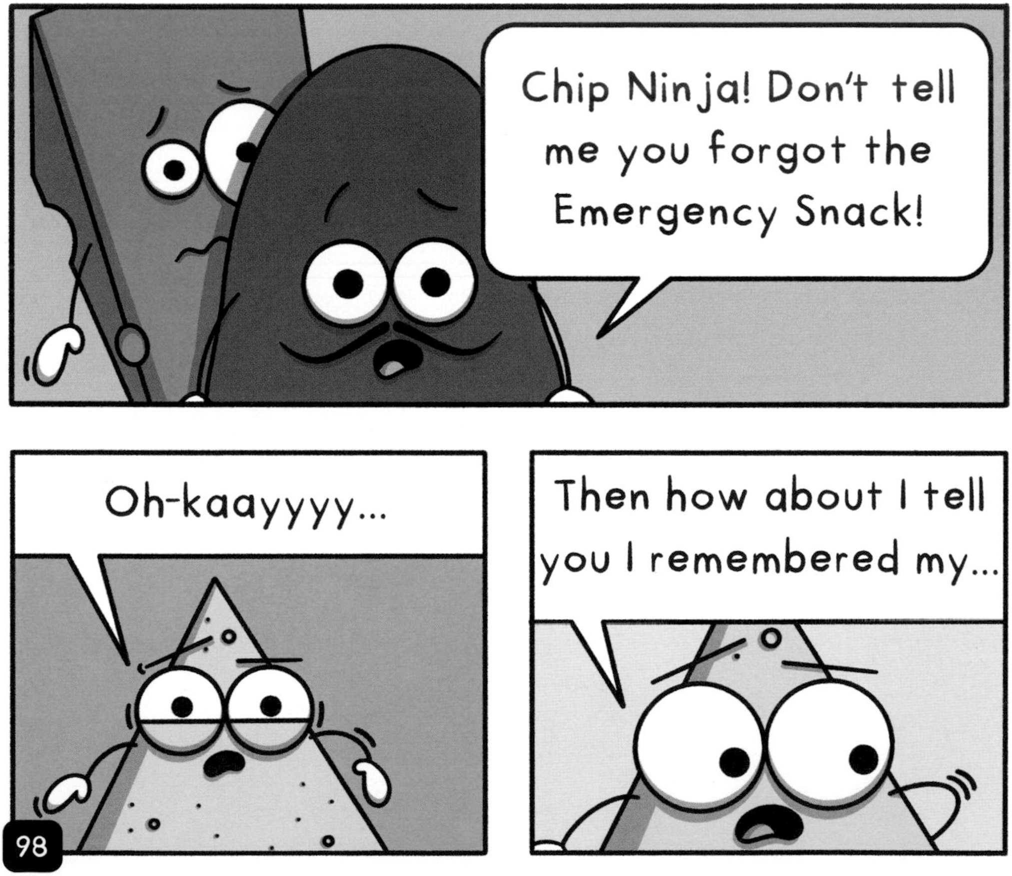
Chip Ninja! Don't tell me you forgot the Emergency Snack!
Oh-kaayyyy...
Then how about I tell you I remembered my...

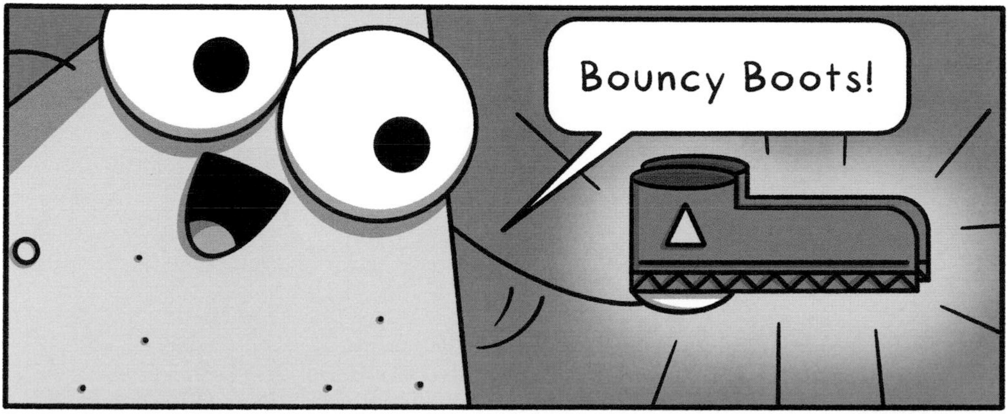
Bouncy Boots!

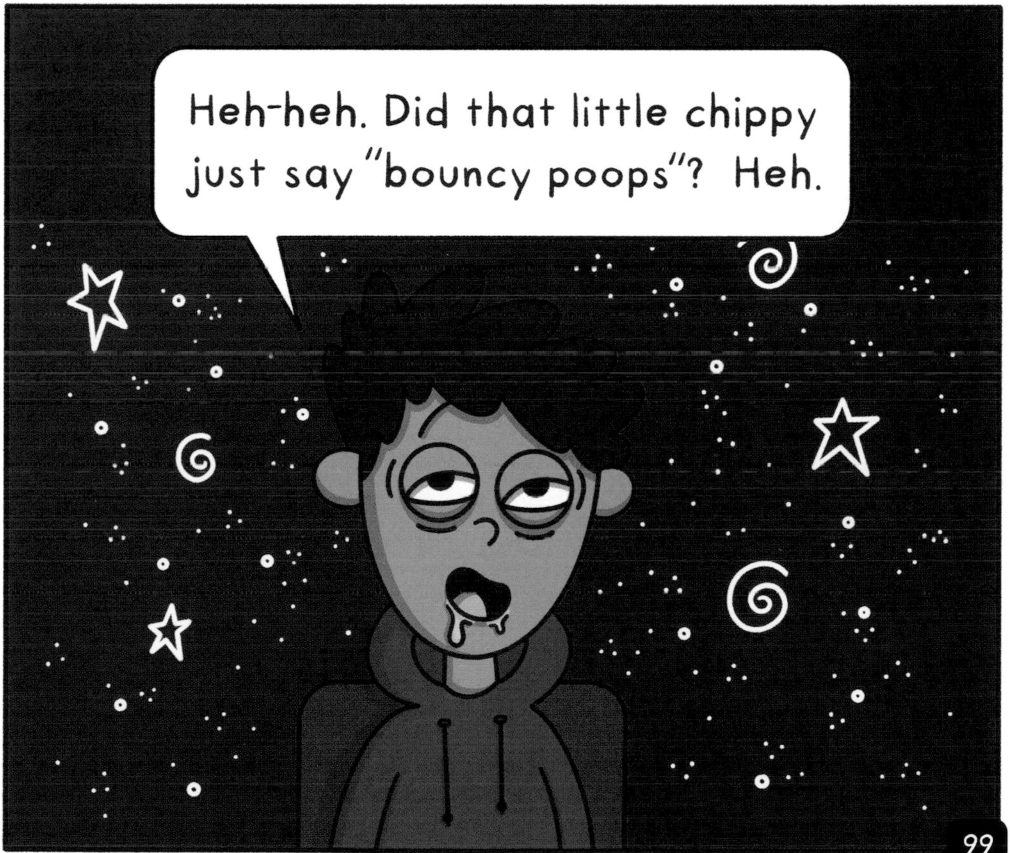
Heh-heh. Did that little chippy just say "bouncy poops"? Heh.

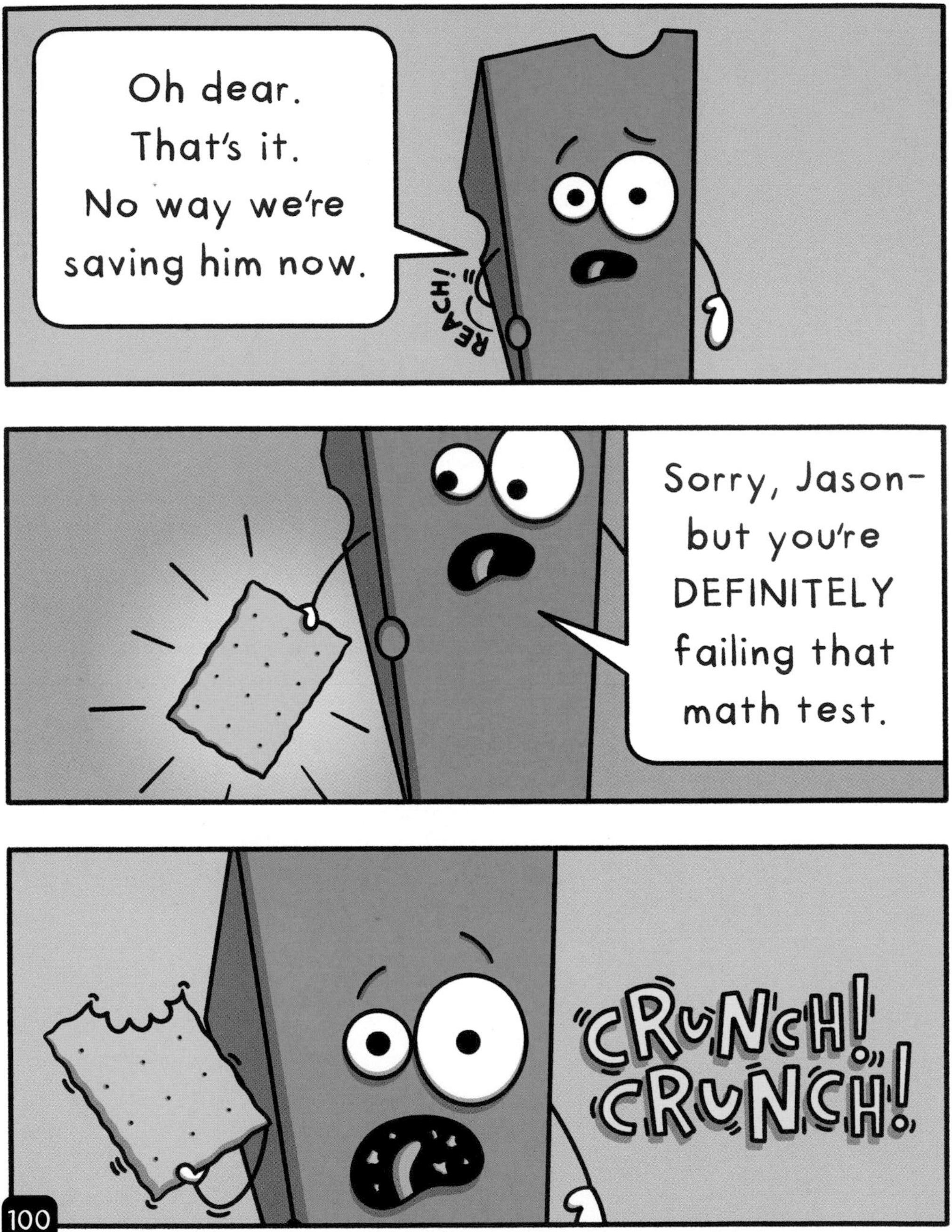
Oh dear. That's it. No way we're saving him now.
REACH!
Sorry, Jason—but you're DEFINITELY failing that math test.
CRUNCH! CRUNCH!

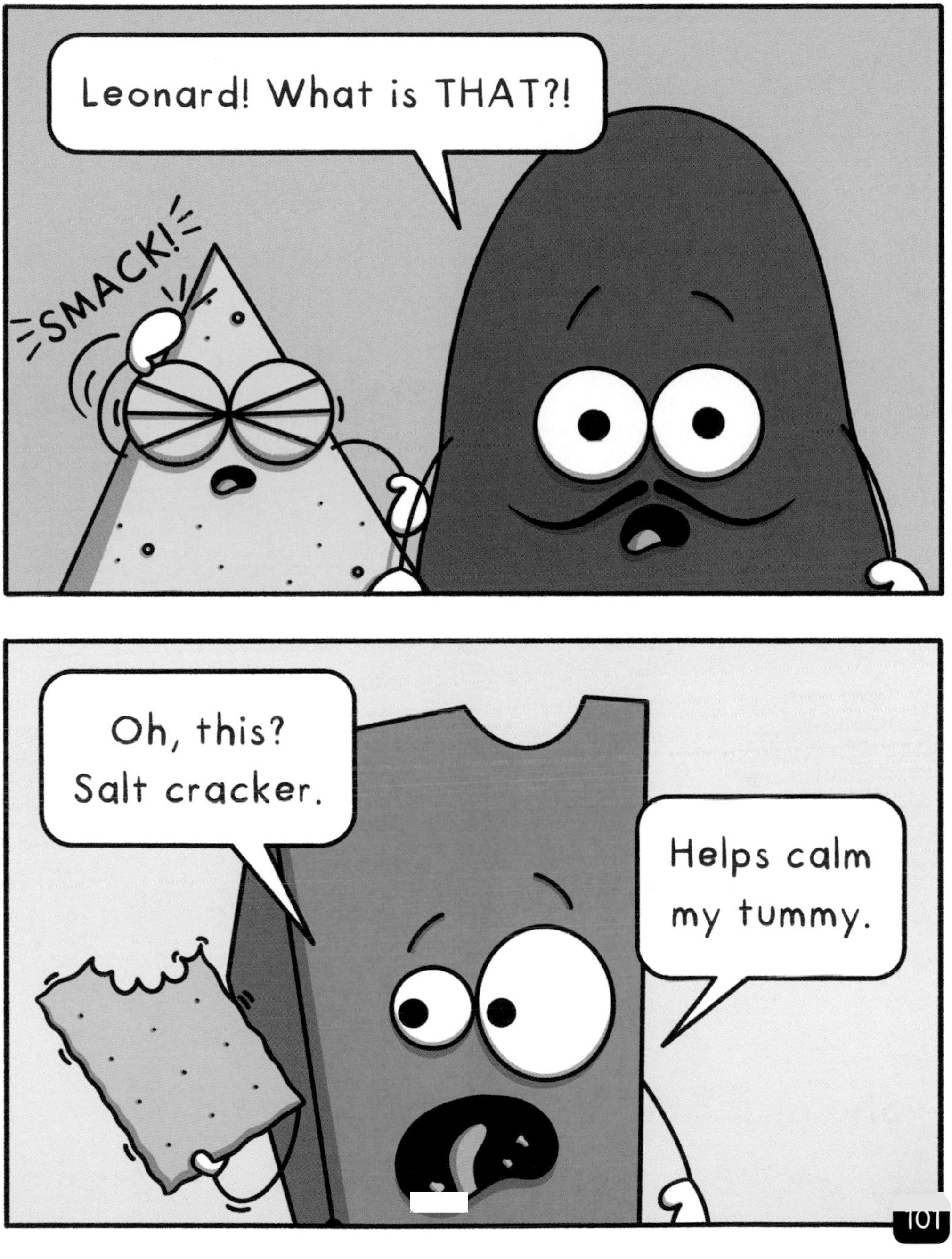
Leonard! What is THAT?!
SMACK!
Oh, this? Salt cracker.
Helps calm my tummy.

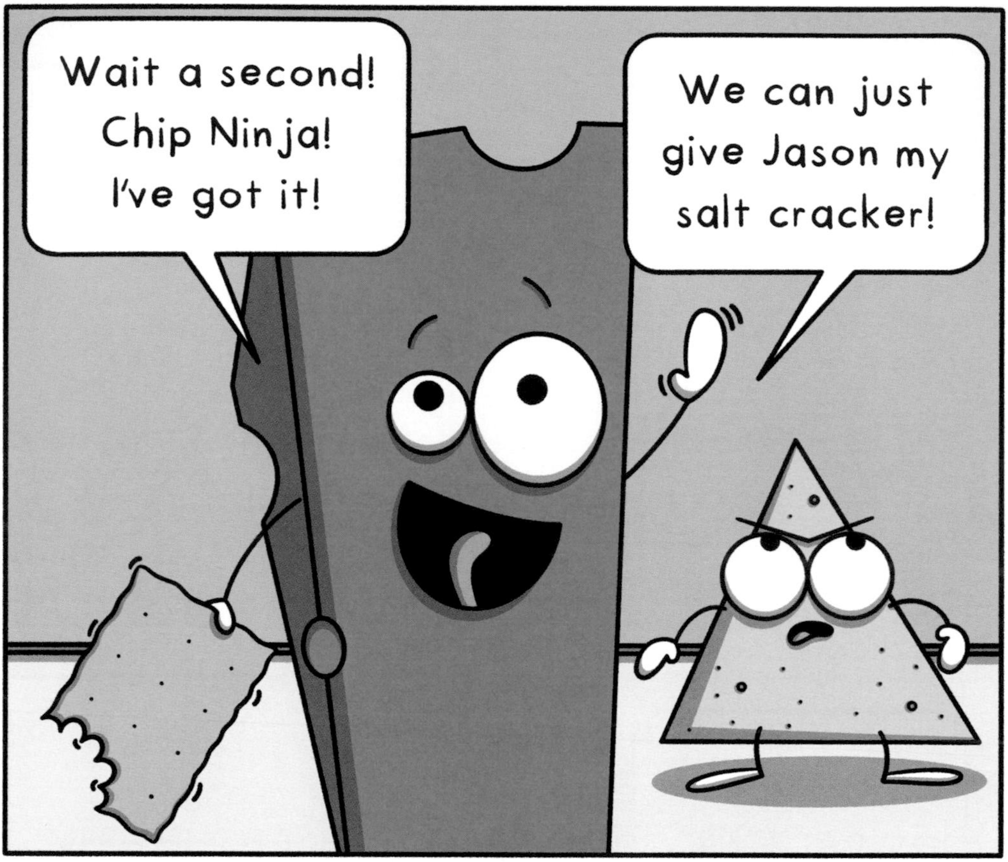
Wait a second!
Chip Ninja!
I've got it!
We can just
give Jason my
salt cracker!

Leonard held the salt cracker out to Chip Ninja.

She grabbed it, then strapped on her Bouncy Boots and rushed toward Jason.

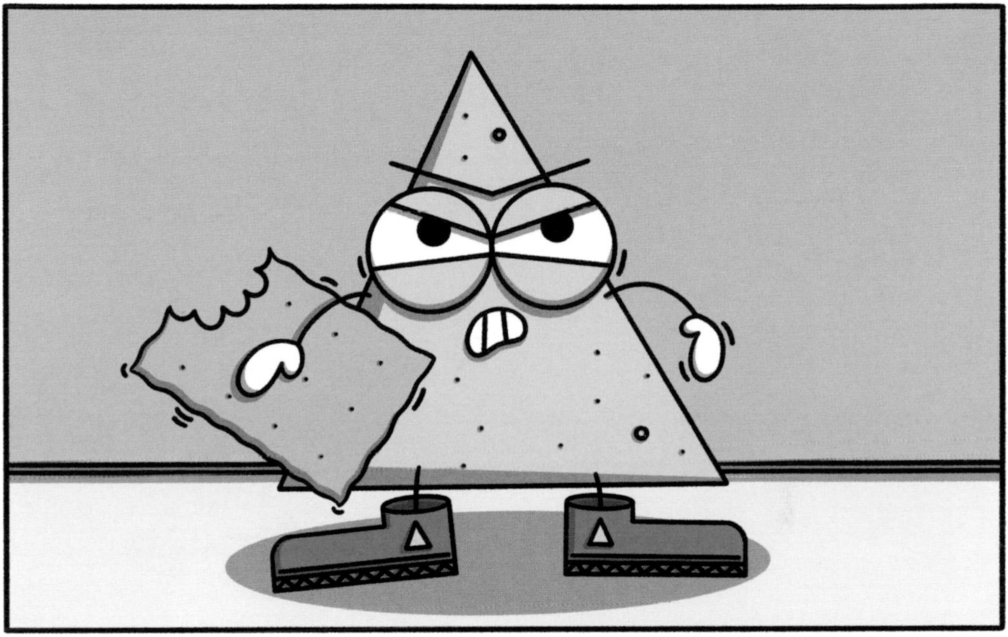

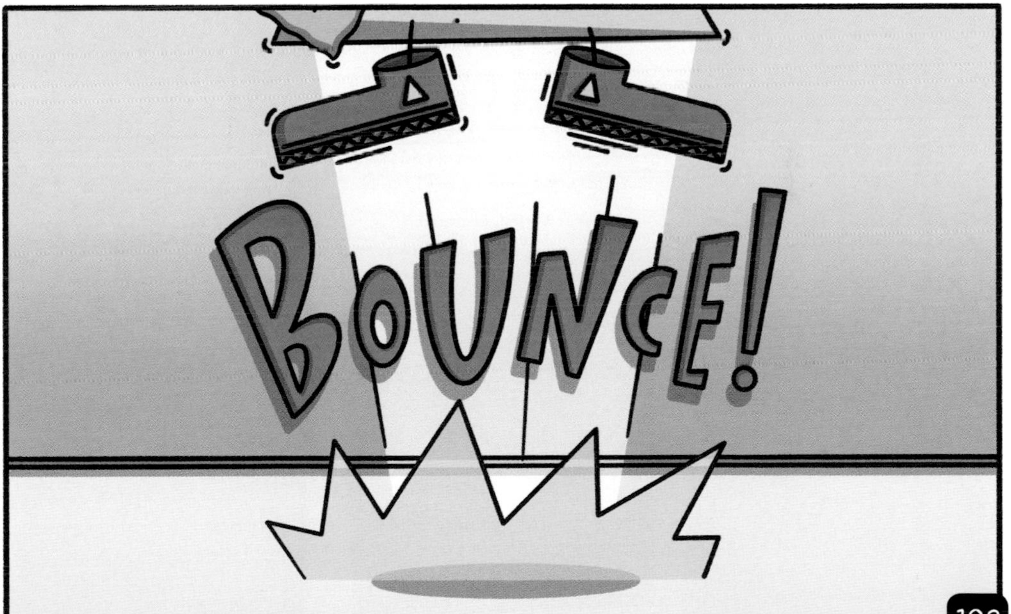
BOUNCE!

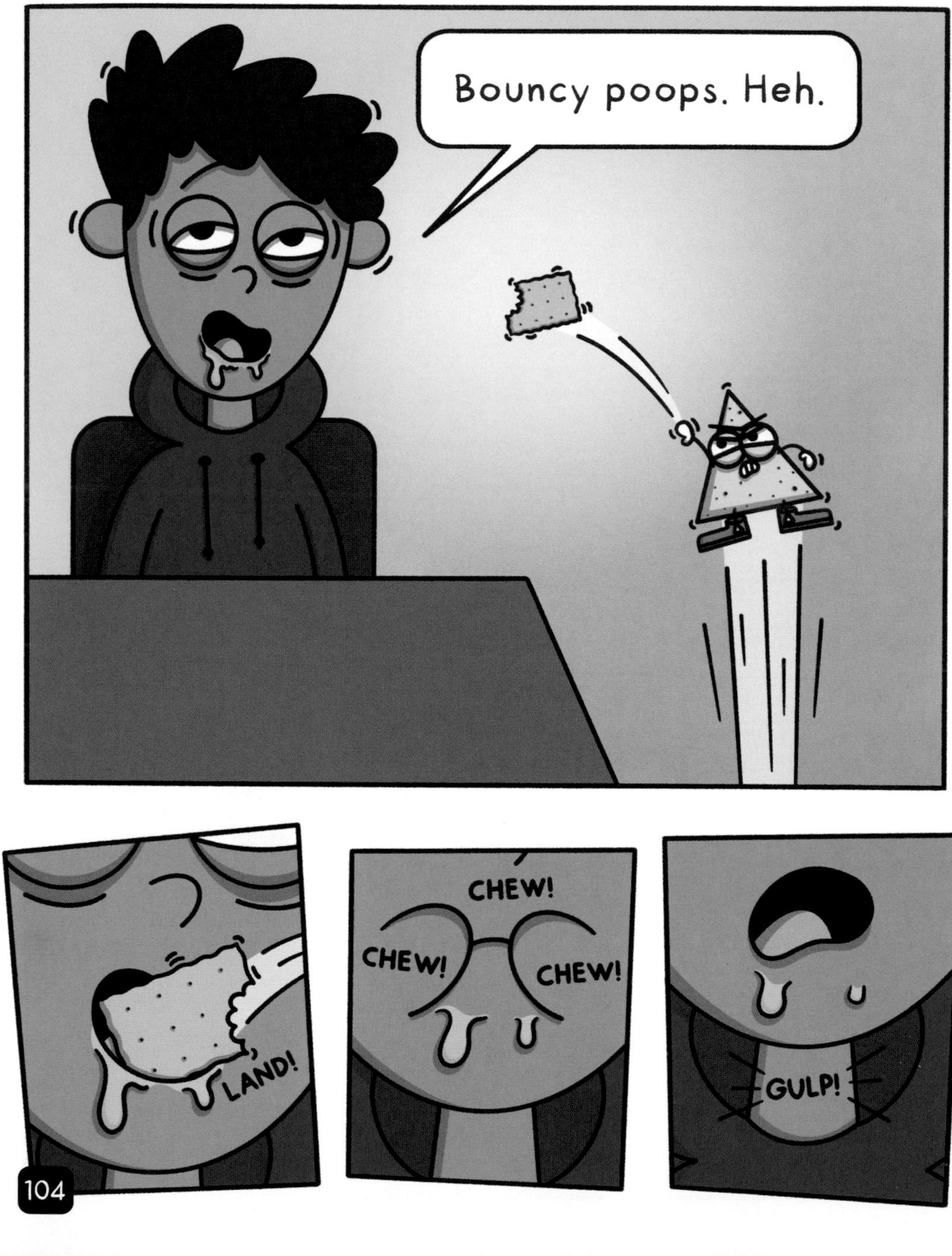
Bouncy poops. Heh.
LAND!
CHEW!
CHEW!
CHEW!
GULP!

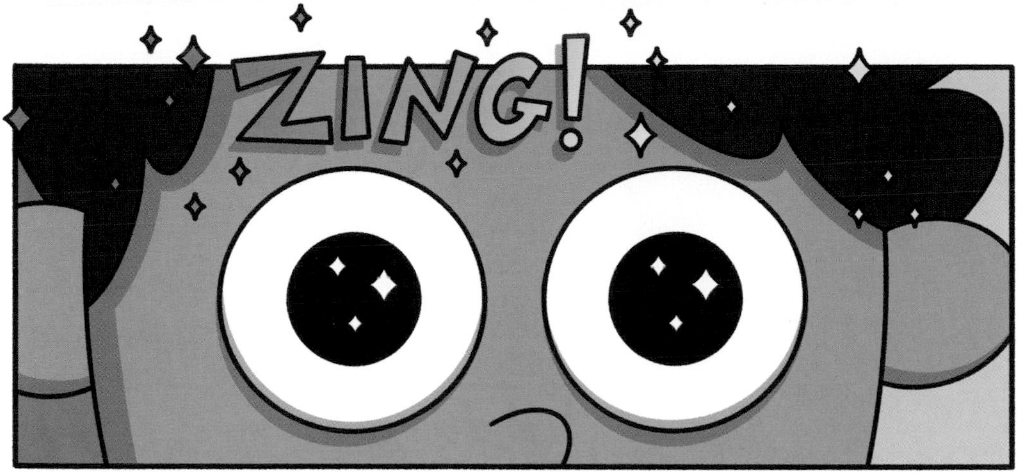
ZING!

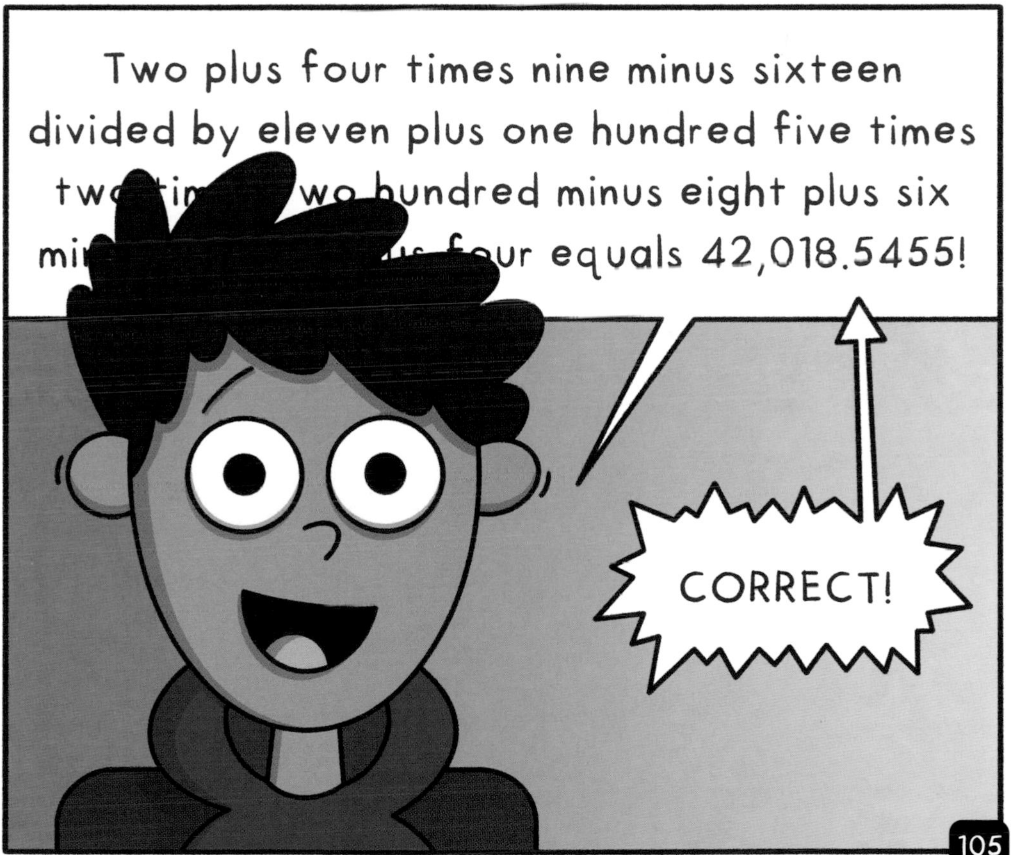
Two plus four times nine minus sixteen divided by eleven plus one hundred five times tw ti wo hundred minus eight plus six mi our equals 42,018.5455!
CORRECT!

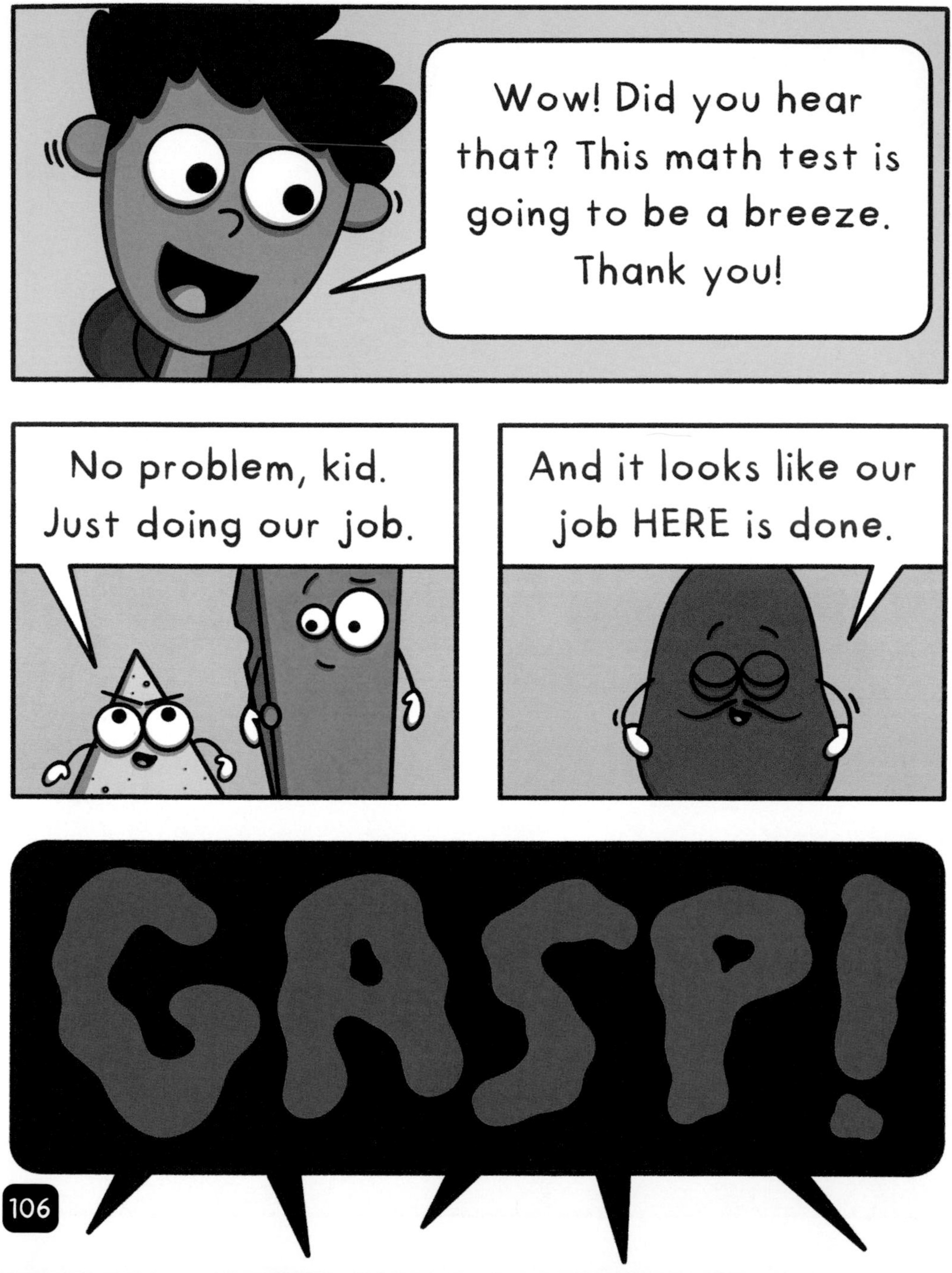
Wow! Did you hear that? This math test is going to be a breeze. Thank you!
No problem, kid. Just doing our job.
And it looks like our job HERE is done.
GASP!

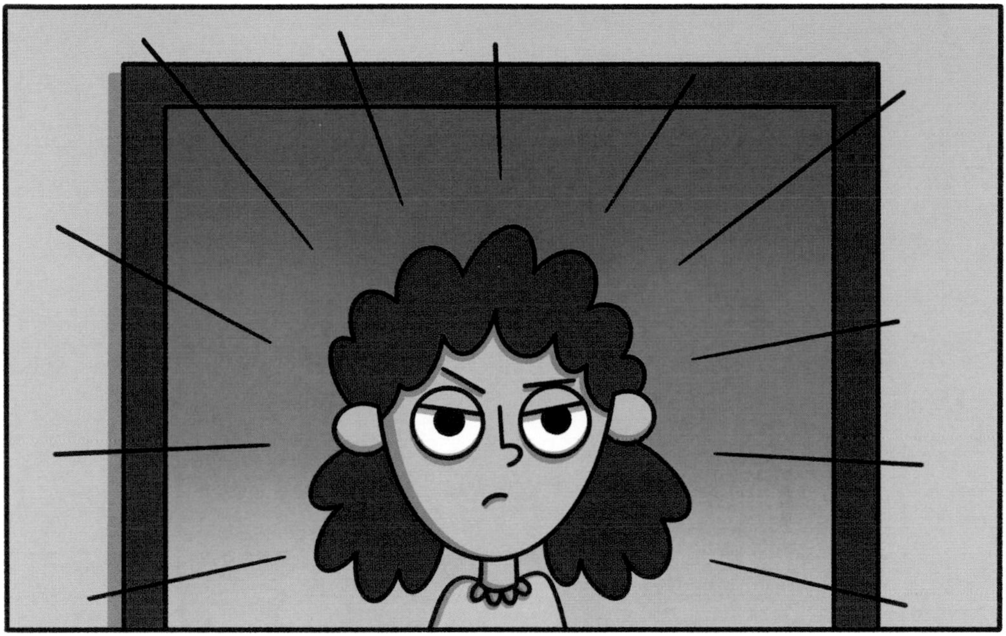

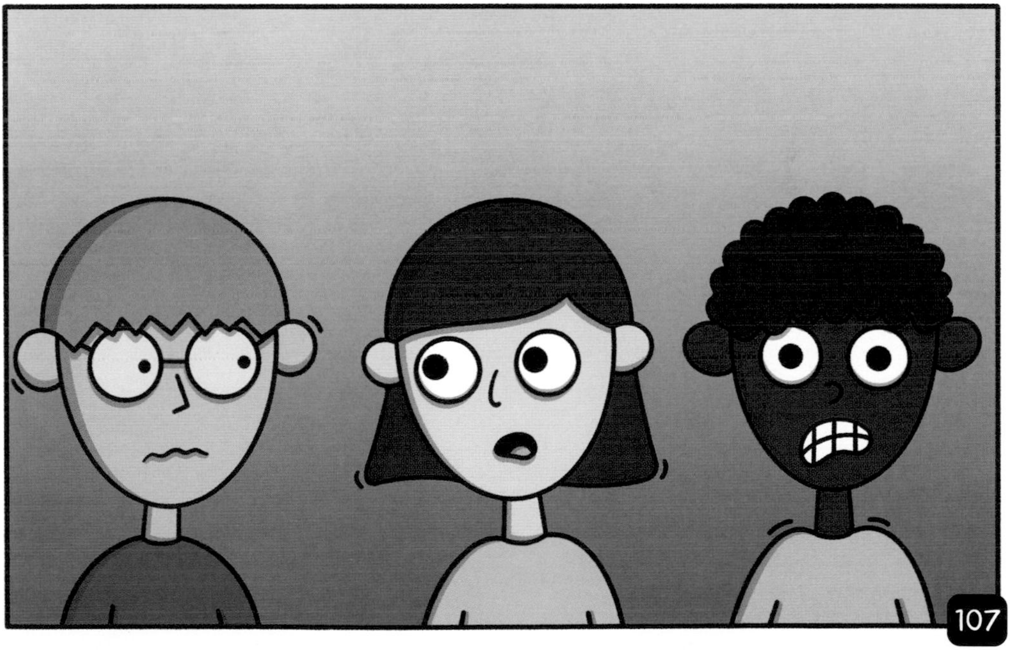

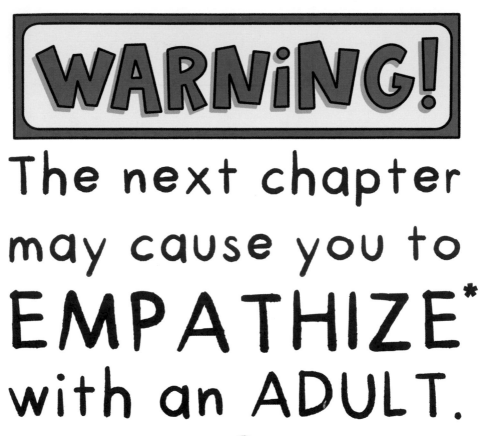

WARNING!

The next chapter may cause you to **EMPATHIZE*** with an **ADULT**.

*To understand and share the feelings of someone else.

READ AT YOUR OWN RISK.

You got this!

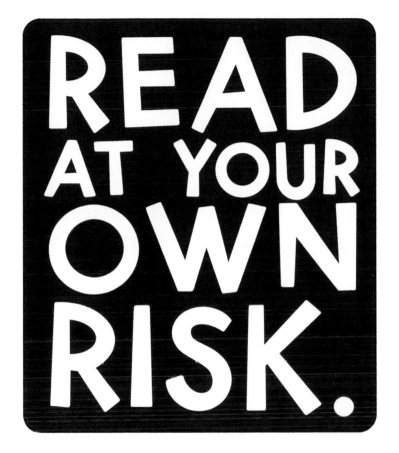

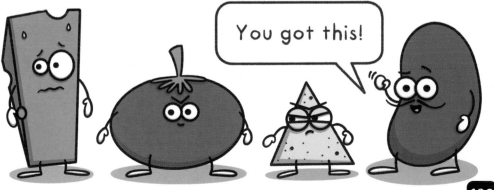

CHAPTER 8

Mrs. Sternbladder stomped into her classroom.

She glared at the Hunger Heroes. Then she glared at the cracker crumbs on Jason's desk....

And then she went from upset to furious!

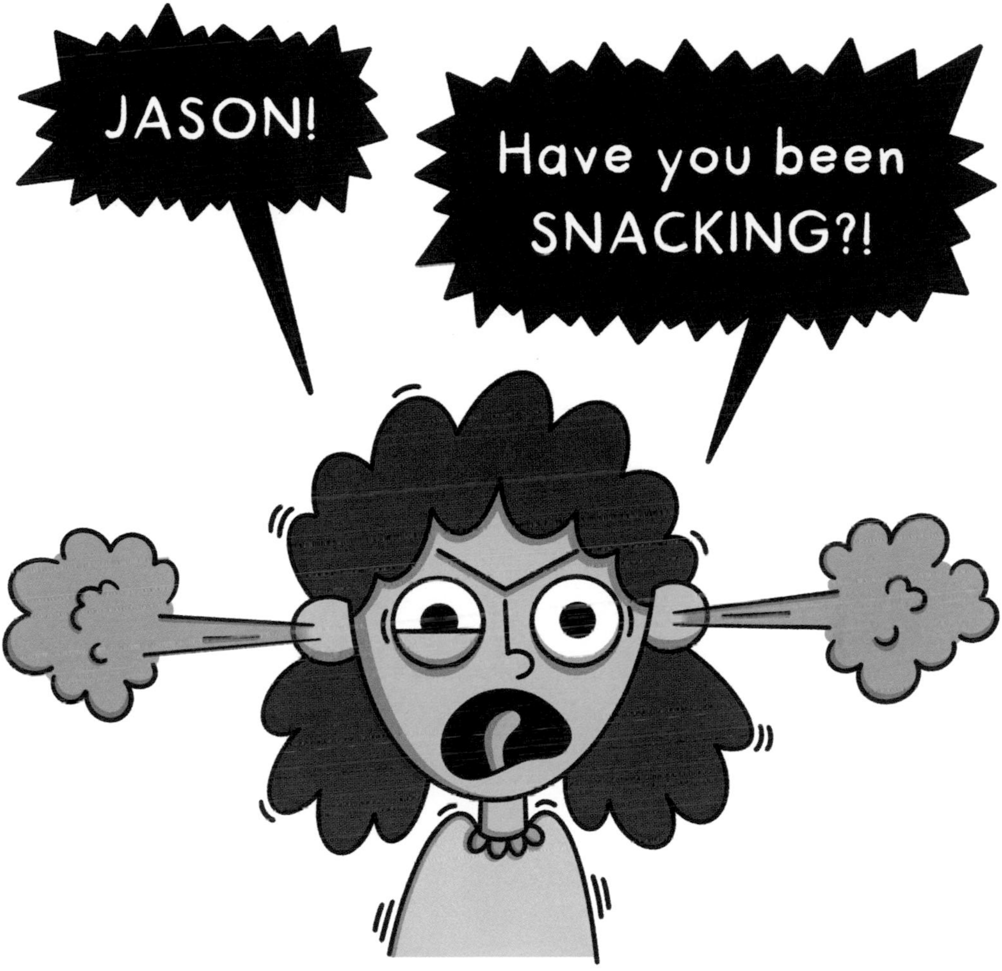
JASON!
Have you been SNACKING?!

What were the Hunger Heroes to do?

They could make a run for it....

But then they would be leaving Jason and all the other kids to deal with Mrs. Sternbladder all alone.

And that wouldn't be very heroic....

Which was why Mr. Toots finally stepped forward.

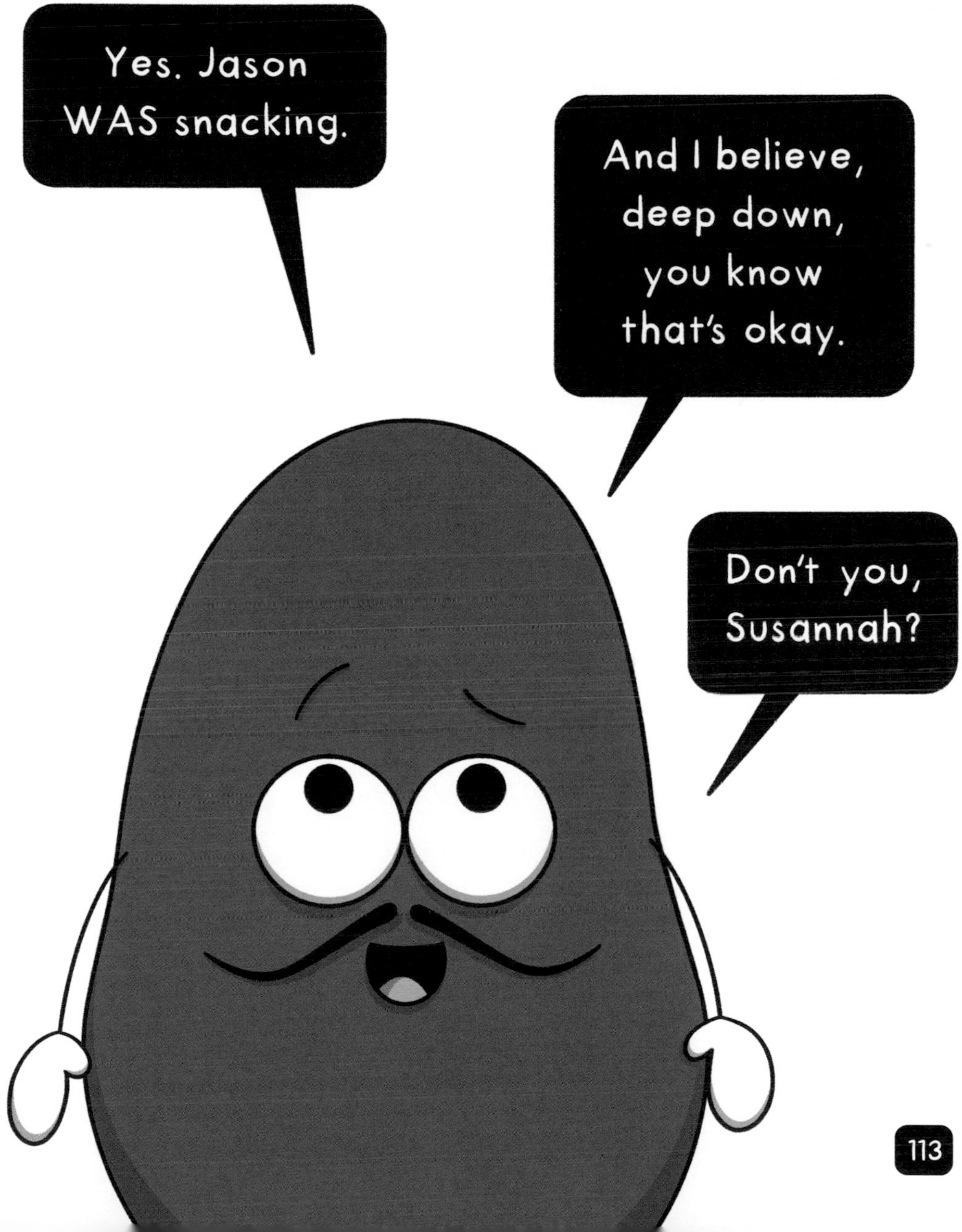
Yes. Jason WAS snacking.
And I believe, deep down, you know that's okay.
Don't you, Susannah?

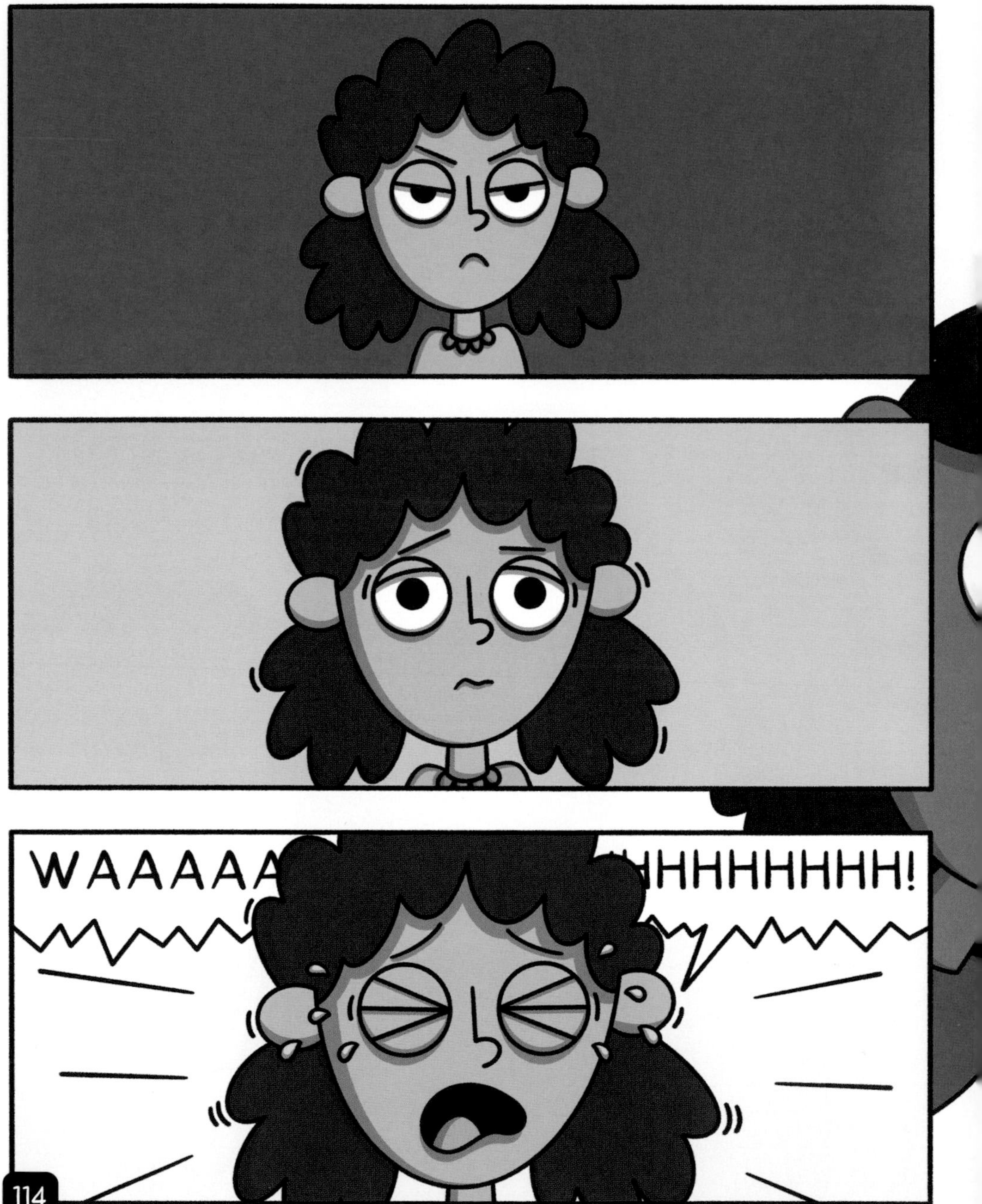
WAAAAA
HHHHHHHH!

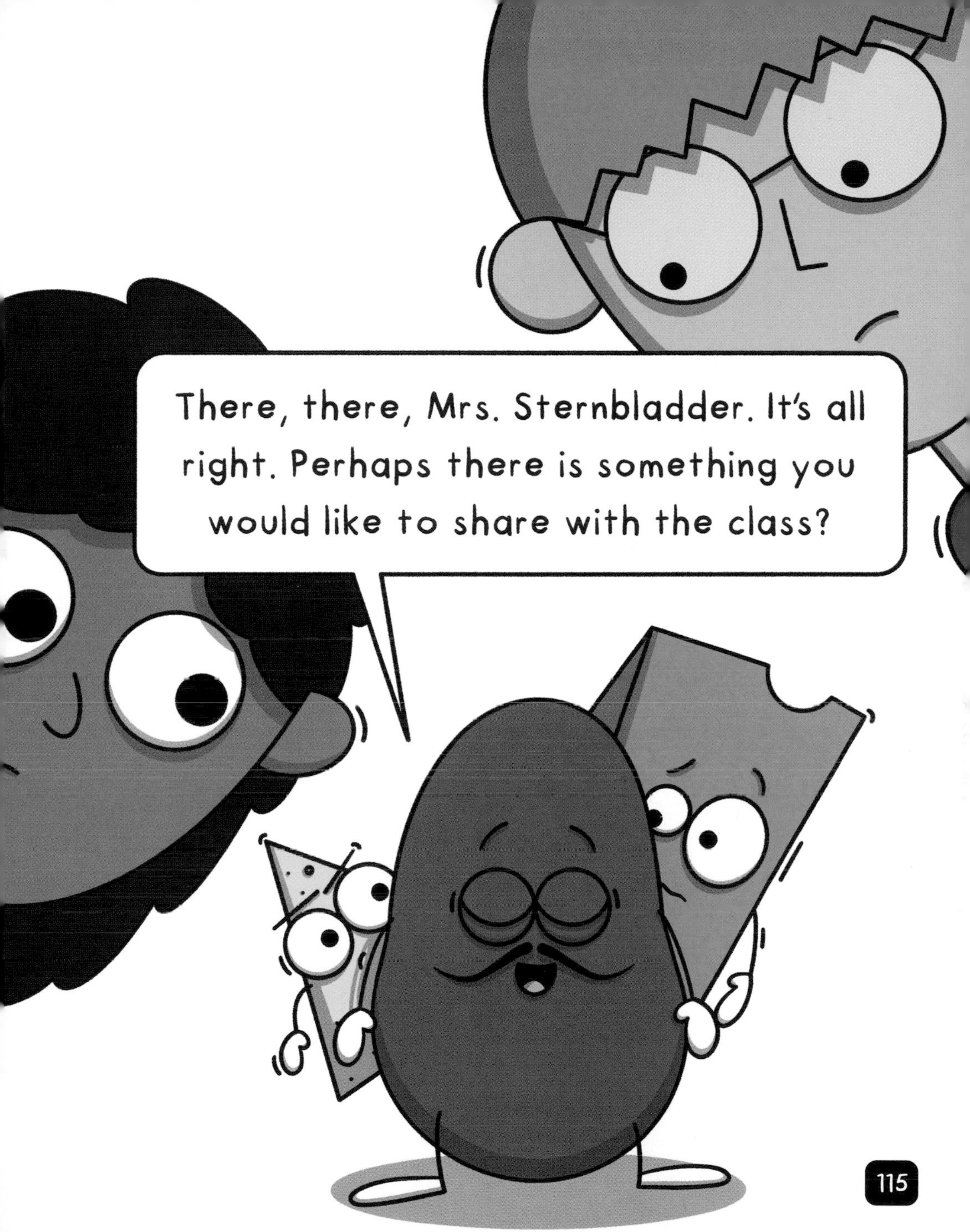
There, there, Mrs. Sternbladder. It's all right. Perhaps there is something you would like to share with the class?

"There is," Mrs. Sternbladder told Mr. Toots.

She took a deep breath and told her students a story....

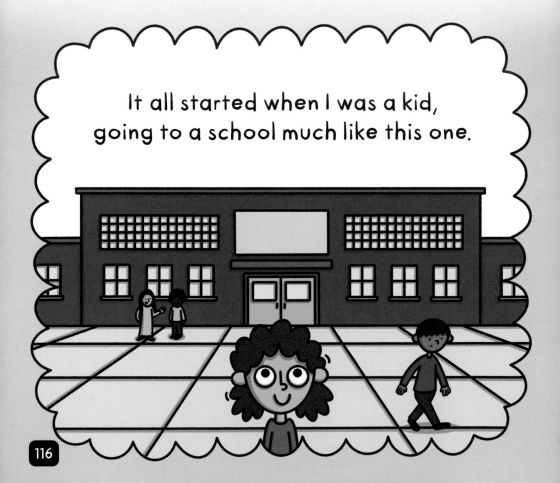

It all started when I was a kid, going to a school much like this one.

One day during class, I got a little hungry. My stomach was growling so loudly that I was having trouble focusing. So... I snuck a few bites of a snack.

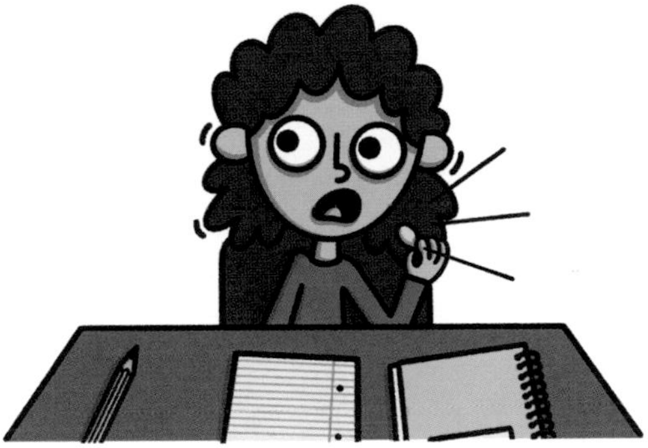

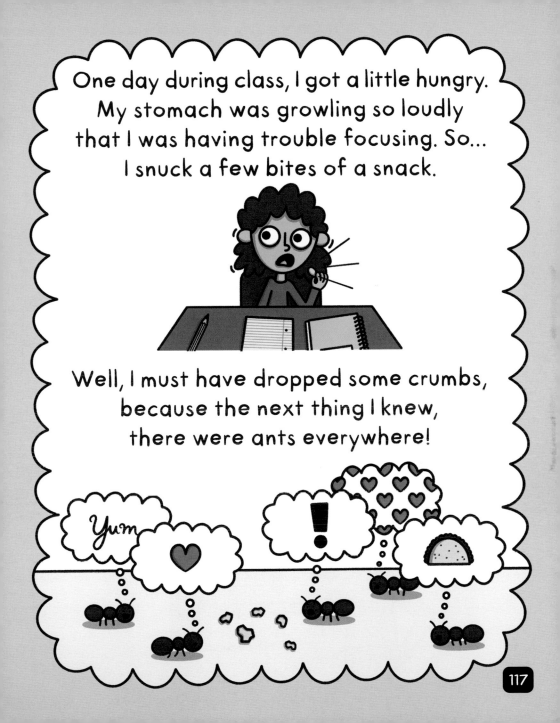

Well, I must have dropped some crumbs, because the next thing I knew, there were ants everywhere!

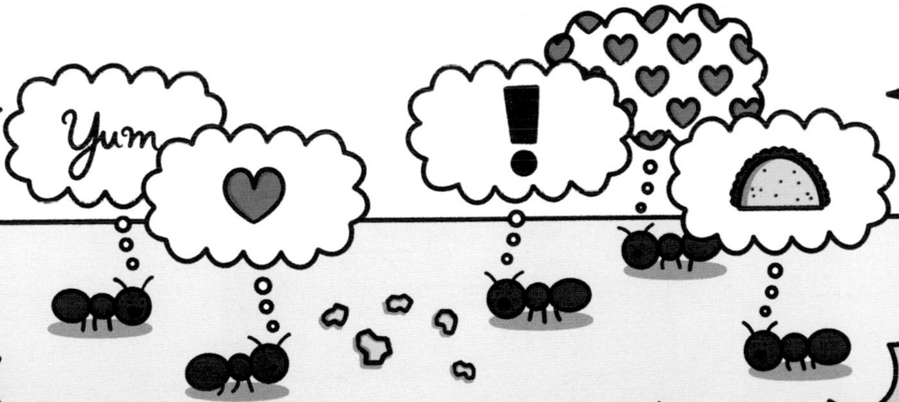
Yum
!

I got yelled at.... And laughed at... It...
It was terrible.

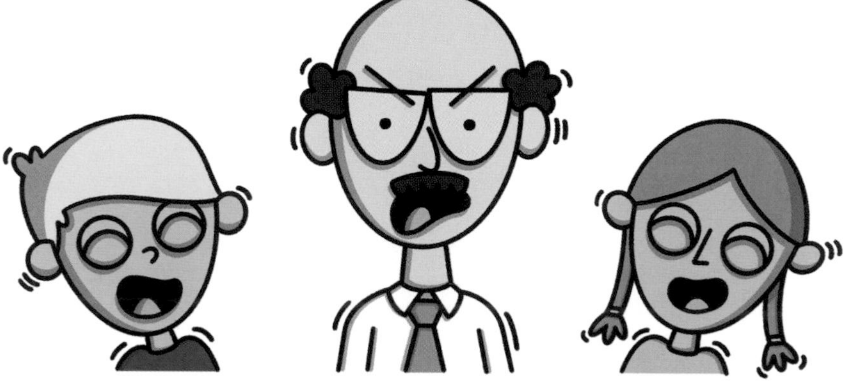

When I grew up to be a teacher,
I vowed to never let another child
experience such a thing.

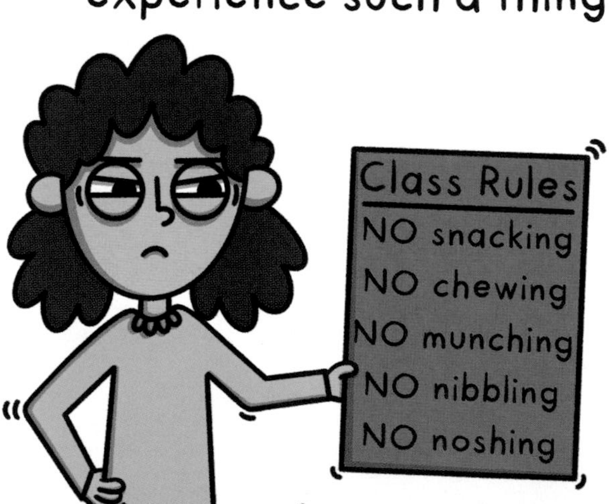
Class Rules
NO snacking
NO chewing
NO munching
NO nibbling
NO noshing

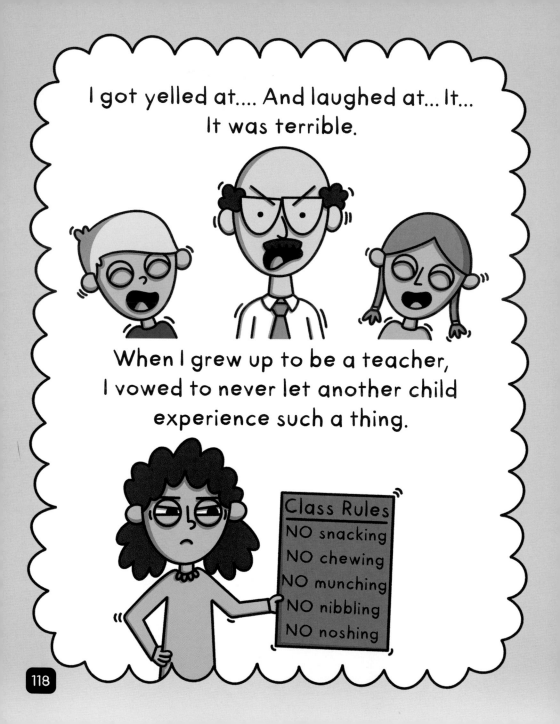

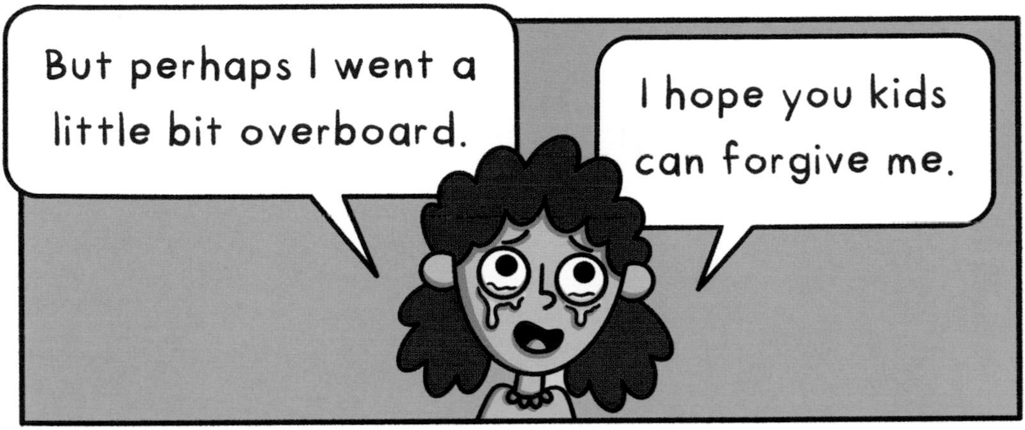
But perhaps I went a little bit overboard.
I hope you kids can forgive me.

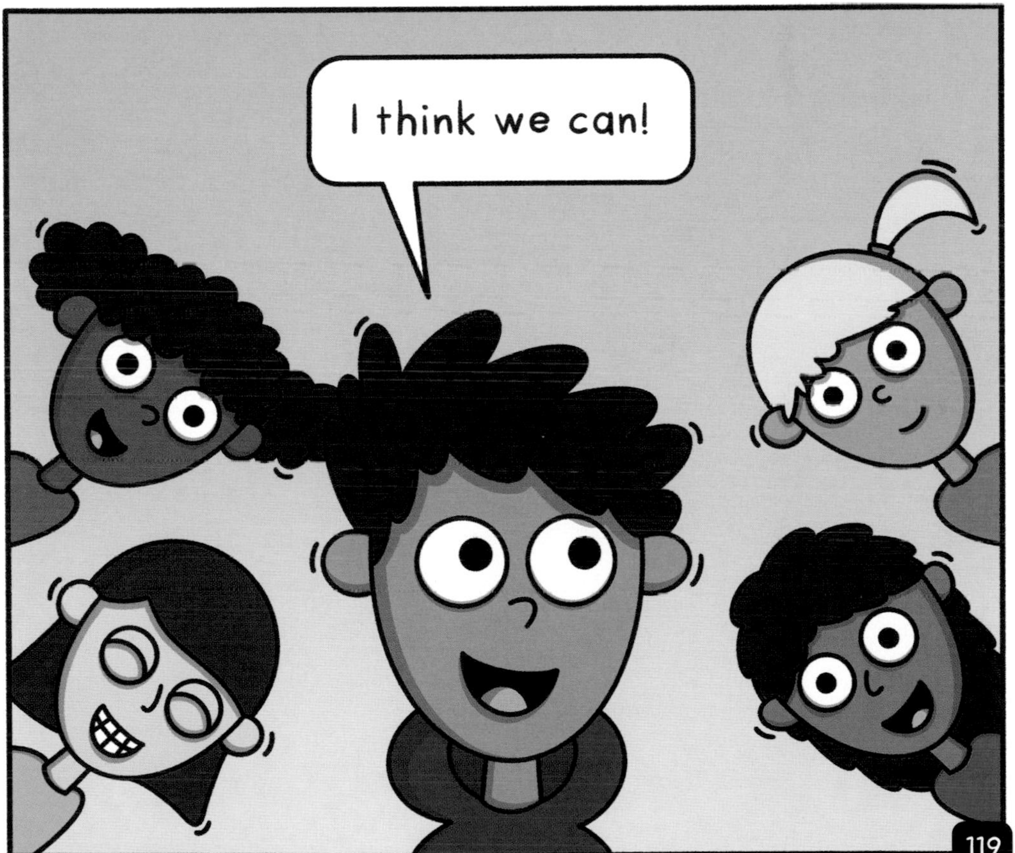
I think we can!

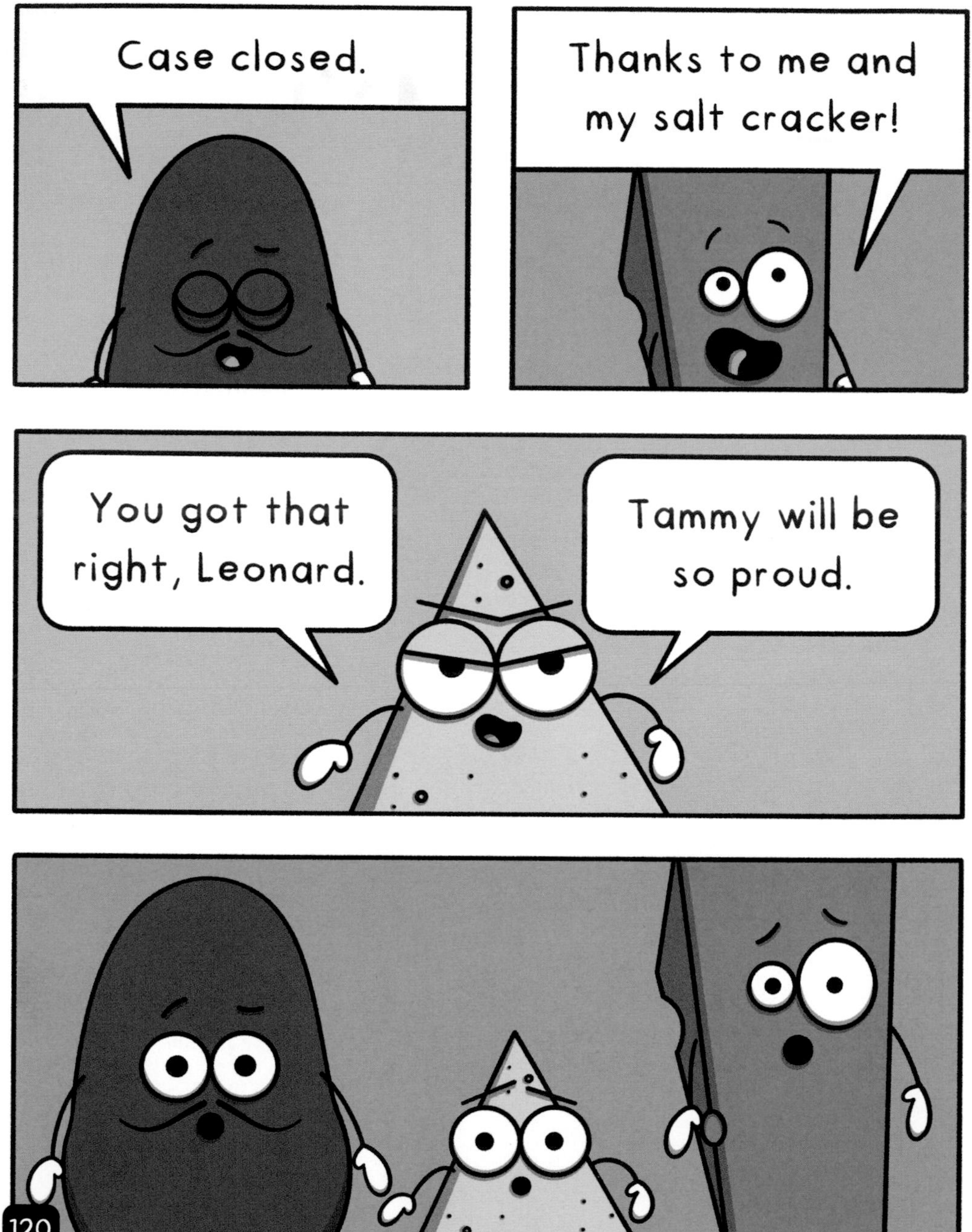
Case closed.
Thanks to me and my salt cracker!
You got that right, Leonard.
Tammy will be so proud.

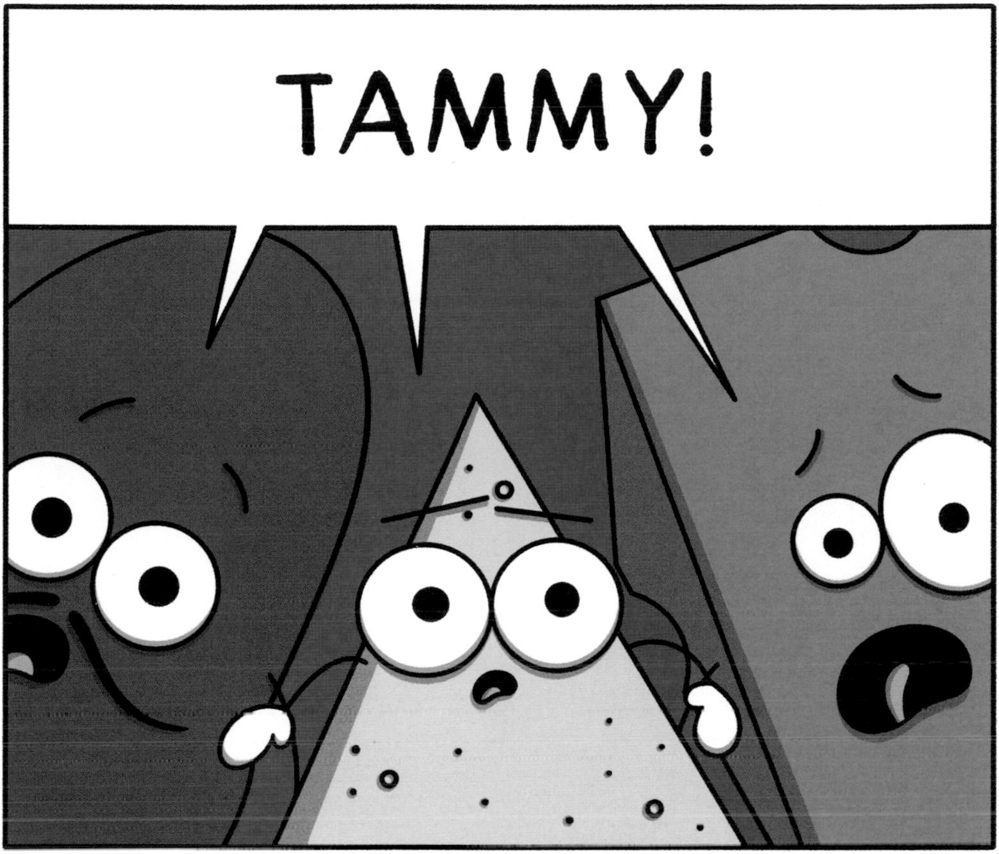
TAMMY!

All at once the Heroes remembered that Tammy was still out in the hallway—and so was THE VACUUM! They scurried out of the classroom to find her.

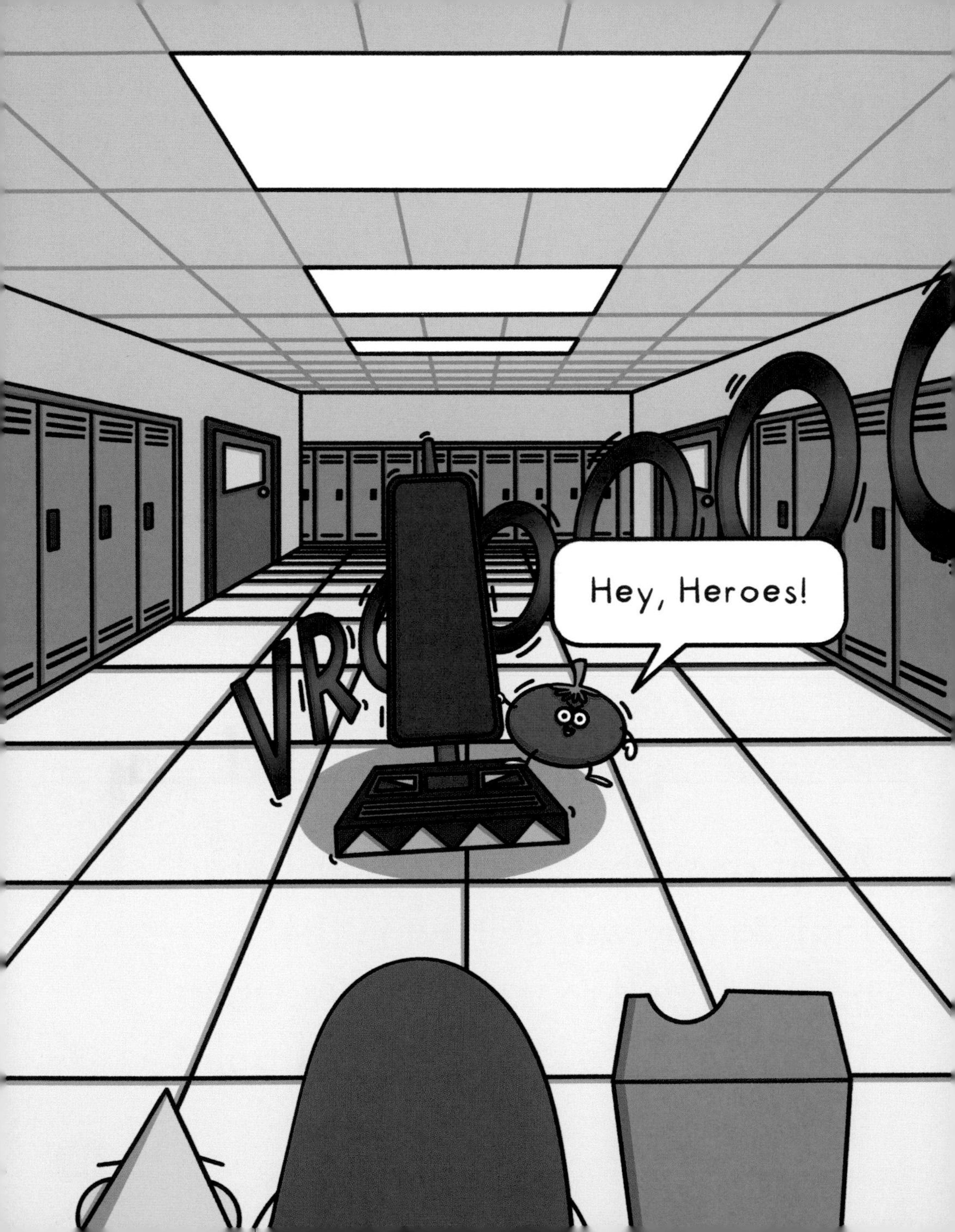
VROOOOOO
Hey, Heroes!

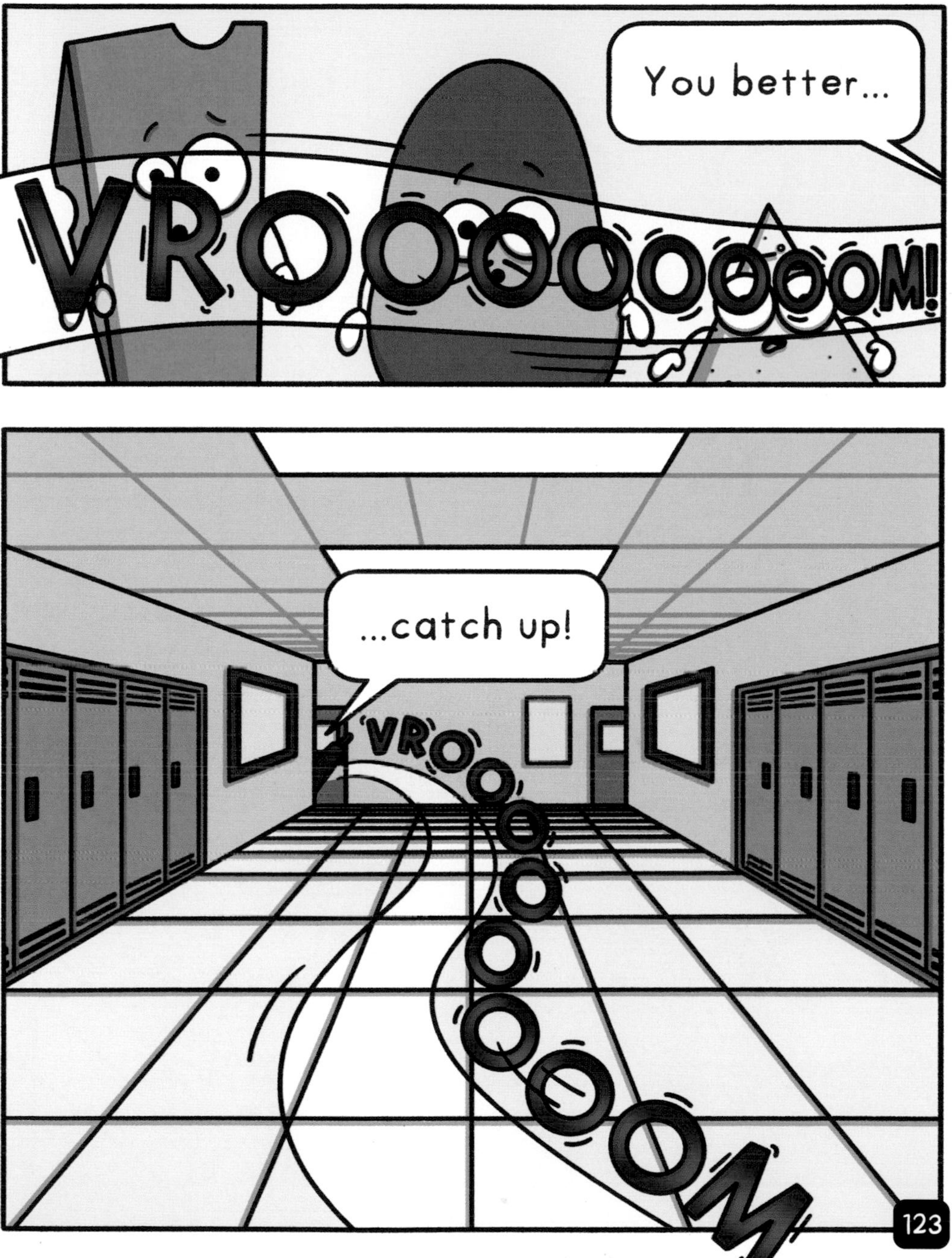
You better...
VROOOOOOOOM!
...catch up!
VROOOOOOOOM

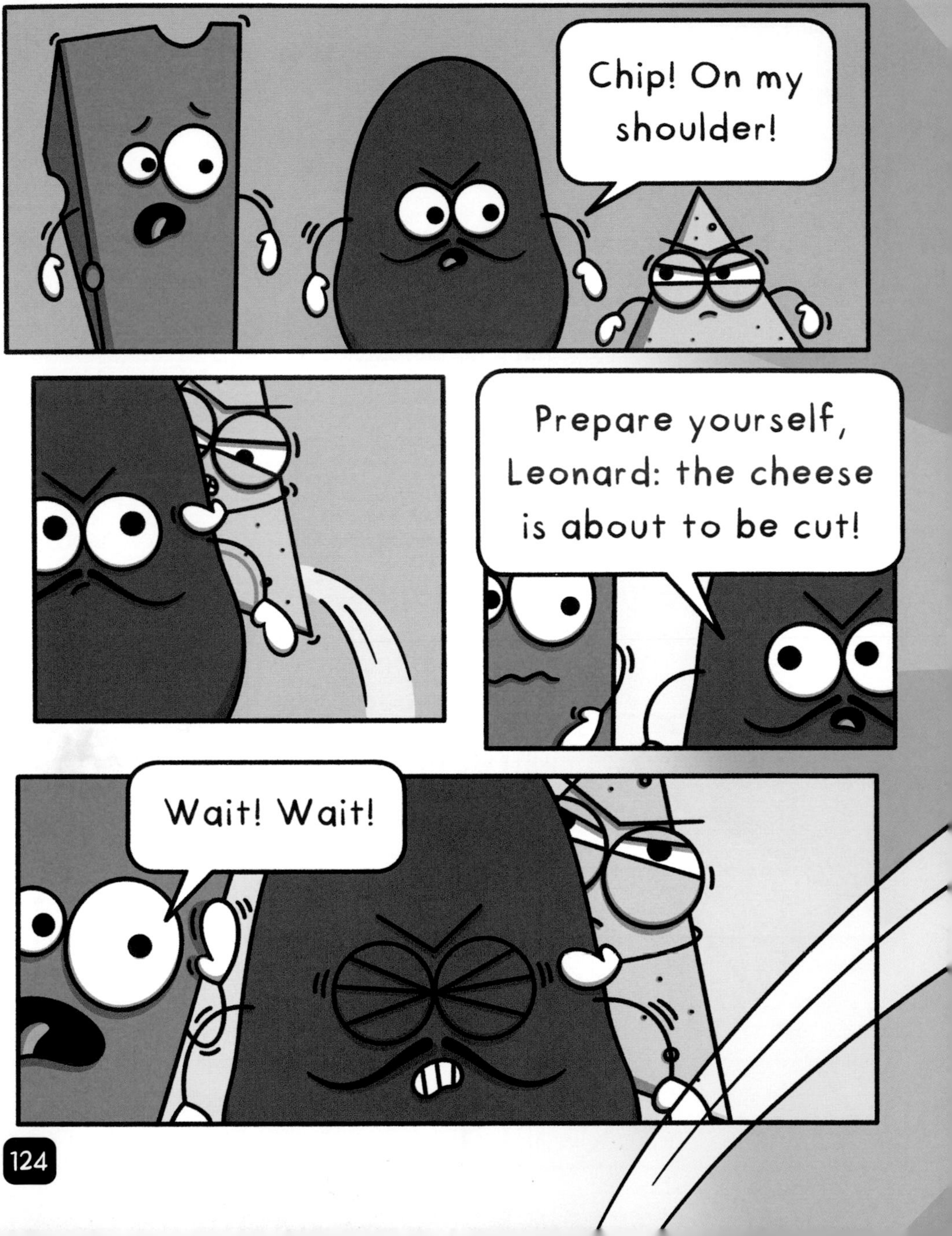
Chip! On my shoulder!
Prepare yourself, Leonard: the cheese is about to be cut!
Wait! Wait!

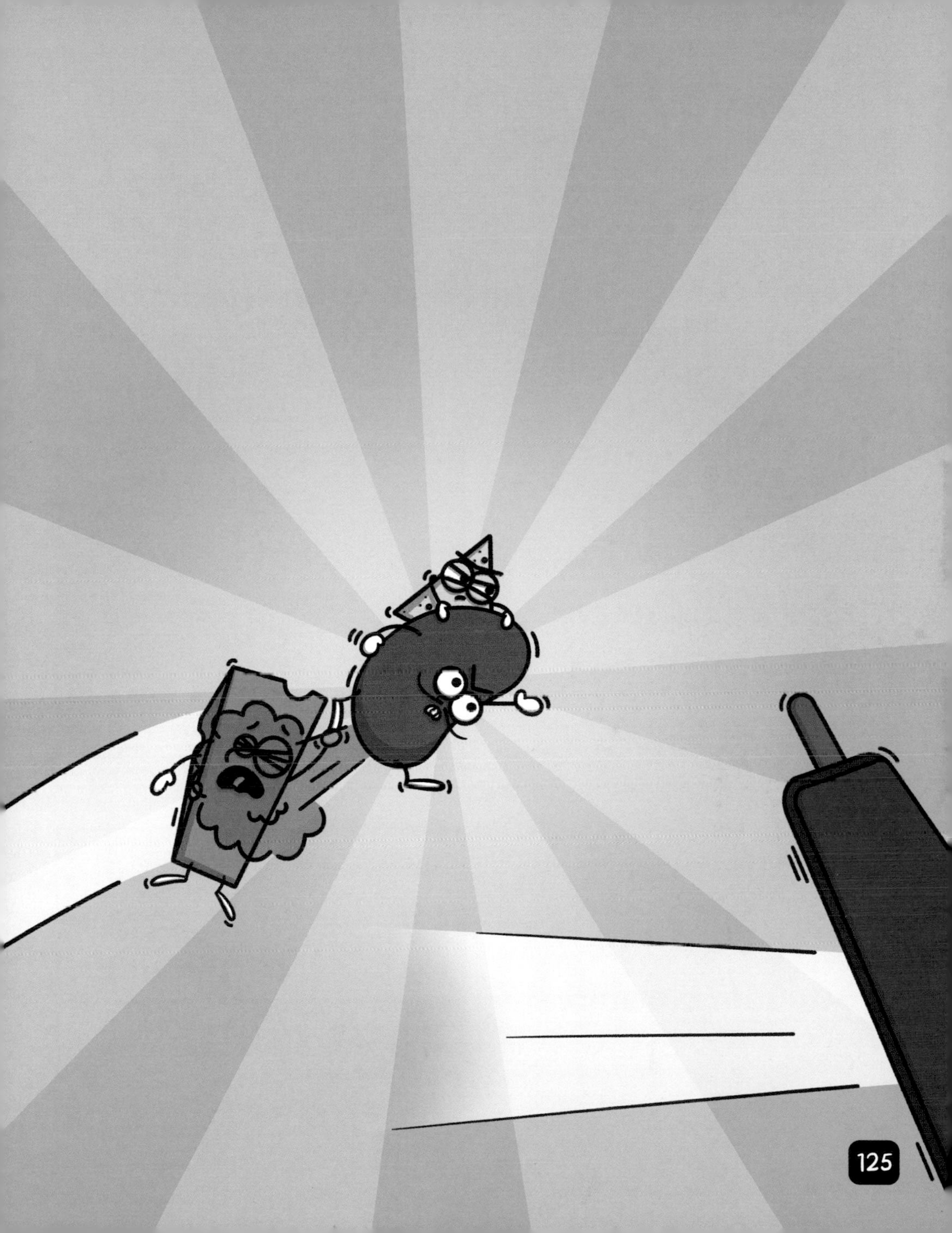

Mr. Toots flew himself and his friends closer and closer to the vacuum.

"Get ready!" he called to Chip Ninja and Leonard. "I'm about to run out of gas!"

And not a second after the words had left the big bean's lips... the Heroes fell.

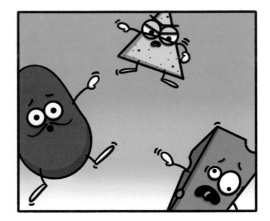

Fortunately, they fell right onto the vacuum cleaner and...

Nice of you three to join me. And right on time. Here's the door!

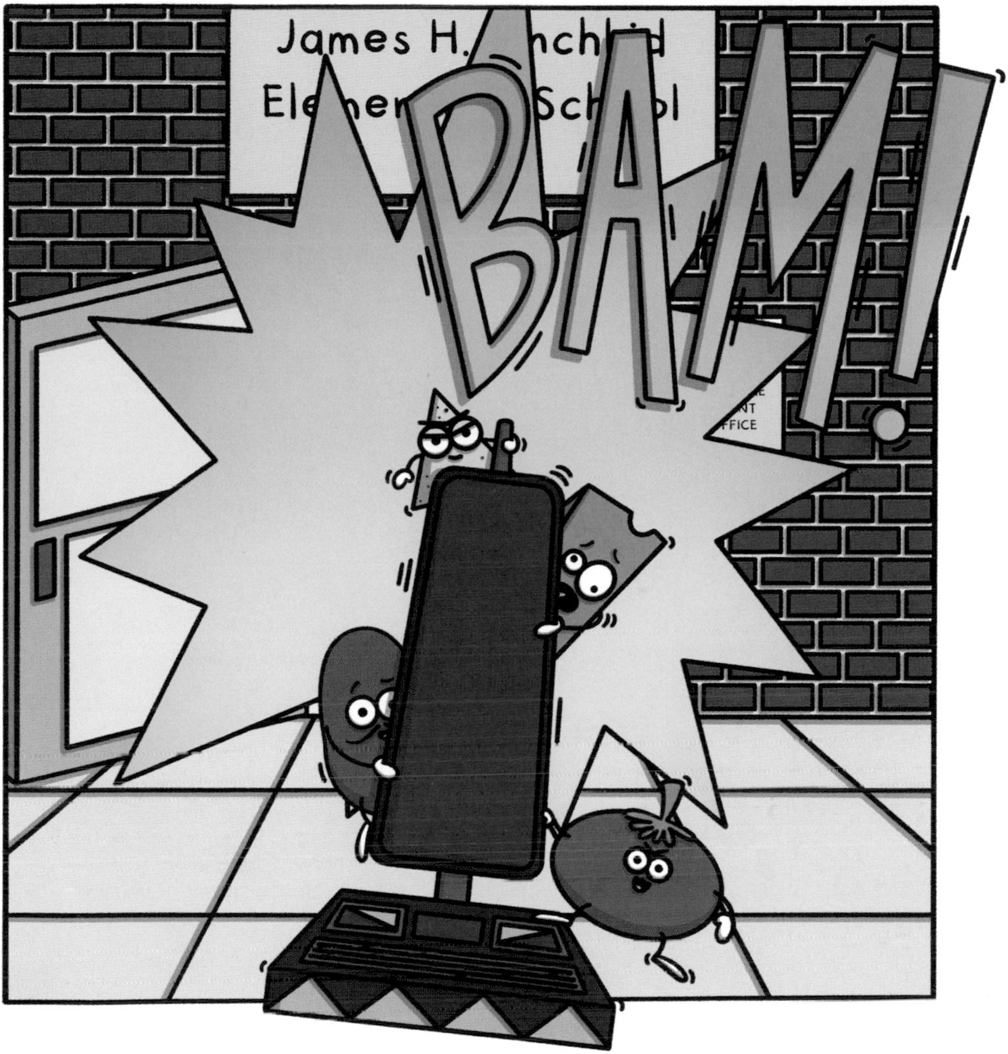
BAM!

burst through the door of the school
and back outside.

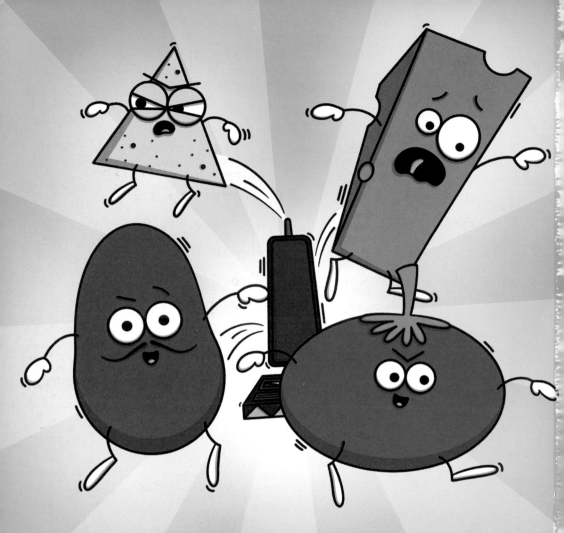

Leaping off the vacuum, the Hunger Heroes hurried to the Hovercraft, ready for their next adventure!